THE SLEEPLESS KNIGHT

JACK WIMBERLEY

For those who were too scared to love, were not allowed to love, or were punished for their love.

THE SLEEPLESS KNIGHT: A PLAYLIST

Realiti - Grimes
Fly To You - Caroline Polachek
Running Out Of Time - Ashe
Supersad - Suki Waterhouse
Eko - Yeule
Free - Florence + The Machine
Human Behaviour - Björk
Pink in the Night - Mitski
A Place You Can Meet Me - Carol Ades
(You) On My Arm - Leith Ross
Sports - Beach Bunny
mona lisa - mxmtoon
Voicemail - MARIS
Simulation Swarm - Big Thief
Hits Different - Taylor Swift
Valentine - Laufey
Say It Back - Luna Day
pretty isn't pretty - Olivia Rodrigo
Hurricanes - Rina Sawayama

Family Line - Conan Gray
Pain and Pleasure - Caroline Kingsbury
Sarah Come Home - Allie X
i love you - Billie Eilish
Beaches - Beabadoobee

CHAPTER ONE

I had always been a dreamer. Not in the sense that I had ambitious professional goals, but that I was incredibly delusional when it came to love. On this particular Monday afternoon, I was daydreaming of my future boyfriend. I couldn't picture a face, but I knew he would be kind, funny, and extremely attractive. A buzzing sensation took me out of my silly fantasy.

The vibration came from my phone, which was buzzing with a call from Maia, my best friend. I swiped across the flashing screen only to be met with a loud shriek. "Zack! Did you see?"

"See what? I've been asleep since noon," I lied. I didn't need her making fun of me for the truth. She would have every right to if she did, because who sits alone in a room for hours daydreaming about a man who will never exist?

"The new game that's coming out!" She screamed, her

volume never getting lower, staying at a steady rate of an ear-shattering high.

"No?" I said, "Are you going to calm down..?" I assumed I already knew what she was talking about. For years, Maia and I have played VR together. Through those three long years, we could never find what we were looking for. It was nice to play together, but we wanted more. More space, more people... more freedom.

"Okay, fine bitch I'll calm down. You know, a year ago you would have been screaming too." Anyway, it's a VR game called *Echoes of the Blade,* and it's everything we have been looking for. I'm talking villages, lots of real players, an exciting storyline, everything. It comes out next month, and there's even a pre-order bonus."

She wasn't wrong. When we first started playing I was the loud and excited one when something new released. I tried to change my tone, "I'm already sold. Let's meet up at your house so we can take a look at the game together. I'll bring my laptop." Part of me didn't want to move, but I didn't want to disappoint Maia. Something we had waited for since middle school was finally happening. I shouldn't be annoying today. I rolled out of bed, stumbling to the mirror to fix my hair. My pillow always flattened my hair out of its normal curl pattern, turning it into a horrific brown bowl shape. I put on my shoes, headed downstairs, and looked in the kitchen. The digital clock on the microwave read 4:29pm. I found my mom in the living room, reading a book.

"Hey Ma, I'm heading to Maia's house for a little bit."

"Not until you take out the trash, young man, you have been asleep all day," she said playfully. Yeah, I'll let her think I was sleeping. No one needs to know I'm just lonely as hell. She wasn't a strict parent, but always made sure to remind me of chores even if it sounded like a joke.

"Of course, I'll take it out when I head through the garage. Love you."

"Love you too Zack. You know, you and Maia would make a cute couple," she said, her voice rising in pitch like a jeering child on the school playground. I forced a fake laugh and smiled, leaving through the garage with a full trash bag in my hand. It wasn't new for her to make hopeful remarks about Maia and I. It wasn't surprising either, as we became friends in middle school and had stayed friends through to our Junior year. But what would surprise her is the fact that neither Maia nor I would ever date each other. Even if Maia didn't have a new "future wife" everyday, I only have eyes for men. Of course neither of our families were aware, and neither of us wished to crush their dreams too soon.

I got in my car, a white Subaru Impreza, started the engine, and headed out of the driveway. I drove past our current high school, a daunting building with rundown bricks and three stories whose stairs would tire anyone, no matter their age or physique. To get to her house, I passed several small shops, turned on Lance Road, and then whipped into her neighborhood. Despite living in Missouri, her neighborhood was named "Liverpool Estates," oddly British for a state formed after the revolution. I went past several cookie-cutter looking houses. Not to say they weren't impressive, but tall, brick, houses with white pillars get less exciting when there are twenty in one glance. I passed her neighbor, whose vibrant garden was filled with thriving florals of all colors. This was in contrast to Maia's dim, grassy yard, which little to no work had gone into, despite her past interest in a "blooming front yard." I pulled to the curb in front of her house and parked. I grabbed my laptop from the passenger seat and headed to her front door.

Before I could even knock, Maia opened the door. "Come in, come in!" Her dog, Tippy, started barking long before I even reached the door. He was ready to greet me, tail wagging as soon as Maia let me in. He was a small Chihuahua with brown and black fur, which meant his bark was high pitched and unlikely to scare anyone away. Maia led me upstairs to her room, past family photos and banisters chewed by Tippy. We entered her room, and I was instantly met with the scent of conflicting candles.

"What are you burning?" I asked, confused about what I was smelling.

"Rose Water and Blueberry Pancakes. Two different candles."

"That explains... a lot."

"If you came here to hate, there's the door. But I personally like the smell," she said, crossing her arms.

"No, no, I want to hear about this new game." We sat down at her desk, which was overflowing with piles of books and papers. Many of the books had bookmarks near the middle, and all of the papers were either joined by a paperclip, or had paperclips hanging loose. Plastered over her walls were posters of her favorite musicians and drag artists. Her computer was already on, its light-lined fans matching her room's LED lights with a neon pink color. The monitor displayed a black screen, with a play button in the middle. I guessed she had prepared something to show me, but I hadn't expected to jump right into a trailer. Maybe some promo pictures, but a trailer did seem more promising, like the game was already a full package.

I sat down in her pink desk chair, and Maia awkwardly stood behind me. She was like a kid who awaited her parent's feedback on a new discovery. She reached over me, took her mouse, and hit play.

My eyes were instantly met with a bright flash of light, and then the appearance of the game's logo, an ornate sword inside a ring of words. The image disappeared, and a city was presented. The view started with a large cathedral-like building, surrounded by many small houses and shops that spiraled around the building, ending with a bridge connected to an indistinguishable land mass. The trailer panned to the inside of the city, the streets hustling with townspeople in life-like motion, with cat-like creatures running around the buildings and into alleyways. Next was the bridge, which was a long, expansive, stretch with lights all over the edges. It appeared that each piece of land was floating separately in the air, the bridge being the only thing connecting the two. The bridge led to a giant plains area, with monsters, outposts, and foliage across the land. The open area seemed gargantuan, with small ponds and flowers for what appeared to be miles. As the view retreated, you could see that the Plains were enclosed by impressively tall mountains, which featured perfectly flowing waterfalls and short ridges. A shot of the sky was shown, show-casing a bright sun and buoyant clouds. Text appeared in the sky, displaying the release date of the game, and the trailer ended.

"So, what do you think?" Maia said eagerly, her nails piercing my shoulders.

"It looks great! Because you found it, I was a little skeptical, but I'm actually really excited now! I mean the graphics are amazing, the architecture is beautiful, and the map seems so expansive."

"I know, right! And that was only the first area shown, they are supposed to have created at least nine whole different biomes! I'll ignore your other comment because you're excited, but I *never* forget, ho."

"How many people can be on a server at a time? I mean yeah, the map is big, but it can't hold that many people." I asked, trying to redirect her focus back to the game.

"You won't believe me, but they are only making around ten servers for each region, with at a maximum of 500 players per server."

"500?" I practically yelled. I had never heard of such a high player count before. "Sorry, will they even have enough players for that?"

"That is the attitude I've been looking for! Don't worry, they keep a running count of their pre-orders for public view on their website, and it's already past fifteen thousand pre-orders."

"That is insane! Speaking of pre-orders, what is that bonus you were talking about?" I asked, getting more excited by the minute.

"Oh yeah, you will get a random dragon mount for the whole game. It is supposed to be special to only those who pre-order, and I guess the later players will have to buy ugly bird mounts or something if they want to fly."

"Kinda sucks that you don't get to choose, but I guess it's cute that way. The dragon kind of picks you I guess."

"Whatever you say, but you sound weird as hell. Anyway, let's get your pre-order done!" I got out my laptop, and went to the ViLar website, the home page for the headset we used. I navigated to the shop page, and entered the name of the game. It quickly popped up as a trending pre-order, instantly soothing any concerns I had over the potential popularity of the game. I pre-ordered it with haste, trying to hide my card information from Maia's intense stare. Maia jumped with glee as I hit "purchase," prompting her cat, Holly, to rush out from under her bed.

Maia and I chatted about school for a little while, and I headed home. Dinner was ready as I walked in the door, and my mom was quick to make comments about my beaming smile as I arrived. "So, I see you had fun at Maia's. Are you two together yet?"

"No Ma, just some really exciting news about our game stuff."

"Okay, you two need to get together someday though. I don't know how you two spend so much time in that 'virtual reality,' I nearly fell over when you tried to show me last time." We both shared a laugh and ate while watching her favorite show, *Gilmore Girls*. I went up to my room and began the countdown to the release of a game that I didn't even know about a few hours ago. In a little over 2 weeks, I would have access to a whole new world.

...

SATURDAY, JANUARY 5

The time had come for the new game to come out, and I was kindly reminded of that by another call from Maia. I had missed three calls due to a dream I was having. This time, it was a real dream, not a daydream. Within this fresh dreamscape, I was holding hands with that faceless boy, but this time, we were in the world of *Echoes*. At least, I thought we were. There was a large oak tree glowing gold, and a white dragon with coral undertones flying above us. Just as I was about to kiss the boy, Maia's rings entered my consciousness, and woke me up.

I answered her fourth call and was met with another high pitched scream, "It's out! It's out! Get online right now!" Before I could answer, she hung up. Despite her childish eagerness, I decided to go get breakfast before I played. The whole meal, my phone was blowing up with notifications from the ViLar app, all messages from her in the game:

. . .

Red_Rider33: Get online! **8:22am**
Red_Rider33: Where r u? **8:24am**
Red_Rider33: Bitch, I will call ur mom. **8:26am**
Red_Rider33: I'm going in w/o u ho! **8:28am**

By 8:30, I was finally ready, and messaged her back to notify her, hoping she hadn't already gotten into the game without me. I got another aggressive and colorful message confirming that she had not entered yet, but that I needed to "hurry my twink ass up" and join her. I put on my headset, which was for once, fully charged, and joined her party.

"Finally! You were taking forever! Now, we can stay in the party until we get to the tutorial, but after that I think we should see it alone then meet up when we're done," she said, her voice changing from anger to excitement as she spoke. We loaded the game, and we were immediately placed into a black void glittered with stars. A menu materialized against the twinkling backdrop. Under the game's insignia shone a large **PLAY** button. I pressed the button and was met with five different servers: *Fervor, Honor, Valiant, Bold,* and *Devoted.* Quite stereotypical server names for a fantasy game, but at least we had a variety.

"So which one should we join?" I questioned, unsure if we would get a choice to change our servers later.

"Let's go with *Devoted!*" Maia said cheerfully. We chose the server and entered a character design hub. To my surprise, the avatars were extremely lifelike, with slight wrinkles, soft skin, and human-like bone structure. We chose our races, both of us going with elves. I edited my avatar to look exactly like me, with dark brown hair, blue eyes, pale lips, and slight freckles. We then chose our classes, me being a support knight, and Maia being a tank mage. Next was the issue of names. Of course, you wouldn't want to use your real name, but you also wouldn't want to use a basic gamertag. I settled on *Mirage.*

"Okay, I think it's time for the tutorial, I chose the name 'Mirage,' what is yours?" I asked, hoping it would be easy to find her in the game.

"I went with Selene. Simple and elegant."

"So unlike you-" Maia, or Selene, quickly cut me off and hung up, leaving me to the tutorial. A star in the abyss began to glow brighter and larger, seemingly pulling me toward it. A burst of light popped before my eyes, and I was instantly inside of a large building with white walls. The walls were lined with stained glass and thin archways, all pointing towards an intricate painting on the ceiling of two dragons, both circling each other. One dragon was black, the other white. In the center of the image hung a large chandelier, which held a dozen tall candles, illuminating the center of the room. The space was empty, with a diamond pattern covering the floor. The diamonds alternated from pink to blue as they reached a large podium. I made my way to the stand, noticing the marble detailing of the lectern, which had edges with scale detailing ascending to the flat surface on which a rolled scroll was found. I reached towards the scroll, and as my hand hovered above it, text appeared, reading **"BEGIN TUTORIAL?"** I picked up the scroll, and a tall woman materialized on a blue diamond in the center of the room. She had long, white hair and tan skin. Her ears were pointed, and she wore regal golden armor with silver gloves and boots.

"Hello, knight." She said, her voice deep and billowing. "You are here to fight a great evil. King Syphon has been using the natural essence of the great land of Velouria for his own wicked plans. He has utilized our very plants to destroy not only their kin, but also harm our treasured creatures. You must join your fellow warriors to liberate these precious beings and free our world." She finished, walking towards the podium.

"Lovely, cannot wait for that," I said sarcastically, to no one.

"The time has come for you to take your blade." The woman presented me with a basic sword, with a leather wrapped handle and a silver blade. I took the weapon with my right hand, and awaited further instruction. "Now, swing your blade," she said. A golden arch appeared in front of me. I swung the blade, following the shape provided, and continued doing so in different forms. Left, right, up, down, in circles, in squares, around me, and in arches, until no more techniques appeared. "You're ready, soldier," and with that, the elven woman disappeared, leaving a trail of stars leading to the ornate chandelier on the ceiling.

I walked towards two large doors, each with a solid hoop doorknob, twisted the left one, and pushed it open. I was instantly met with a flood of light, which illuminated a circular courtyard. I paced to the center of the courtyard, and waited for something to happen. The yard was surrounded by bushes and small streams, each with roses on their banks. I heard the sound of disturbed wind, and looked up to see the silhouette of a dragon flying above me. The shape moved its wings in place for a few seconds, and began to dive straight down towards me. I moved back, and the dragon landed where I had been standing. It was slightly shorter than myself, and had mint green scales with blush undertones. I reached my hand out to its snout, and it nuzzled into my palm. Text appeared before me, **"PRE-ORDER BONUS ACQUIRED, PLEASE ENTER YOUR DRAGON'S NAME."** A keyboard appeared, and after a short period of consideration, I settled on the name *"Jinkx."* I pet Jinkx once more, and headed out of the courtyard. Now that I was outside of the building, I could confirm that this was the Cathedral from the main town. I found the path leading to the town area, and headed down a stone path with Jinkx in tow.

I reached the first few buildings, and immediately saw a player pacing back and forth. As I got closer, I immediately knew it was Selene. From her miniscule height to her red and black hair, her avatar very closely resembled Maia. Her elven ears were the only real distinction between Maia and Selene. I began running towards her, yelling and waving my arm. She immediately turned and went, "Took you long enough! Where were you? I've been standing around here for at least ten minutes."

"Just naming my dragon and learning the mechanics, did you not?" I replied defensively.

"Well I named my dragon, her name is *Dawn*, but no I skipped the tutorial. The mechanics can't be *that* hard."

"I would agree if you were a melee player, but you're a mage..."

"Oh shit. I didn't even think of that." She shrugged it off, then we headed further into the town, walking past bustling NPCs and brick houses. We passed through a produce market, both of us being too poor to buy anything, and got to an area buzzing with the speech of dozens of players.

"Well, this sucks but I have to go, can we meet here tomorrow?" I asked, realizing I had plans with my mom in less than half an hour.

"You are so boring, but yes, I will get off too." We said our goodbyes and turned off our headsets. I plugged it in and headed downstairs.

My plans with my mom consisted of dinner, cheesecake, and several rounds of *Mario Kart*. I was purposefully vague with Maia when I left, as I knew she would have some snide comment about why I was taking my absence. Since I was about ten years old, my mom and I had been playing the game together, the only game she played other than *Candy Crush*. She loved playing as *Rosalina*, and I as *Daisy*. It had become a tradition and an expected event every week. We could play for hours, playing through most courses that we liked, and even some we didn't. Tonight consisted of several different *Rainbow Roads*, *Mario Circuit*, *Toad Harbor*, and the dreaded *Cheese-land*. After eight rounds, we decided to call it a night.

I returned to my room, set my alarm for 8:00am, and went to sleep.

CHAPTER TWO

I awoke to the sight of at least a dozen messages from Maia, as she obviously had not gotten the same amount of sleep that I had. I made sure to get a bite, say "Hi" to Ma, and take a shower before quickly strapping on my headset.

I loaded into the game, and my audio kicked in before the visuals. I was staring at the starry void while I heard the voices of several players, including the standout voice of Selene. Once I had fully loaded into the game, I was met with Selene staring me down, hands on her hips. "Took you long enough."

"Sorry?"

"I have been waiting here for five minutes. Five whole minutes!"

"Girl..." We both laughed, then started heading further into the plaza area we had found the previous night. We walked past butchers, tailors, blacksmiths, and more vendors we couldn't afford to buy from just yet. Eventually made it to a small circle of players; two elves, a druid, a sylph, and an orc.

"Oh. My. Gosh. More players!" The sylph shrieked, throwing her hands up and waving at us, despite how close we were. "My name is Sylvia." Sylvia had dark skin that complemented her green eyes and blondish white hair nicely. She then pointed to the orc, "His name is Rufus." Sylvia next turned her attention to the green skinned druid, "Her name is Apha." Apha's black hair fell over her back as she waved at us. Before she could announce the elves' names, the one on the right spoke up.

"My name is Rampi, and I wanted to actually introduce myself," said the red haired, blue skinned elf with a pointed tone, glancing at Sylvia.

"And my name is Lali," the other elf, with a more natural, olive skin tone and black hair, interjected.

"Sorry guys, I guess I got carried away..." said Sylvia, now looking at the cobblestone floor.

"That's okay," I said, lightly laughing, "My name is Mirage–"

"And I am Selene," my friend said, glaring at me as if to say *I will not let you introduce me like that sylph did to them.*

"Where are you guys headed?" I asked the group, hoping for some guidance.

"Off to the Dusted Plains of course!" the orc spoke up. He had pale green skin, pointed ears, a muscular frame, and a large hammer attached to his belt. "Would you like to join us?"

Selene and I stared at each other for a few seconds then Selene said, "I think we are okay, we know each other in real life and want to explore together at first. We could friend you guys though, you all seem so nice!" And with that, we added each of them as friends, and started heading back on the path.

We passed more shops, players, homes, and stray animals, and eventually reached a large bridge. The bridge had a smooth stone texture, with pillars lining the walkway. It started from the edge of the city, which also happened to be the edge of a floating island. Beneath the bridge laid a thick fog, with no end in sight. The structure must have been held up by magic, as there were no supports aside from where it attached to the islands. At least it was assumed both sides had the hexagonal supports jutting out of the land, as the other side was too far away to be seen. Selene and I stepped onto the bridge, our shoes making a light *click* as we hit the stone. We walked for what seemed like ages, passing lamp posts and birds that circled the bridge. We began running out of excitement. Our steps got louder as we sped across the stretch of stone. After at least five minutes of running, we reached a large arch. The arch was made of the same stone as the pillars all across the bridge. It was detailed with intricate carvings of snakes and scales; the scales appeared unlike those of a dragon.

Selene and I walked through the large gate, and the woman from the tutorial materialized just as she had before, stars falling down from the sky. This time however, there was text above her that read *"Illia."* She walked closer to the gate, almost walking past us, and said, "Welcome, traveler. The Dusted Plains are in desperate need of your help! What once used to be a blooming range of flora and fauna has now become a dry stretch of dirt. Not only did this drought endanger all of the creatures in the area, but the toxins in the soil killed off all of the foliage." I looked around, and saw exactly what she was talking about: withered trees fallen on the ground, cracked dirt all around, and no trace of anything alive. "This is due to a great evil that has rooted itself inside of the Plains. It is a subject of Syphon, and must be destroyed to restore this land to its previous splendor."

"That bitch!" Selene exclaimed.

"Girl calm down..." I said, burying my face in my hands.

"Go ahead warriors, and find the root of this tragedy." Illia evaporated into hundreds of flying stars. Selene and I headed down a path to the left, if you could even call it that. It was a thin line of land that was slightly less cracked than the rest of the dirt, and had obviously been used as a path before the drought. We walked for a while, taking in the devastation around us. One small field mouse crossed our path, but swiftly ran to cover before we could try to pick it up. We continued on, and heard steps.

We thought we would see more players, but instead saw our first enemies. The path opened into a small circle, which was surrounded by some worn down fencing. Inside this circle paced four slender lizard-like creatures. They were tall, with dark green scales, eerily triangular heads, and thick, spiky tails. Each had a strap across their chests, with either a bow or sword sheath attached. As we approached, they immediately stopped walking, their attention swerving to us in unison.

"Oh shit," Selene whispered, "I do not have a clue what to do."

"I think I have a plan?" I said, not meaning for it to come out sounding like a question. "I say, you try to pull their aggro using your tank-i-ness, and I'll chase them down and hit them from behind."

"Sounds like a plan." The plan started out great, her extra defense and health stats easily pulled the lizards' attention, but the problem came with defeating them. They only did minimal damage to me, but I also only did minimal damage to them. As a general rule, supports don't get the highest attack stats. This was obviously true in *Echoes* too. As she distracted, I slashed and slashed, but to little end. I tried every type of swing I knew, even the one that accumulated light before releasing the energy, and only one lizard was close to half health. I turned to see Jinkx, just sitting there watching.

"Hey Selene! Do you know if our dragons can attack?" I asked, praying for an affirmative answer.

"I am about fifty percent sure!"

"Great…" But then I saw it, an option above Jinkx, a very small elegant piece of text that said *Battle*. I reached for it, one hand extended to Jinkx, and the other swinging at a lizard. As soon as I made contact with it, Jinkx hopped into action. She couldn't fly yet, but she could bound around like a leopard. She pounced on a lizard, biting its ankle and dragging it to the floor. While she didn't do too much damage, the lizard was stunned for fifteen seconds. I hacked away at the creature until it was almost defeated, and was disappointed to see it get up. Luckily, the small amount of damage Jinkx could do was enough to finish it off, and one lizard was down.

"Dawn, get the hell in there!" Selene shrieked, obviously stunned by how helpful Jinkx was.

"Damn, no need to be so rude to her," I jeered. We went back to fighting, our dragons each quickly taking down one of the lizards. While they were down, we finished them off, each of us focusing on our respective lizards as determined by Jinkx and Dawn. Tanks and supports are not really suited for combat. Together we survive, but we are not the fastest fighters. After what felt like hours of suffering, we took down the last remaining lizard creature, and a notification appeared for the both of us. It seemed to be part of the tutorial. The message read "**NEW LOG ENTRY: SCALOSOS.**" I opened the highlighted journal tab, and noticed a rundown of the creatures:

Average Height: Six feet, seven inches
Area Found: Plains, ???, ???
Color: Green, ???, ???
Origin: ???

"Selene, we are going to have to deal with these things in two more areas..." I said, shaking my head.

"Hell no! I am not dealing with THAT again!" Of course, she knew that wasn't true, and if she disliked the first enemies that much, I wondered how badly she would take the next ones. A chest appeared in the middle of the circle, and we both opened it. Inside were some coins and scalosos scales. We took our bounty, and headed further down the path. We eventually reached a ruined village, with only players present. The roofs of the buildings were caved in, and there were only eerie holes where the windows once were. The ground was similarly cracked to that of the rest of the area, and the town's well was dried up. As we reached the center of this abandoned town, we saw some familiar faces.

"Selene! Mirage!" Sylvia screamed, jumping up and down.

"Hey!" Selene and I said in unison, walking towards the group.

"So where are the two of you headed?" Rufus questioned.

"No clue actually. We've just been following this trail and hoping for the best," Selene responded, obviously worried we may be going the wrong way.

"Same here, but we heard of a public event in that giant dust storm," Rampi said, pointing to a large cloud, "Apparently it unlocks the boss room for the area."

"Well that sounds like something we should go to as well, has anyone started the event yet?" I asked, hoping we could be the first to get to it.

Lali spoke up, surprisingly sounding a lot like Rampi, "Not yet, but we are kind of hoping we can get a larger party together before we go in." Selene and I nodded, and quickly received party invites from Rampi. We accepted, and began walking further into the town. We passed dead rodents, broken glass, lost swords and more before finally reaching the outskirts of town, where we found a small pond. This was the first sight of water since entering the Plains, and we were all surprised to find it. We filled up some bottles with the slightly muddy water, and kept advancing towards the dust storm. We passed more players, some even joining our group as we crossed the dry land. By the time we had reached the storm, we had an extra two eleves, an orc, and another druid trailing slightly behind us.

"Is everyone ready?" Lali awaited everyone's confirmation, and we headed into the storm. Only now did it dawn on me that Rampi and Lali appeared to be the leaders of this little group. Despite Sylvia's loud voice, Rampi and Lali had been the ones organizing everything. Everyone, including our new companions, followed Lali into the storm, and immediately the event began. Text appeared in the center of my screen: **"EVENT START: THE FIRST STORM,"** and under that, ***"Place 20 scalosos scales in the pot before the timer runs out."*** The mentioned pot was a green piece of pottery sat in the middle of the dusty field. Very quickly after the announcement, our first wave of those irritating lizards spawned in. Selene, Rufus, and I took the first team of two, which proved to end faster than when Selene and I had fought our first few. Rufus being a damage player, or DPS, helped defeat them faster, his quick cutting moves packed the punch needed to harm them, and we could divert their attention and keep him alive. Our teamwork was much needed, as our dragons couldn't do much but flail around due to the dust. After only a couple of minutes, the first two scalosos were down.

Rampi, Lali, Sylvia, and Apha took down another four, making it seem painless with their evenly matched numbers. I watched in awe as Rampi summoned a pool of electric energy at the scalosos, paralyzing them and allowing Sylvia to swoop in with her own bit of magic. The four of them quickly took the reptiles down. We noticed that our added travelers were struggling with two more scalosos as the final two of the first wave approached them from behind.We all jumped in to aid them, and had the last four of the first wave down in a flash. Each lizard had dropped a scale, and we had harvested a total of ten by the end of it all. As soon as we added the first half to the pot, eight more spawned in, but this time their scales were a deep red color.

We could immediately tell that these scalosos would not be as easy to take down as the first ten. We split into teams based on class, trying our best to evenly dish out support, tank, and *DPS* players. Rufus, Selene, and I were on a team again, this time with one of the travelers that had joined us on the road. We fought for almost ten minutes trying to take down the eight lizards, running down the clock to only a minute. They were all defeated, and we grouped up around the pot. Each group had one member drop in their harvested scales. Sylvia dropped in two, I dropped in three, and Lali dropped in her three. I noticed something was wrong, "But that's only–"

"Eighteen. I know. I think we were too slow." Rampi interrupted me, sounding defeated. I refused to give up, that was too much work to have to repeat it. I noticed that despite the different levels of scalosos strength, both had dropped the same green scales.

"Wait! I have an idea. Selene, get your scale out from the chest earlier!" We both raced to empty our inventories, revealing our scales from our last run-in with the dreaded creatures, and threw the scales into the pot.

"Whew. I hate to give up my hard-earned possessions but that was close," Selene announced, throwing her hands up in a sarcastic celebration.

"How did you already have some? None of us have ever seen those things."

I turned to answer Sylvia, but Rampi interrupted me, laughing, "Oh, well I think I know. I saw that there were some of those lizards on the way to the town, but I didn't think we were ready yet. I chose to walk around that area. Sorry guys." Rampi shrugged, obviously harboring a sense of guilt for robbing her friends of that experience.

"You have no right to be sorry. Thank you *so* much for not making me fight those bitches earlier than I had to," Sylvia replied, almost on her knees as she thanked Rampi. We all started laughing, but quickly stopped when a sharp light erupted from the pot. In a flash, the clouds dispersed, and a woman flew out of the green ceramic piece. She was draped in a flowing white dress, with billowing sleeves spiraled with flowers. She drifted down, barely hovering above the ground and spoke.

"Warriors, you have made great progress in restoring this great land to its previous vigor, but there is much left to do." She pointed towards a circular building lined with gold trim and lit by three ghastly blue lamps. "Venture there, and you will find what is plaguing this soil. Please warriors, destroy the creature that has its filthy grip on this land." With that, she floated back into the sky, and dispersed into a soft green light. Similar to how Illia had, but without the stars. Did all the NPC women in this game evaporate when they left? After she disappeared, our first true quest finally appeared: "**SONIQUE'S GRACE.**"

"So I think that woman was Sonique... and she was kinda..." Selene started, not realizing the others probably did not want to hear her thirsting over an NPC.

"Anyway..." I said, "Let's go in, I guess." We moved towards the building, and Rufus opened the door. It led into a small chamber, with windows and a small lever in the back. We all piled into the space, viewing the scaly gold floor surrounded by tall walls etched with snake-like figures. After we were all confirmed to be inside, Rufus pulled the lever, and we began to fall.

The chamber turned out to be an elevator, and we tried to look through the windows, but only saw pitch black. After about three minutes of falling, Sylvia spoke up, "I see something!" We all looked out of the same window, which was impractical but made the moment more dramatic. Through the window, we all saw the same chilling sight: one tall candle, lit the same eerie blue as the lamps outside. Soon after acknowledging this luminous monument, the elevator came to a stop. We spilled out as the doors opened, and found ourselves slightly elevated on a stone surface, with stairs leading down to a cobblestone path. It was too dark to see past the first few feet of the path, so Selene looked through her spells to find something to help. It quickly became apparent that we were lucky to have brought mages with us.

The illumination spell was a skill only available to mages and only appeared in the guide when you were in dark places. Selene, Rampi, and Sylvia all deployed the spell, and we headed down the path. As we neared the blue flame, chills went down my spine. It may be just a game but the developers had made the atmosphere so realistic. Even the air from my ceiling fan made me turn around.

We reached the candle, and the ground began shaking instantly. As if we weren't already extremely deep into the ground, the dirt beneath us gave out, and we plummeted into another chamber. After we landed, candles lining the walls lit one by one, revealing a large, sleeping snake. There were at least one hundred candles to be lit, and with every new spark, the reptile twitched more and more. The snake was at least twenty times the height of our tallest player, Rufus, and many times more wide. It had mustard yellow scales, a trapezoidal head, and large fangs hanging out of its mouth.

The last candle lit, and the snake hazily rose, expanding from its coiled position into a looming threat, stretching towards the ceiling of the chamber. The snake hissed loudly, opening its mouth, and started off our fight by lunging at Selene. Its deafening rattle filled the silence with a deathly ring as it lunged. Selene dodged, and ran behind the snake. "Tanks! Surround this ugly ho!" Following Selene's demand, Lali, the extra orc, and another mage all got on different sides of the snake. This worked for a few seconds, confusing the creature, but it quickly diverted its attention to one of the supports. *Me*.

Not even Sylvia. *Just me*.

"Hey!" I yelled, "Why don't you guys all take it in one direction and run it around the room?"

"Oh. Well that was my next idea!" Selene yelled back, trying to save face. The tanks did so, and the snake quickly shifted its attention to them. They ran it around the room, allowing the brawlers: Rufus, Apha, and the two extra elves, to attack its rattle, which helped take its health down. Rampi and the other remaining mages stood in a circle, casting distance spells at the snake's head. I hadn't had a chance to look at its health bar, but when I did, I finally saw its name. Above a mostly full health bar was the name "*Ralios*." Ralios then spun around to shake the brawlers. They all jumped back unscathed, but its body had hit Rampi. She went flying towards one of the walls, and I quickly ran to her side. I stabbed my sword into the ground, which created a healing pool around the two of us. I emptied my inventory to find my only health potion, and used it to heal her. I retrieved my sword, and swung it into the shape of a star, restoring the rest of her health, and even some of mine. As quickly as she got up, we lost our hope of a quick re-entry into battle. A shadow hovered over us, and we knew we were about to get another smack from Ralios. We tried to roll out of the way, but the tail was still headed for us.

Before I could react, I was in the air. However, the tail hadn't touched either of us yet. I looked up to see a greenish figure holding me, its large wings flapping in the blue tinted room. It was Jinkx, and she had somehow learned to fly. She brought Rampi and I up above the snake, and dropped us on its head. We slashed and cast away, aiming for Ralios' maroon eyes and loose scales. He shook us off, and Jinkx caught us, only this time she was too tired to bring us back above. Jinkx dropped us off by the other mages, who were still casting away, and retreated to a dimly lit corner.

How Jinkx even got into the cave was a mystery to me. No one else had their dragons, why was she here?

Our head-on assault had dropped Ralios' health down to far below half, and our hope returned.

Rampi and I joined the fight once again, and things ended quickly after that. Everyone got in a few more hits: the mages used paralyzation spells, the tanks threw everything they could while running, and everyone else charged the reptile. Once the health bar hit zero, Ralios collapsed, its body evaporating into dust particles, and sinking into the floor.

In its place, Sonique now stood. "Thank you warriors. You have restored the Plains, evicted Ralios, and reclaimed my sacred temple. There is much more for you to do to save this world from *Syphon*. Ralios was only one of his many manipulations. But for now, I hope you can accept these gifts as a token of my everlasting gratitude." Sonique waved her hands, and each of us had restored health, an "Essence of Ralios," new armor, and a new weapon.

The new armor was pretty bland, just a leveled up version of the old armor. Though my attention was first drawn to the drab armor, the sword was definitely the best part. The flower-wrapped blade had a description to go with it: **THE SPRING'S VIGOR;** *A blade once trapped under rubble has been restored to its former glory. New roses bloom with each swing, and the blossoms dictate the player's heightened stats.* After I read this description, I noticed the pink and white colors of my flowers. After some searching, I learned that white amplifies my shield stat, and the pink amplifies my support stat. I looked around at the other knights, and noticed they only had roses of one color on the tip of their blades. I watched as the flower flew off, and sprinkled dust onto the players, apparently giving them some sort of boost. My flowers however, did not disappear. I reopened my inventory, checked the sword, and saw its rarity: **¼ found in all of Velouria: LEGENDARY.** Okay, so I wasn't the only person who could get this sword, but I was still special.

I looked up again, and saw Sonique leaving. She didn't float away like before, but was walking in the temple. She opened a door at the end of the room, and exited, the door disappearing behind her. I mean, she did say this was *her* sacred temple anyway. Where she originally was, now stood a rectangular, golden portal. The party walked through one by one, and came out in the Plains. This time however, the Plains were beautiful. Just like the trailer, the Plains were covered in grass, with flowers covering almost every inch of the green expanse. Where there used to be deepened patches of dirt, were now small ponds of water filled with small fish. The mountains now came into view, still distant but no longer obscured by clouds of dust. I hadn't remembered the mountains, believing they must have changed the layout of the world after the trailer came out. But now, seeing the restored Plains, I saw the same beauty that had influenced my pre-order.

We all decided this was a good place to end today's session. Not only did Selene and I get off, but so did the rest of the party. We made plans to play again tomorrow night, and said our goodbyes.

Before I logged off, I checked my map, and the previously undocumented area had been filled. The words **DUSTED PLAINS** appeared over an intricately drawn model of the area we had just freed. As I was about to close my map, the first word split into several pieces, flew away from the map, and fell back down, shaping a new word: **RESTORED.**

CHAPTER THREE

The previous night marked the last day of Winter Break. Both Maia and I had no desire to return to school, but it had to happen. It was kind of hard to skip school with five AP classes.

I threw on some clothes and headed downstairs. I packed my "lunch." A cold pack and a Dr. Pepper, just like every other day. My mom likes to complain about my eating habits, but they really only get "bad" at school. Something about the depressing environment at the school immediately eliminated any appetite I could've had, and I usually could only stomach a drink.

I microwaved a leftover piece of pizza from two nights ago, then double checked my bag. I had my books for AP Language, my four different binders, my laptop, and my headphones. I was missing something. I ran back upstairs, leaving my pizza to get cold, and retrieved my pencil bag. I had been sketching The Spring's Vigor last night, and had forgotten the bag upstairs.

Atop a sketch of a shining blade with flowers blooming all over laid at least ten of my pencils. I scooped them into my bag, and ran back downstairs. While getting my pizza, I checked the clock on my microwave, which read 8:02am. *Shit*. I grabbed my bag, keys, and water bottle, then ran out of the garage.

The only good thing about being a Junior was being able to drive. I ripped open the door of my *Subaru*, threw my bags in, and backed out of the driveway. I drove to the school, one hand on the wheel, one hand eating my slice. I reached the back parking lot, and parked next to Maia's *Kia Soul*. As I turned to my right, I saw her mouthing along to a song with intimidating passion. I didn't have to guess what song it was, as her car radio was on full volume, serenading the parking lot with *Naked in Manhattan* by Chappell Roan. I got out, and tapped on her window. No response. Knocked. Again, no response. After those attempts to get her attention, I just got out the spare key she had given me, unlocked the car, and got in the back. I poked her in the back and yelled. "We have five minutes to get across the entire school!" She jumped forward, honking her horn.

"Bitch! Do not do that ever again!"

"Sorry that I didn't want to be late!"

"Don't you dare put this on me, I have been sitting here for twenty minutes! What took you so long?"

"I either slept in too long or just had no motivation to get here, could be both." Maia glared at me, and we got out of her car. We sprinted towards the back entrance, rushing past a short girl who was holding the door open. Passing dark hallways lined with navy blue lockers, we crossed the entire school, and separated into our classrooms. Maia and I had our first periods in the same hall, but not the same classroom. I scrambled to find my chair, which had my name taped to its back. I had made it before the bell, and had time to look around. In front of me sat a boy with dark brown hair and tan skin, and next to him a blonde boy with pale skin. They were both dressed in sportswear, basically a guarantee that they were straight. I looked next to me, and on both sides were people I could not stand. On my right was Linda Pertone, a girl who had once spread rumors about Maia being a "lesbian freak" who was "obsessed" with her. Little did Linda know, Maia despised her and often compared her to Dr. Suess's *Horton*.

To my left, was *Connor Price*, a boy who had broken my heart despite never having dated me. He was my first acknowledged crush, and the first "gay" man I had met. I met him in Freshman year, and started really talking to him last year. He entertained my interest for a few months, parading me around enough to have people asking questions, then ditched me. He wrote me this long message detailing how I was obsessive and obnoxious, and then blocked me. A few months later, he got a girlfriend, took the pride flag out of his instagram bio, and went back to being straight. Maia did her research, and discovered he had been lying about his sexuality for years to cover up how poorly he had treated his last girlfriend. After I was done crying, I built up anger and jealousy that never went away. There I was, unable to come out at all, but he could do it as a facade for his own shady convenience.

A deep voice interrupted my scan of the room, "Welcome to AP Lang, I'm Mr. Wills. I doubt many of you did the Summer assignment, despite having two extra seasons to do so... but let's see a show of hands. How many of you did it?" Hands all around the classroom went up, including mine. Two did not. The couple of hands that remained down belonged to the two boys in front of me. "Okay, what are your names?" Mr. Wills asked, a notepad in hand.

"Uh, I'm Alex. Alex Greene," the brown haired boy said.

The blonde followed, "I'm Ben Troy."

"Disappointing as expected. You two, see me after class." Mr. Wills rolled his eyes, and went straight to instructing. We went over the summer reading, discussing Capote's use of imagery and O'Brien's diction, and left with two essay prompts. As I left, I got a glimpse of the two boy's faces. Ben was not very attractive, but I had never found blondes too attractive. Alex however, was very cute and definitely my type. If he ever needed help, which seemed likely, I would be more than happy to oblige. Once I exited the class, I saw Maia staring at me with a shimmer in her eyes. She hooked her arm into mine, and practically skipped me to my next class.

"Got something to share with the class?" I said, slightly fearful.

"I'll tell you during lunch!" She winked, and leapt to her next class. My next class was AP US History, with Ms. Tati. This class wasn't new to me this semester though, as it was required for the whole year. The class covered two credits worth of content.

Upon entering, I saw the submission basket, slid in my outline for our most recent reading, and took my seat next to Bostyn. She was an acquaintance of mine whom I'd been sitting next to all year. We had little in common aside from music taste, but one dark force tied us together. Bostyn happened to be the ex-girlfriend that Connor had left so shattered he had to assume a new identity. Our shared hatred brought us closer, and even provided slight comfort.

We resumed our unit from the previous semester: The Gilded Age. I absolutely despised this unit. Tycoons, trusts, labor, blah, blah, blah. It was all so boring, confusing, and to me, pointless. I was never a huge fan of history to begin with, but I needed the AP credit to get into my dream school, *Harvard*. Basic, but to me, a magical choice. I toured the campus the previous summer with my mom. It was beautiful, with lush trees, old fashioned buildings, and of course, outstanding academics. Part of me wants to go to get away from the horror that is the midwest. The other part feels an obligation to let my mom live out her *Gilmore Girls* fantasy, which I would happily be a part of. After an hour and twenty-minutes of the Standard Oil scandals, APUSH was finally over, and I could get to lunch.

Maia found me again, this time almost sprinting at me. She dragged me to the art room, home to our favorite teacher, Ms. Bash, and sat me down in the corner. "Okay, so I found another girl for me. Correction, *woman*. She is everything. She has these beautiful goddess braids, perfect lips, and is even taller than me."

"That's not hard..."

"Shut up! Anyway, she has the cutest laugh and she is in my science class."

"Do you think she-"

"I don't want to hear the 'is she gay?' speech, let me live for a day. I have no idea, but I know her name is beautiful too, Sierra." As she said her name, she stared off into the distance like a lovestruck cartoon character.

"That's great. Truly, I hope she is into you, but let's see what your other classes have to offer, then we can fixate on one girl. *Sorry,* 'woman'." I threw my hands up sarcastically, and opened my Dr. Pepper. After a few minutes of awkward silence, I got up, and walked over to Ms. Bash's desk. Atop stacks of sketches and tax forms were photos of her and her wife, some with their new baby. I wrapped my knuckles on an open part of the desk. "Excited to have me in two classes this semester?" I decided to take both AP 2D and 3D art, hoping it would be an escape. I already had some pieces for my portfolio for both, and I had always been an artist -at least to my mom.

"Why, of course, Mr. Catrone!" she replied in a fake British accent. "Sorry, that was horrible. Yes, I hope I don't get sick of you..." She smiled, and went back to sorting her papers. I nestled back into the corner with Maia, and saw her rummaging through my lunch box.

"Really? Just a Dr. Pepper again?"

"Girl, don't try it, you know my appetite disappears when I enter this hellhole."

"I don't think that's normal, but you do you." Maia rolled her eyes, and went on her phone. We sat in silence for about ten minutes. Maia gorged on her bento box, stalking Sierra on Instagram while I stared at the ceiling sipping my Dr. Pepper.

"Find anything?"

"Not yet, she has a private account and hasn't accepted my request yet."

"Well, it has only been like twenty seconds. I *just* watched you send the request."

"Never mind! She accepted it. Oh. My. God. She wants me."

"Oh yeah! She is totally planning your big fat gay wedding as we speak!" To prove a point, I requested to follow her, was accepted in around thirty seconds, and shoved my phone in Maia's face.

"Damn. Just kill my dreams like that. I will never help you find a man again."

"I was kidding, she probably saw that you were following me. Also, when have you ever helped me find a man?"

"Uh, Connor?"

"You convinced me he wanted me and said 'womp womp' when he switched up..."

"Everyone makes mistakes, including someone as amazing as me. Deal with it." The lunch bell rang, and we raced to our next classes. Mine was in a completely different building, because for some reason, the science classes are separated from everything else. My first day in AP Biology, and it was ten times better than the first day of the preliminary course, Honors Biology. For starters, my new teacher, Mr. Ralph, didn't start off with a quiz on material we hadn't learned yet. In honors, I had gotten one out of five questions right, and started crying, using the test paper to hide my tears. The new teacher was also a lot more relaxed and kind than that devil who ruled the dungeon that was Room 212. He seemed a little unusual, but was still pretty chill, for now at least.

I finished the first science class I had enjoyed in a long time, and headed back to Ms. Bash's room. I expected to find the usual art students, aka the furries, the emo gays, and the anime fans. I did. But I also saw a familiar face sitting at the only empty table. Well, the only empty table that I could see. There was definitely some tunnel vision once I saw Alex. I took the seat next to him, and awaited instruction.

"Okay everyone, welcome to AP 3D Art. Today, I would just like to introduce myself and pass out the syllabus." Ms. Bash went over her expectations, personal interests, and the basics of the curriculum. After a short Q&A session on how the course would work, she passed out blocks of clay. "Even though this is an AP class, I am guessing most of you have no idea what you're doing. Play around with that, you're going to have to get used to it." Normally, at any other school than Hill Crest, this would not be necessary. However, the admin here trusted the students to choose their own electives, eliminating art prerequisites.

She proved to be right when Alex turned to me and said, "So, am I supposed to shape it with my hands or like with a pencil?" His question, while valid to a degree, didn't show a high level of understanding or self confidence. I gave him a few pointers, and began working on a sword. I usually don't care enough about games to think about them during school, but

Echoes was all that was on my mind. The bell sounded, and I wrapped up my handle with some saran wrap. Unfortunately for me, Alex did not have AP 2D Art after this. He left, and I stayed in my seat.

The new students piled into the room, and Ms. Bash gave a speech similar to her AP 3D one, and told us to sketch. We were expected to have sketchbooks, so no material was handed out. I continued to work on my sketch from last night, and was relieved to hear the final bell.

I went straight to my car, only to find the spot next to it empty. Maia had already left, probably so she could make fun of me for being "late" to our in-game meetup. I got home quickly, and strapped on my headset.

CHAPTER FOUR

"Mirage!" Selene's voice echoed in a sing-song tone.

"Yes?"

"Hurry up! Your internet is so slow, there is no reason for me to be able to see you hovering there like that."

"My bad?" I finally loaded in, and saw her staring me down. We headed towards the old village in the Plains, which looked stunningly different now. After freeing the Plains, the town became filled with villagers. Bakeries, smithies, and libraries hosted countless numbers of players and NPCs. The walkways were now cobblestone, with patterns in the shapes of waves. We walked down the winding road and found the others.

"Selene!" Sylvia ran over to us, "You too Mirage!" It was like she had forgotten me, but maybe Selene's behavior was just more memorable. With the shouting, cursing, and embarrassing moments, it is hard to forget her.

"Hey guys, where are we headed today?" I asked, the question pointed towards Lali and Rampi, as I expected them to have a plan.

Lali unsheathed her sword, raising it to the right, "To those mountains. The storm had obscured them before, but we have reason to believe that is the next area. I checked out the beach to the left of us and barely escaped alive. The enemies over there were too powerful, so I'm hoping those across the mountain are more our speed." Lali pulled out her log, displaying a hologram of a shark-like creature, the only information available was its level: **LVL 56.**

"Oh yeah, I am not going to that beach anytime soon." Even with getting the legendary sword from the last boss, I was only level eight, and everyone else was either level six or seven. Before heading to the mountains, we made a stop at one of the local bakeries. The building was small, with vines covering the sides and flowers blooming on a sign that read "Sonique Sweets." It showed how important Sonique really was around here.

"I'll take three cream puffs!" Selene yelled excitedly.

"You have to click on the menu, the worker isn't real..." I said, already having been assaulted with a flood of second hand embarrassment. After I got four croissants I headed out. The rest of the group paid for their pastries, and joined me on the path to the old temple. The contrast of the lush grass and sea of vibrant blossoms to yesterday's dark and dirty landscape was shocking and beautiful. We followed a similar cobblestone trail out to the mountains, but stopped when we saw a sign that read **"TURN BACK NOW OR FACE DEATH."**

"So cliche," Selene said, sighing, "This is literally still a part of the first area, calm down." She led everyone into the mountains, which started off as a relatively flat forest. Squirrel-like creatures brushed past us in a large herd, all running from something further down the path, eliciting a scream from Selene. Soon enough, a boar came charging at us. It was far enough away that we could get a good look before taking any action against it. Jammed into its left hind leg was an arrow, prodding it to run in pain. Sylvia and Rampi acted quickly, Rampi paralyzing the animal while Sylvia removed the arrow and healed it. The boar got up, produced a puny squeak and ran back into the woods.

While this solved the mystery of the herd, it only led to another: where did the arrow come from? The developers had discussed an archer class, but it hadn't been finished. "So... I'm guessing we are dealing with archers up here?" Sylvia said, throwing the arrow into the trees. We all grunted in either confusion or agreement, and headed further down the path. As we went on, the terrain got steeper and steeper. We eventually reached the top of the smallest mountain, which unfortunately, was facing another mountain. This disappointment started our trek across the taller mountain. There was only a very slender trail jutting out of the side of the steep bulge. We were almost to the top when we heard a scream from behind us.

"Help! I'm falling!" Rampi shrieked as the ground around her started falling, taking her with it.

"Coming!" I summoned Jinkx, and flew down to Rampi. We had decided not to keep our dragons out for spatial convenience, so my rescue was almost too late. I rode Jinkx down to a smaller mountain, and she grabbed Rampi with her claws. We flew back up to the path with the others, and Jinkx dropped us off, and took a spot in the sky next to us.

"It's so unfair that your dragon can fly, " Selene remarked, crossing her arms.

"Maybe you just aren't good enough, you know...with that lopsided eyebrow and water bottle ass figure." I retorted, rolling my eyes sarcastically.

"I know you aren't talking. Just because you have a fancy dragon doesn't mean you don't look an absolute mess," Selene clapped back, stirring even more confusion amongst the rest of the group. "This is normal for us, ignore it…" We continued up the mountain, eventually reaching a small clearing in the center of some spruce trees. The sun was setting, creating a pink and purple hued dusk that rested upon the Plains below. The moon was shining above us, quickly rising to take the place of the formerly beaming sun.

"I think we should camp out here until dawn, the nights here are only around ten minutes long. I think it's safest to take a break anyway." Rampi instructed us as she rested her staff against a tall spruce tree.

"Great idea Rampi, I'll set up some lights," Sylvia replied, waving her staff in a whirlpool motion, stirring a collection of miniature stars into a single orb. She placed the orb in the middle of the clearing, and we all sat down around it as if it were a campfire. Looking past the far edge of the clearing, the Plains were visible. Even in the dark, the warm lights from the village illuminated some of the Plains, displaying an array of cool toned flowers that sprawled over the terrain. I turned my attention to the old temple, which displayed an even more thrilling sight. Surrounding the circular building were hundreds of small flowers, all shining golden in the night. The temple itself was barely lit by its three lights, but the ocean of gold provided the otherwise drab temple with a sense of prosperity. The only thought that crossed my mind was how romantic the Plains appeared whilst cloaked in darkness. Selene took out Dawn, and sat next to me.

"So, how's it going?"

"Oh, yeah, I'm fine, just thinking."

"If it's about a boy I am going to throw you off of this mountain."

"Not a boy specifically, just how exciting it must be to be in this world with a lover. Look at the Plains, wouldn't that be romantic?"

"Ew. But yeah, it may just be a bunch of pixels but it's beautiful."

"As beautiful as Sierra?"

"Never. Some fake, boring ass grass or the woman of my dreams? Give me a challenge." Selene started laughing, getting a laugh out of me. We looked insane, but our fit of laughter was cut short by a loud noise. ***BOOM!***

We all snapped around, abandoning our respective conversations to stare at the trees. More booms followed, twigs snapping with each sound. Each *step*. Soon enough, two large yellow eyes were visible in the treeline. Before we could make out the figure, it lunged at Selene. A large troll with big, floppy ears, a humongous gut, and warts all over was revealed. Selene dodged the creature, "Damn that's big!" She ran it over to Sylvia's light, seemingly blinding it, and allowing me to knock it over. Despite its size, its reaction time was extremely fast. "Mirage, this whore has a bigger back than you!"

"Haha. So funny, bitch!" I yelled back to Selene. It quickly got up, stomping out the light before summoning a daunting ball and chain. The troll swung its chain, whipping the ball towards Lali. She blocked the hit, and the ball went flying towards me. "What are we supposed to do? We have so little space and this thing is taking up most of it!" I screamed while dodging the spiked orb.

The ball seemed to have a mind of its own, it predicted my movement, and oriented itself to where my jump would land me. I raised my sword, bouncing it back but it still took over half of my health. I ran around until I found somewhere to heal, taking out a croissant and stuffing it into my face. My health was full again, and I was ready to make a plan. I stayed put for a few minutes, analyzing the troll's movements and attacks. The creature appeared to only have three main attacks: stomp, slam and swing. It would use its heavy feet to shake the ground and crush anything in its way. Then it would slam its ball and chain downwards to create a similar effect, and swing it to get in a horizontal attack. By using our swords or shield magic, we could send the ball in a certain direction, taking the chain with it.

"I have an idea! Everyone, surround the troll, and hit the ball away when it swings!" We all gathered around the monster, taking our places at least three feet away from each other. The troll did its stomp and its slam, and as predicted, moved on to its swing. First Lali hit the ball, sending it towards me again, then I sent it to Selene. We bounced it back and forth until the chain surrounded the troll, confining its limbs and taking it down. This time, it didn't get up, but just laid there, defenseless.

We took turns getting a hit in, which took about three rounds of attacks due to its size and health. With a final slam of electricity from Rampi, the troll turned to dust, and its weapon dissolved into the ground. We all leveled up; some people leveled up twice, based on their contributions during the fight. We didn't gain any items, but we were relieved to be done. "And I thought the lizards were bad..." Selene mused, staring at the ground where the troll once laid.

The sun was up again, making the sky glow an orange and teal shine. We began heading back down the mountain, finally getting closer to the next area. Our group moved down the last stretch of steep rock, walking into another steady-grounded forest. The forest was filled with bright green trees, with birds singing atop the branches. That was, at least, for the first few trees. As we ventured further into the forest, the trees started turning a sickly raisin color. The leaves weren't falling off, but they assumed a similar brown-purple tone. The songs of the birds turned to ravenous screeches, and the once fluffy grass turned sharp and dangerous.

We eventually reached the end of the forest, which opened into an expansive valley surrounded by mountains.

The valley housed a large village, with houses and taverns for miles. What was likely a once lively and vibrant town was now a rotten wasteland. The buildings and paths seemed intact, but the natural essence of the valley appeared drained and infected. The grass was almost black, the air was tinted with a purple mist, and even bugs were scarce. We walked down the old path, and stumbled across a small inn. We walked inside, only to find the owner crying in the corner of the room. I approached the NPC, being careful in case it was actually hostile, and heard it muttering something. "He took it. He took it. He took it!" On the final utterance, the NPC shot up, grabbing my hands and shaking me. "Help us please! That beast has stolen our light! And we can't get it back ourselves!" A new quest appeared: "**FIND THE HEART**."

"What is that bitch on? Girl, calm down. You aren't real." Selene scoffed, getting ever more annoyed by the dramatics of these NPCs. We exited the inn, and began traveling further into the town. We reached what appeared to be a fountain, with two dragons dancing at its center, heads up. The mouths however, were not producing water, but a bubbling purple substance. "Ew..." Selene mumbled, "let's keep going." We continued down the path until we saw another troll. It had a similar appearance to the one from the mountains, but it was slimmer. It had the ball and chain, but also a cage in its other hand. We hid behind a building, and looked down the street. We could see five trolls attacking the squirrel-like creatures from the mountains and forcing them into the cages. The sight made my stomach churn.

"Oh my god. Do you remember what Illia said? Syphon is

using the land's flora and fauna for power, these must be some of his minions." I said, stunned by the atrocities in front of us. As I made the realization, a side quest appeared: "**SIDE QUEST: FREE THE QORLINS.**"

Selene started whining, "No! I know I just got mad at that NPC for being dramatic, but I draw the line at animals."

"You literally screamed out of fear the last time you saw a qorlin..."

"Shut up Mirage, you know I care for animals. They just caught me by surprise earlier." This was true; all of her honor society service hours were from the animal shelter. She even liked to work at rescue facilities over the summer. It wasn't surprising that her kindness extended to pixels.

"You're right, sorry, but how are we going to take on five of them? We barely took down one!"

"Leave it to me!" Selene hopped in, and pulled the attention of every single one of the trolls. They started swinging their chains menacingly as they rushed towards Selene. "Shit! Nevermind! A little help here?" We all jumped in from behind the building, and started fighting the trolls. They had less health than the large one on the mountain, but they were still tough to beat. Somehow, Selene was evading their attacks with the ease of a falcon. She turned, jumped, and even slid, throwing her staff into the air and collecting it when she got up. She summoned a pool that harmed both her and the enemies, and weakened two of the poachers down to a fourth of their health.

I quickly swooped in, "Here, Selene!" I stabbed my sword into the ground, watching five flowers grow in a star shape, filling Selene with health. Rampi was paralyzing the trolls left and right, really solidifying electricity as her favorite element. Lali drew some of them away, and Rufus chipped away at their health while Sylvia and I healed everyone.

Within minutes, the trolls were down, and the qorlins were free. The three animals jumped out of their cages, and headed towards the forest. As they were leaving, one turned around and ran back. The creature sprinted towards Selene, jumped onto her shoulders, and wrapped around her body until she held it in her hands. "Oh. My. God." Selene sounded like she was about to cry, "It's so cute!" We all got another message: **"QUEST COMPLETED: FREE THE QORLINS."** We all got some cage scraps and acorns deposited into our inventories, but Selene obviously got the rare bounty. "The pet naming menu is up..." Selene turned to stare at us, and jumped up and down in glee, "I'm naming you Holly!" I was the only one who knew it, but Holly also happened to be the name of her ten year old tabby cat.

Just as we were ready to go back to exploring, a loud noise filled the village. It was as if a piece of metal had been run through a shredder. The sound pierced our ears and left us stunned, shifting our focus to where it originated: the dragon fountain. From the poison filled well, a large mechanical rod emerged. It was slow at first, but as it got higher, it began ripping apart the earth around it. The object revealed itself: a large mechanical tube system, with shoots running like roots throughout the whole town. Its pipes were filled with steaming purple liquid, and the machine had a large deposit chamber on its... head? The chamber appeared large enough to fit one of the cages held by the trolls. From its body jutted large, ornate swords with circular carvings lining the way down to their vicious points. Above the swords was an alarm, with what appeared to be eyes above it.

It saw us, and its alarm began blaring, spinning with a red light reminiscent of a siren. It summoned three more trolls, this time without cages. One held a large hammer, and the two behind it held metallic bows. These bows must have been what was used to shoot that boar in the forest. Sure enough, the arrows the trolls drew looked exactly like the one found in the boar's leg. The troll heading the pack rushed towards us, and we all jumped back. I looked over to Selene, and Holly had hidden herself in Selene's robe. To my surprise, everyone seemed to have an idea of what to do. The melee players jumped at the frontrunner, and the mages focused on the two archers. Lali, Rufus, Apha, and I quickly finished off the first troll, and split up to take down the archers. I slid and jumped around arrows before ending up behind one of the beasts. Lali and Apha took the one on the left while Rufus helped me finish off the one to the right. The trolls were defeated at the speed of light, and we all regrouped.

The large robot let out a roar, which sounded more like pots and pans banging together. It threw down a sword, aiming for me. I leapt out of the way, and ran behind it. We had now initiated the boss fight.

I checked over its head, and saw its name "Metious: Syphon's Collector." So, this robot really did transport those poor animals through muck and grime to get to Syphon's lair. Metious swung its swords around like a mad-man, hitting anyone and anything in sight. This unpredictable attack pattern was bad for planning, but kept us safe if we maintained a good distance. At the base of each sword was a purple ring. "Hey! Can anyone with a ranged skill set try and hit those purple rings?" I asked.

"You've got it!" Rampi yelled back, summoning a bright amber ball and sending it flying towards the top right sword. The ball sharpened into a point as it flew, and hit the purple streak spot on. The sword went from being held at a sharp stance to going limp, but quickly flickered back to life. The other mages followed, striking the same sword's weak point until it fell off. The exposed joint took three hits, and the sword fell off the body. Unfortunately, this was only one of twelve swords. I tried to go for the joints, but got a slice to the ribs for my efforts. We waited, defending the mages as they took down each blade one by one. The removal of the blades had weakened the robot heavily, leaving only a sliver of health behind.

I knew this was my chance to do my part. I called for Jinkx, and flew above the robot. I jumped off of Jinkx's scaled back and flipped down onto the robot's head. Summoning Jinkx also brought some lag. I fought through the glitches and drove my sword into the area I assumed to be a deposit chamber, and watched my flowers do their magic. Metious' health dropped to zero, with flowers taking over its body. Roses, lilies, and other flowers bloomed across its body and extended into its roots. The entire mechanoid became covered in blossoms and vines before turning into dust. The head was the last to go, and it didn't dissipate like the other parts. Instead, it burst open, revealing a golden light. It was like a sun, with wavy light emitting from every inch of it. The light floated up into the sky and exploded, filling the land with a blinding light. Once the light had dissipated, the valley was transformed into a charming vale. The grass was green, the trees were covered in pink flowers, and the fountain was filled with water. The earth had been resettled and qorlins roamed freely across the outskirts of town. A message appeared: **"QUEST COMPLETED: FIND THE HEART."**

"Thank you, warriors," Illia's voice boomed over the valley, "I cannot be with you to celebrate, but you have restored yet another area to its past valor, and destroyed one of Syphon's hubs for trafficking. You have returned the core of Hearty Valley to its people, and provided the fauna with an oasis in which to frolic. Thank you."

CHAPTER FIVE

Tuesday, January 8th

It was a new day, and my first english essay was due. Well, not exactly due, but being written in full today. In AP, it's all timed and in class, so we can't work on the essays at home. I rushed out of my house, hopped in my Subaru and raced to the school. To my surprise, I beat Maia this time, and had to wait for her. I turned on a Yeule song and people-watched. There was a girl in the stereotypical lululemon get up, a girl with clothes adorned by dripping chains, and – ew. *Connor.*

Just as I was about to look down at my phone, Maia came speeding through the parking lot and spun into her spot. Her Kia Soul slammed between the white lines and landed danger-ously close to the passenger side of my car. She squeezed out, "Jeez. Couldn't have parked in a little more?"

"Me?" I pointed to my chest. "You're asking me? This isn't targeted to you? I am evenly inside the lines, that's all you." We made our way to our first classes of the day, and I was instantly met with the sore sight of Connor grinning at me. It was an impish grin, one that implied mischief and malintent. He stared at me until I got to my seat, and then jumped me with his petulant ass voice.

"So, have you found a man to deal with your obsessive ass?" I remained silent. "Yeah, didn't think so." I hadn't talked to him since sophomore year, but now he was messing with me again, why? Why did he have to fuck with my head, especially right before an essay? Part of me hoped that Alex would get his perfect-looking self out of his chair and pin Connor to the floor, but I knew my life wasn't that movie-esque. I barely knew Alex, and he was definitely too straight to help me out.

"Okay everyone, take your seats," Mr. Wills' voice filled the room, causing any chatter from my classmates to cease. "Today is your first in-class essay, so get out four pieces of paper, your books, and a pen with blue or black ink. A pen! I don't want to see any pencils. Pencils are for idiots!" He said it with a playful tone, but I knew he was serious. For the exam in May, we would only be allowed to use a pen, so why not start now? I got out all of my materials, grabbing an extra blue pen for safe measure.

I heard a tap on the front of my desk, "Hey, can I please have one? I didn't read the syllabus..." It was Alex, looking at me with fear in his eyes. I slid him a pen, trying not to blush. God, he was so stupid. I couldn't help smiling at the back of his head.

Mr. Wills found his way to the front of the room, and grabbed his manual timer. Somehow, in the twenty-first century, he was still using a manual timer. He cranked it to one hour, and waited for everyone's attention.

"Okay, get ready. Go!" He released the dial, and the timer began ticking down dramatically. I opened my book to its first blue annotation tab. Our essay prompt dealt with the literary principles used in *In Cold Blood* by Truman Capote. We were to find pieces of evidence that supported different themes, and write an essay in an hour. I found my quotes, and organized them by paragraph. I quickly wrote my introduction, and began flying through the body paragraphs. By the time I reached the third body paragraph, I still had thirty minutes left. I finished the rest, and had ten minutes to spare. I checked over everything twice, and just sat there waiting for the time to run out.

"Pens down!" A series of pointed thuds followed, and the room quickly fell silent. We all stood up, and deposited our essays into a metallic tray on his desk. As I left, I found Maia in the hallway, and made a horrified face at her.

"Essay was that bad, huh?"

"Oh no. The essay was fine. The people weren't," she looked confused, "I'll tell you during lunch." I got to Ms. Tati's room, and greeted Bostyn with a similar expression. "You will never believe what happened in AP Lang..."

"Oh no, what did Connor do?" I had told her about having first period with him, and I secretly loved that she expected him to be the problem.

"He asked me if I had a man yet, specifically one that could put up with my 'obsessive ass,'" I responded, cringing as I finished the sentence.

"That bitch! Oh my god, I am going to beat him up next time I see him. Who says that? It's been over a year, oh my god! He is so annoying, I actually hate him so much." As much as I loved having someone to degrade Connor with, once Bostyn starts, she doesn't stop. "He is actually so ugly, inside and out. Have you seen that nose? It's giving *Pinocchio*, even more so because he is such a liar!"

"Yeah... I agree," I sank into my chair, hoping for an end to this conversation. Sure, it was fun to bring up new advancements, but talking about Connor for too long made me nauseous. It reminded me of all he did, and how stupid I was for finding him attractive.

Ms. Tati came to my rescue, "Today, we will be writing a DBQ! Well, you will, I won't. Thank god." She mumbled the last part, but made sure we heard it. She passed around seven documents, some paper, and a rubric. She started a timer - digital because Ms. Tati lived in this century - and we started our writing. To no one's surprise, it was over the Gilded Age. I looked through the documents; various reports on fraud, corruption, and even charity. As per usual, I flew through the essay. The time was called, and Ms. Tati collected our papers. There was still some time left in class, but thankfully, Bostyn was too occupied by her phone to bring up Connor.

The bell rang, and I rushed to Ms. Bash's room. I saw Maia waiting at a table, and took a seat next to her. "So what happened in Lang?"

"Connor did."

"Oh! That's never good..."

"Yeah, he decided to ask me if I had found a man yet."

"Ew, why?"

"I don't know, it was so abrupt. He also made sure to bring up my 'obsessive ass.'"

"He probably wants a piece of *that* ass..."

"Maia!" My face turned to an expression of sheer horror.

"Just saying, I don't believe he was just straight the whole time. But anyway, he isn't worth it, so don't let him get to your head." She seemed to house excitement behind her eyes, which conflicted with her sincere tone.

"How has your day been?" I asked, trying to see how quickly she could crack. It was immediate.

"So glad you asked! So sorry about that Connor stuff, but I have good news!" She paused for dramatic effect, "I got Sierra's number!" She let out a squeal, and grabbed my hands, locking our fingers and shaking them with glee.

"Go you! How though?" While Maia was very open and bubbly with me, she was shy when unfamiliar people were around - at least in the real world.

"We are doing a project together."

"So, did she pick you as her partner?"

"At some point in our lives, yes she absolutely will, and we will likely hyphenate our name. No, Ms. Robinson did, but like I said, we are meant to be. I will be her partner sooner or later."

"I need a man to be so blind about..." I responded, slightly jealous of her crush. Our delusion-filled discussion ended, and Maia ate her lunch while I drank my Dr. Pepper. My phone was propped up on an easel so we could watch an episode of *Dance Moms*, and Maia searched through forums on *Echoes*. Our lunch period was soon over, and I headed to biology.

Mr. Ralph didn't have an essay for us like my other teachers, but instead had a project. It was a slideshow, on whichever organelle we were assigned. I was given Golgi, and the assignment was due on Thursday. Only two days to finish it. We were given time in class to do research, and I got to learn all sorts of thrilling information about the organelle's packaging skills. The bell finally went off, and I could get to my escape. Art classes were the only things helping me suffer through these long school days.

The handle to my sword was laying at my table as soon as I entered the room. I made my way to Ms. Bash's desk, "Thanks for setting my piece out, that was so nice."

"Huh?" She looked up from her book, "Oh, I didn't do that, must've been Alex." Alex? Alex brought my piece to the table, our table?

I found my seat, "Thanks for bringing that over, Alex." I gave him my best straight-bro nod.

"No problem! I need a favor though." So that's why he went out of his way to get my sword. "Can you show me how to sculpt?"

"Uh, sure? I mean, it really depends on what you're making. What is it that you're trying to make?" He pulled out his phone, and to my surprise, opened Pinterest. I didn't know straight men used Pinterest. He navigated to a board he had saved, which showed a small collection of oak trees and what I believed to be... pixie dust.

"I want to make a magical looking tree," he said, obviously getting embarrassed, "I know we can't really sculpt the dust but I would just paint with gold trim or something." The tree idea reminded me of something out of *Echoes*, or really any basic fantasy world.

"Okay so..." We began working out how to make the trunk, and I provided him with some sculpting tools to cut pieces and manage the clay as he wished. He had worked up a small lump, which came to a rounded point, and had some swirls in the sides, "It's... nice!" I said, grimacing. Despite how long it took him to make, it fell down in a second.

"Dammit. I really hoped it would stay!"

"It's okay, you can definitely do better than that. Here," without thinking, I grabbed his hands. Like game controllers, I used his hands to mold the clay into a log shape, and after I realized what I was doing, I immediately threw them down. How was I so dumb? Not even Maia would do something so idiotic. I became pink in the face, "Sorry!" I went straight back to working on my sword, and Alex just kept trying to get his tree to work, seemingly unphased by the interaction. I caught him staring at my sword handle a few times, sometimes with awe and others with confusion. I couldn't tell if he liked it, wanted to know how I was making it, or was trying to place exactly what it was. I brushed off his varying glances, and added more details to the piece until the bell sounded.

Alex got up, and left the room with a short, "Bye, thanks!" For the rest of the day, I worked on a new piece for my portfolio. I decided my portfolio should be rooted in what I enjoyed, so the topic would be titled "Where the Virtual Bleeds into the Truth." For the first piece, I chose to draw Holly. Well both Hollys. Holly the cat started from the left of the paper, running to the right. As she neared the right, she began to turn into Holly the qorlin. Her setting shifted from Maia's living room to a field of pixels. Not like those in *Echoes*, where you can't make out individual pixels, but a more matrix-y look. I only had part of the sketch done by the time class ended, but I had high hopes for the project.

As the day ended I entered the parking lot to find that Maia had already left. It surprised me because we had no plans to continue our virtual adventure tonight. I got in my car, and left. As I passed the soccer fields, I noticed Alex on the green turf holding a ball in one arm. I could've sworn he waved at me, but I couldn't be sure. Whether it was a wave or not, it brought a smile to my face. After getting stopped at an annoying amount of traffic lights, I got home and was quickly greeted by my mom. "Hey honey, how was school?"

"It was fine, boring I guess."

"I get that same response everyday, tell me something exciting!"

"Well I got to write two timed essays! Isn't that thrilling?"

"Okay, never mind. That does sound boring."

We curled up on the couch and loaded up Mario Kart.

"I can only play for a little bit, I have a biology project due on Thursday."

"Ew, I am so glad I'm not in school anymore." I was sure this was true. She had been to three different schools while getting her PhD, and had endured enough academic trials for three people. We selected our normal characters, and did our four courses. To my surprise, she actually beat me. "Yes! It has been a hot minute since I beat your ass! Bad wording, that makes me sound abusive." I laughed, and gave her a hug before heading upstairs. I spent about two hours on the project, producing a twenty page slideshow with polished visuals and at least three sources. I would've pushed off this assignment til the next day, but I had too many other assignments to be procrastinating. I read ahead in our next AP Lang reading, *The Great Gatsby*, and went to sleep.

In my dreams, the white and pink dragon was back again. It was flying this time, with its pale scales glistening in the moonlight. Upon it was now a rider, flying side by side Jinkx and I. The rider was obscured, with only a stocky framed silhouette, I could not make out any details. The two flew away, doing a flip that eclipsed the bright moon above. They disappeared, leaving Jinkx and I floating in the sky. We stayed like that for what seemed like hours, watching as the stars twinkled above. After a while, I decided to look down. What I saw made me practically stand up on Jinkx's back. Below us was an expansive forest, consumed in a flame that almost reached the clouds.

CHAPTER SIX

Thursday, January 10th

The school day was nothing short of boring. We went over our essays from the previous day, which Mr. Wills made sure we knew he had stayed up until *3:00am* to grade. I had gotten a 5 on the essay, and was more than okay with that. I didn't mean to, but from the corner of my eye I noticed that Alex had only gotten a 2.

All my other classes were similarly boring, producing little academic value, and only brewing anticipation for the ring of the final bell.

As soon as I got home, I ran to my room. The group had plans to take on the next area, and I refused to be late again. We had agreed to meet in the base town with the cathedral, which Sylvia had informed us was named Wysteria. I traveled to the plaza that we had all first met in many days ago. Quickly, I found Rampi and Lali, and waited for the others. "Hey Mirage! The others aren't here yet, but we have some news once everyone is here." Rampi's announcement confused me, but I was also excited. Part of me expected her to be announcing their departure from Selene and I, another wished they would ask us to stay.

"Hey!" Sylvia came strutting down the town center with Apha and Rufus in tow. We all circled around, awaiting Selene's arrival. After five minutes of awkward silence, Selene came barreling through the plaza. If the shops weren't fixed, she would have knocked them down as she ran barbarically towards us.

"I'm here! Sorry for the wait!"

This was my opportunity to mess with her. "Oh my god, Selene! We were waiting five minutes for you! Five whole minutes, what is wrong with you?"

"Okay *smart ass*. Sorry for being impatient in the past. Happy now?"

"Actually, yes. I am."

"So..." Rampi started talking. "Would you all agree that we work pretty well together?" Everyone nodded in affirmation. "Well, Lali and I were doing some thinking."

Lali took over, "We would like to create a guild! It doesn't have to be big, just us. We believe it would tie us all together and make it easier to organize play sessions. We can also create a group on the ViLar app to keep in touch!"

Rampi spoke again, "Our different skills have combined beautifully in the past two areas, and we would love to maintain that energy."

"I think that sounds great, do we have a name?" I asked, and everyone turned to Lali and Rampi for an answer.

"Yes, actually. We were thinking 'The Sleepless Knights.' Now, I know not everyone here is a knight, but I think it's cute. I thought of it when we were playing at 1:00am last week... Which just proves the 'sleepless' part." Rampi laughed wryly then looked around the circle as if she expected opposition.

"You know what? I know I'm generally pretty snarky, but I love that!" Selene exclaimed, rushing towards Rampi with excitement. We elected Rampi and Lali as our leaders, and the guild invites were sent out. Shortly after the metaphorical paperwork was finished we all went down to the nearest tavern and bought drinks to celebrate. Of course, they were pointless, just a use of five coins. However, the act made us seem like a group of real friends.

In one quick, fake swig, we finished our drinks, and headed out of town. Now that we were all past level 8, our dragons were ready to be ridden. We got to the bridge, and summoned our companions. Apha had barely missed the pre-order menu, so she got on Rampi's lavender toned dragon. We flew above the bridge, and found our way to the plains.

We passed the glistening fields of pastel flowers, reaching the mountain range. We all pushed our dragons to go even higher up, passing the mountain tops and reaching the valley. Just as we were about to push past the far mountains, our dragons got forced back, sending us spiraling. With haste, we rushed to regain control of them, and Apha almost fell off. "I guess there's a boundary? Probably because we haven't cleared the next area yet." Rampi verbalized what I was thinking.

Most games were like this, they'll give you a perk but it has its limits. "That reminds me, and I had completely forgotten, let's limit our dragon use from now on. I think it's okay for travel, but we all experienced that lag when Mirage attacked the boss in the Valley."

Everyone turned to look at me, most of them crossing their arms. "My bad," I said with a wince. I didn't know they had felt it too.

We eased our dragons down to the land and dismounted, dismissing them as we walked towards the mountains. Luckily for us, we didn't have to cross any more tall peaks. The path inside the valley's village extended to the outer mountain range, and cut through two mountains. There was just enough room to walk to the next area on a flat surface. We walked past the large rocks until it all blended into a forest. Tall spruce trees surrounded us, with small beams of light shining down upon us. After several minutes of travel in the woods, we reached a tattered fence. There were two gates that read **"KEEP OUT."** The fence was adorned with red and white mushrooms, which also lined the grass we walked on.

"Well, I'm going in." Selene pushed open the gate, and we were instantly met with a very different scene. The bland forest transformed into a teal-hazed woodland with fog grazing the ground. Moths fluttered from the trees up into the shining sun. We continued further into this new forest, and saw a tiny village. Not tiny in the sense of acreage, as it expanded over several miles. It was tiny in height. Short mushroom houses lined a complex series of pathways. These houses only reached our knees, their chimney smoke dusting our faces.

We followed the stepping-stone paths until we reached a larger, more dignified building. In front of the structure was a small gnome, pacing back and forth. "Thank the heavens! You're here!" He squeaked, stopping his pacing and turning to us.

"You have to save our land! Our Forest used to be a haven to a diverse population of creatures, but Syphon has ripped us apart. He installed two walls, separating our beloved home into three sections. In doing so, he tricked our neighbors in the center forest. Who once used to be our friends now view us as a wicked evil.

They can't see what's behind the two walls, but they still think it's Syphon." The gnome pointed to a large wall further back in the forest, to my surprise, a flaming rock was being hurled over it, and into the mushroom forest. Rampi was quick to throw a spell at it, redirecting it far into the sky. After she deflected the rock, a quest appeared for everyone: "**REUNITE THE FOREST**."

We ventured over to the giant wall, which was reinforced by iron and barbed wire. The mix of metals and spikes was contrasted concerningly with the rest of the Forest's architecture. We used everything we could; from attack combos and ice spells to first barrages and electricity, it would not budge. Just as we were about to give up, Rampi spotted something atop the wall.

"Look! Up there!" On top of the wall sat a large green wolf. It was watching us struggle intently, but with no visible reaction. Rampi shot a beam of lightning at the dog, and it turned its head to dodge the attack. After a few seconds, the wolf got up, and leapt down from its perch.

The creature rolled on the ground, got up, and bared its teeth, growling. Now that it was closer, I could get a good look. It had a mainly black coat, with glowing green swirls. Its teeth were as sharp as knives, and its claws stretched out to a gnarly curl. It jumped into the air, gaining height above our heads, and crashing down onto Lali.

"Why me?" It grabbed her ankle, and started dragging her around. "I guess this is what I get for being a tank." Rampi threw lightning its way, hitting its stomach and causing it to whine in pain. The attack caused Lali's captor to release her, and she quickly jumped back to where I was standing. Unlike the past enemies, the wolf did not have a name. Its health bar however, was already at half from Rampi's hit.

"Good job Rampi!" I shouted, and then watched as the wolf knocked her down. "Well..."

"Thanks? I think..." Rampi yelled back as she was pulled around in the dirt. I hit the creature with my sword and grabbed Rampi, taking her to safety and healing her. After a few more hits, the wolf collapsed with a whine, and stopped breathing. It did not turn to dust or seep into the dirt however, and before we could investigate, the wall began to rumble.

The metallic block shifted down, making a clicking sound and pausing every few seconds until its top was level with the ground. Even more barbed wire lined the top of the wall. As we cautiously stepped into the next part of the forest, I looked back. The wolf was still there, but it didn't show any signs of life.

Quickly after entering the second forest, we were met with another fireball. Rampi countered it again, and we readied our defenses. A small humanoid creature flew towards us with rage, and came to a quick stop as soon as it saw us. "You're here! Oh my, you're here!" It was a faerie, or pixie, or something like that. "We are getting attacked from both sides, and we could really use your help, warriors!" The faerie flew closer to us, and stared at us awkwardly. It took us almost a minute to notice a chat log option next to it. Our options were:

What?

No! You don't understand!

How can we help?

"I say we go with '***What?***'" Selene joked. After some deliberation, we chose the second option.

As soon as we clicked it, the faerie knew everything. "What? The gnomes are still over there?"

On cue, the gnome from earlier came tumbling into the faerie territory. "Valia! Please tell your troops to end this madness, it's just us!" He panted and took a seat on a small stone.

"Hester? Oh my, I am so sorry! I thought Syphon still had forces around us. That wolf up there kept terrorizing us at night, and I assumed he was one of yours. The same thing has been happening from Amethyst Woods." Valia turned to the other side of the faerie forest, and pointed to another wall. Just as she had said, there was a wolf right on top of it, this time appearing more orange toned.

Before the two got in another word, an arrow came flying over the wall. It made contact with a nearby tree, and let out a purple fog. The tree lost its leaves immediately, and turned a deep raisin color. Hester looked stunned.

"Oh no, I think they are fighting back now. The kiri have access to some of the most poisonous flowers. They may be beautiful, but when cultivated correctly, they pack a punch." So the habitants of the other part of the forest, or Amethyst Woods, were scared enough to fight now as well. If we didn't lower all the walls soon, this forest would go up into flames and ruin.

A chill went down my spine as I remembered the dream I had the previous night. My grandmother always claimed to be a prophet, and it was how she caught her ex husband cheating. It felt like a hate crime that I could know about the events of a game the night before, but not how I would get screwed over in real life. So much for familial privilege.

"Warriors, you have to bring that disastrous wall down. There is no way the kiri will trust us if they can't see us." Valia was crying now, floating down to Hester for comfort. We began our trek to the next wall, passing a war ravaged town. Beehives were smashed on the ground, mushroom and acorn houses were cracked and dying. The children of the faerie forest were shivering under leaves as they mourned the loss of their homes and families.

"I know they aren't real, but it just makes my heart hurt, you know?" Sylvia mused. "It makes you think about those in our world, doesn't it?" My heart dropped, I had never thought of games that way. That they maybe took inspiration from the atrocities occurring in the real world. I shook off my discomfort, and sped up to rejoin Selene at the front of the group.

"What do you think is going to happen?"

"I have no clue, I can just hope the Kiri are as understanding as the other two. I mean, what if they're real bitches?" Selene was obviously being dumb, and it brought a smile to my face. We finally reached the wall, and Selene took it upon herself to taunt the wolf this time.

"Come on bitch!" She sent a focused orb of red magic at it, and missed it. Before her next blast, she beckoned towards herself with her hands, moving back and forth as if to ask the dog to square up.

"Really? Get down here!" This time, she hit it, and instead of gracefully leaping down, the wolf fell off of the wall. The wolf had a similar pattern to the green one, the only difference being its deep orange swirls. It got up, shook off the fall, and circled us, fangs out. The wolf leapt at me, with foam flying out of its mouth as it soared.

"Ew! Keep your rabies-prone ass away from me!" I squealed as I blocked it with my sword, and it used the blade as a platform, bouncing off me and redirecting its attention to Rufus. The orc hit his attacker square in the jaw, sending it flying towards Lali.

We all surrounded the monster to get in our final attacks, but it shot straight up, soaring above us and behind our circle. It knocked down Lali and Rampi, then jumped on Apha. Rufus pulled the wolf off of her, only to be met with a bite to the face.

"Wow. This one is a little feisty, goddamn." Selene sent another ball towards the wolf, knocking it to its feet. While she distracted it, I healed the others, bringing them back to their feet. We raced back to the fight, only to find Selene with the wolf under her heel, looking at us triumphantly.

Valia and Hester regrouped with us, ready to talk to the kiri. Just like the last wall, this wall lowered with a few clicks. To my surprise, the lowering of the metal veil revealed an industrialized town. The duck-like citizens were riding zip lines that reached the highest peaks of orchid colored trees.

The duck creatures were built just like those in the real world, with bills, wings, and webbed feet. The only difference was their ability to use machinery. I saw ducks, or kiri, driving small segway-like platforms into construction sites.

Bright purple flowers were being harvested left and right, and it even appeared they had been over cultivated; next to sparse collections of vibrant flowers were gray patches of grass. Hester pushed through us, running towards a busy construction site. "Himi! Himi! Where are you?"

A burly kiri came crawling out from under a stack of logs, and his eyes narrowed. "Hester? What are you doing here, traitor?"

"Wait!" It was Valia. "I thought that too, but the attacks aren't from him, or any of us. Syphon left around some watchers, and they are the ones who came in and tore up our belongings in the dead of night. I made the mistake of attacking both of you, but my fear was misdirected. These heroes have helped us lower the walls, and defeat the wolves. Please, Himi, stop with the attacks, the forest is free now!" I expected a quest completion notification to appear, but nothing popped up.

A loud galloping sound came from the faerie forest, and it sounded doubled. We all turned around to see the two wolves charging at us. We readied our weapons, but the wolves bounded over us, taking a place before our group.

They snarled at us for a few seconds before jumping in the air again. The two leapt and stationed themselves midair, spinning in circles as they did so. It was as if they were dancing. They took a short break, stared at each other and howled. It was their encore. They smashed into each other, emitting a sharp light.

Once the light waned, a larger wolf was revealed. It had too many teeth to fit into its snout, making its snarl even more menacing. It maintained the stark black coat as its predecessors, but had deep red swirls that stretched over its lanky body.

Above its health bar, no, health bars, finally read a name, "Grimsolad." Grimsolad growled, its drool searing the ground, leaving burn marks. We all took a step back. "How are we supposed to beat something with three health bars?" I asked, dumbfounded. Almost in response to my inquiry, a herd of faeries and kiri came rushing to our aid. The faeries hurled large flaming rocks at the beast, aiming with the utmost precision.

After a relentless assault on the wolf, the faeries raced back to their slice of the forest. It was time for the kiri to step in. Dozens of kiri archers drew their bows, and released a haunting barrage of purple tinted arrows. The giant yelped as the arrows turned it into a porcupine. The arrows dissolved, taking down the last half of the first health bar. The arrows left behind a withering effect, which took a small amount of the wolf's health every few minutes.

We were now in a good position to take down this hellhound. We charged the beast, each melee player taking a leg. As we attacked the paws, the wolf came tumbling down. With a blitz of mage attacks, the second health bar was down. I had been pushed to the offensive, and couldn't do much to heal others.

We were hanging by a strand, and I had to get out of the front lines. I waved my sword in a series of angled strokes, which created a sharp rose shape, and slammed the blade into the grass beneath the wolf. A large light burst from under the sword, taking the outline of a rose, and filling everyone's health.

Selene took a leap, and slammed her staff to the ground. She created a damage pool, putting herself at risk to take down the boss. I ran to her aid, slicing thin air with my blade to send small pink petals her way, healing her while leaving the wolf defenseless.

Selene's trick worked, causing the last health bar to dwindle down to a miniscule amount of health. She herself was also left with little health, and due to my continued aid, I couldn't refill it. She blasted another orb at the creature, hitting it straight on the forehead, and collapsed.

Sylvia created a healing pool around her as we watched the wolf lift off of its gigantic paws. It spun around, less elegantly than in its dance from earlier, and burst into light.

The kiri leader walked up to us, smiled and delivered grim news. "Great job warriors, but I must warn you. Syphon has taken most of our amethyst blossoms, and is using their power for malicious purposes. If used correctly, they are an amazing and renewable source of energy.

However, they hold poisonous properties, and if in the wrong hands, could create horrific weapons." I immediately realized that we had dealt with the poison before. Metious must have been powered by the flowers, and the poor extraction of their essence had resulted in the leak. I shuddered as I thought of what that meant for the animals taken from the valley.

A new notification appeared: **"QUEST COMPLETED: REUNITE THE FOREST."** We all got the usual payout, some materials and coins, but it was apparent that Selene got a little something extra. "Oh my god! Guys! Look, I got a staff!" She stared at her new staff in awe. It was an unpolished piece of wood, chiseled to a sharp point at the bottom. Spiraling the wood were mushrooms and a few amethyst blossoms.

"Selene, quick, check the rarity on that thing." She obliged, and was shocked when she found out.

"Holy shit! 'Legendary.' It says there are only four in the game!" She ran around the town in circles, almost destroying a campsite. She took a break and checked its abilities. "This is perfect. It drains the enemy's health just like those arrows did. It doesn't say anything about hurting me though, so this is gonna be a game changer!"

CHAPTER SEVEN

Saturday, January 12th

The weekend had come, but we had no plans to liberate any virtual worlds. The guild had established a weekly time to play *Echoes*: Thursday. Sylvia, Selene, and I all had school, and the rest had jobs. Somehow, everyone who was employed had Thursdays off, and none of us students cared about staying up late, so we could easily adapt to that schedule.

I was headed out to Maia's house when I saw a cat in my yard. It was white and fluffy, with a soft pink nose dotting its tiny face. The cat had a silver glittery collar, so I just took a picture and posted it to our neighborhood page.

My neighbors were a little too trustworthy of their cats; you could find at least one cat roaming the neighborhood per day. I guess they were right to trust them, as I never once saw a missing poster go up. I got into my car, and headed out of the neighborhood. While we lived in a gated neighborhood, the gate rarely worked, and usually just stayed open. However, the gate was now magically working. I pressed the dark green button with "exit" sprawled across it in aggressive lettering, waited for the buzz, and drove through the flimsy gate.

I drove past the school again, dreading going back in a day. I loved academics, but the stress of my current classes had made that passion wane. Ruining my routine drive to Maia's house, I checked the soccer fields as I passed. For some reason, I was disappointed to not see Alex there. Not like I would have ever gone to say hi to him - I would never willingly step foot on a soccer field. As cute as Alex was, soccer was still the second most unattractive sport to me, only losing to golf.

I turned into Liverpool Estates, and found Maia's tall house. I walked up to the front door, and waited for her to let me in.

Instead, her mom opened the door. "Hello Zack! So great to see you, come on in!" I accepted, petting Tippy as I walked towards the kitchen. To my surprise, I found Maia sitting on a barstool. I had assumed she was upstairs given that she hadn't been the one to meet me at the door.

"Hey." She mumbled, obviously consumed by her phone.

"Maia, don't be rude, get him a drink."

"I'm okay, really." I said, giving her mom a quick hug then walking closer to Maia. I peered over her shoulder, she was stalking Sierra's instagram.

"Ah. I see we are in our Ricardo López era.."

She looked up from the dim screen. "Huh? Who is that?"

"Sometimes I forget you aren't very cultured. He's the guy who stalked Björk."

"Oh yeah! The watermelon guy. You made me watch a documentary on YouTube about that. Ew! I am not like him. What the hell?" She laughed, closing her phone. We headed towards the stairs, passing a narrow hallway and some family photos. We reached the stairs, grazing the wrapped garland around the rail.

It was a couple weeks into January, and they still had their Christmas decorations up. Not the outside lights and inflatables, thank god, but the indoor accessories. The walls were lined with warm fairy lights, the banisters were wrapped in light up garland, and the tree stood tall with flashy ornaments in the foyer. It was a Christmas tradition bred from sloth. For the past three years, the "difficult to take down" decor was removed first, and the indoor was left up until February.

After ascending the festive flight of steps, we reached Maia's room. As a response to the piercing afternoon light, her curtains were tightly drawn. Her LED lights were set to a soft pink, and her tapestries hung elegantly from the ceiling. Maia's bed frame was light gray, with tall posts forming a canopy. The frame was draped in star-lined tulle, which lit up with a sparkling golden hue. It finished the aesthetic of Maia's room with a dreamy glow.

Maia pulled back the tulle and motioned for me to take a seat. I sat down, placing a pillow behind my back, and pulled out my laptop. We turned on *Dance Moms*; it was the episode where Abby made the girls dance around with golden guns. We laughed at how clunky the guns looked, and how insane it was to make kids spin with firearms in hand. We managed to finish the whole episode before Maia went back to stalking Sierra.

"So..." I started, trying not to sound rude. "Got anything to share?"

"No, she's just really pretty." Maia spaced out, and I had to snap at her to get her attention.

"Do you think she could be into girls? Like has she said anything to make you think that way?" We sat in silence as Maia racked her brain.

"Yes actually!"

I was already scared. "Let's hear it..."

"She said Rina Sawayama was hot."

"Okay, well I'm gay and I agree. But it is surprising she knows Rina. I mean, she is for the gays." As I thought through it, my confidence in Maia's hope-driven gaydar increased. "I haven't heard of a straight person who likes her now that I think of it."

"See! I'm not that crazy. I am still scared she would shoot me down though." As gay kids, we always wanted to take chances on love. Books and movies made romance seem possible, but we also knew it wouldn't be picture perfect. We always ran the risk of accidentally approaching a straight person, and if they were ignorant enough, getting outed or used.

"Why don't you ask her to hangout?" If this ended poorly, I knew I would have to pay the consequences.

"Yeah what a great idea!" Maia barked, rolling her eyes.

"No, I'm serious. You don't have to make it sound like a date, just ask to go shopping or something. See what happens." I realized I was being naive, but still pushed it. Hoping that maybe one of us could experience teenage love.

"You know what? I'll do it, but you have to talk to that boy."

I knew who she was talking about, but I played dumb. "Who?"

"Bitch, you know who I mean. That lanky soccer player that makes you drool."

"Okay, I do not drool. Also, there is no way he is gay."

"First off, yes you do. You look just like that fatass downstairs when I'm making her food." She was talking about Tippy. "And don't tell me about gaydar, you know how I feel about my chances with Sierra. Come on, I won't make a move if you don't." She grabbed my phone off the foot of the bed and threw it at my face.

"I don't know..." I had been scared to make a move since the Connor situation, and it showed.

"Okay, let's settle it." Maia whipped out her switch, and connected it to her TV. I was always jealous of her switch. We both had one, but she had the Animal Crossing edition, and younger me desperately wanted it. I shed a tear when she face-timed me with an unboxing five years before.

Maia got out two pro controllers - we were not single joy-con people - and opened Super Smash Bros. We selected our characters, choosing polar opposites. She chose the menacing dragon from Metroid, Ridley. In contrast to her dark and threatening beast, I chose Princess Daisy. She didn't have any unique moves, as she was a mirror character of Princess Peach, but I thought she had the better outfit and hair. She selected the basic map, and pressed play.

We decided to play three rounds, one life each. First to two wins got their way. I started off strong, Daisy used her body-guard, Toad, to send Ridley flying. Unfortunately for me, the dragon could actually fly. He quickly bounced back, flapping back up to the platform. Maia skillfully grabbed my character by the throat, and threw me off of the platform. My parasol could not save me, and I fell into the void. It was now 0:1, in favor of Maia. We started the next round, and I planned an assault. I bumped into the monster, and as he flew back, I smashed a turnip into his face. The score became 1:1, an even match. The final match was a harmonious disaster.

We both hurled impressive attacks at each other. Switching from special attacks to punches, quickly running down the clock. We evaded every attack we could, and those we couldn't, we countered with powerful blows. The time ran out, and it was time for a death match. My heart raced as the fake announcer yelled "sudden death," and dropped as he said "go." It was all too fast for me. Maia grabbed me, and instantly threw me off of the map. We finished with the score 1:2. I had lost.

"Well that was fun!" Maia exclaimed, finding my phone and shoving it into my hands.

"You first. What am I doing? I don't even follow him."

"What? You don't follow him? Why did we do all of that? Just follow him, that's enough for today. You would look desperate as hell if you followed him and immediately asked to hang." Such kind and helpful words.

"Okay, we can do it together. Get your message ready." Maia typed out her message, and I found his account: *Alex_-Gre.ene13.*

She counted down from three, and we made our moves. In harmony we let out deep sighs, then waited impatiently. Within seconds, I got a follow request back from Alex. "Well, that was fast."

"What? He already followed you back? Maybe he is into you... or just really nice. That is your weakness, nice straight men."

I glared at her. "So where is Sierra?"

Maia responded with a horrified look. "She is typing." She let out a shriek, and threw the phone into my lap. "I can't look, read it for me." I took her phone, and accidentally let a pained expression slip out.

"Oh shit. What did she say? Probably 'leave me alone you freak.' She did say that, didn't she?" Maia shot up, and started pacing around the room.

"Uh, well... it could be worse, or better, depending on how you view it. She did not call you a freak, but she did say 'OMG of course bestie!' with a collection of different cat emojis. So, good luck!" I put a special emphasis on "bestie," just to show why I reacted the way I did.

She snatched the phone out of hands and began typing. "You know, maybe she is playing it safe." I wanted to believe she was as calm as her tone, but the panting proved otherwise. I hung around for another hour, and headed home. My mom had spaghetti ready, and we settled down to watch *Gilmore Girls*.

CHAPTER EIGHT

The weekend was soon over, and AP Lang was calling me back. Mr. Wills passed out our most recent assignments. Luckily, we didn't have to write a whole essay, but we had to write three paragraphs. Again, I got a high A. I felt bad doing so, but I looked up at Alex's paper. To my surprise, he had only gotten one point less than I had.

For the first half of the day, school went on as it would any other day. Ms. Tati gave us some short answer practice, which was finally over a new unit, Unit Seven: Imperialism.

Maia and I ate in the art room again, but this time, Maia spilled watercolor paint into my Dr. Pepper, rendering it inedible.

We got our scores back from Friday's presentations in biology. I only got a 95 because my "slide style was distracting." I wondered what was distracting about an off-white backdrop with slate pink accents, but took my high score with resigned glee.

The true twist came in the first art class of the day. I continued working on my sword, this time constructing the main blade. I was deep into the curvature of the shape when I felt a soft tap on my shoulder. "Yes?" I asked, scared he may have been wanting to berate me for how I acted last week.

"Sorry to bother you, but I had a question, if that's okay?" So this was it. He would either confess his love for me or tell me to kill myself.

I braced myself for either outcome. "Sure, shoot."

"I was hoping you could help me with Lang. Like tutoring or something? It's so embarrassing, but I haven't been doing too well, and Mr. Wills said you were his best student." That was weird, not only because I had seen his recent scores, but because Mr. Wills does not talk to students unless he needs to. Mr. Wills had not called Alex to his desk since the first day.

I brushed it off. "Sure, if you think it will help you."

"Great! Thank you so, so much. Does Thursday work?"

I almost forgot about *Echoes* when he said that. "No, actually, that is the one day I am busy."

"That's okay, what about Friday?"

"That should work, my house?"

"Sounds great!" As we wrapped up our conversation, the bell sounded. He waved, and took off, leaving me there dumbfounded. In a few days, I would have a boy over at my house.

CHAPTER NINE

Thursday, January 17th

Thursday afternoon had rolled around, and Rampi had a surprise for us. She took us back to Wysteria, leading us past tall buildings and a concerning amount of smithies. We passed chattering groups of NPCs and players alike, trying to ignore their conversations for our own sakes. To my surprise, we passed the cathedral, heading to the outskirts of the city. Rampi took a quick left turn, squeezing us into an alley, and making a stop at a short building to the right of us. "Ta da!"

"What are we looking at?" Selene asked, with a hint of fear in her voice.

Rampi searched for something in her inventory, and pulled out a light blue key. She stabbed it into the center of the door and twisted the handle. We all filed in, finding our places around a long table. "Now that we are officially a guild, I thought we should have a guild hall!" Despite its small exterior, the inside was at least ten times larger.

"How did you afford this? Buildings are like twenty thousand coins." I asked, my eyes checking out the intricately-designed chandelier above us.

"Lali and I went to the Plains and farmed last night! It was all my idea, but Lali was nice enough to help out. That's what younger sisters are for!" It all made sense. No wonder they worked so well together, they had been doing so their whole lives.

Selene was staring at her, I could only imagine how quickly her jaw had fallen to the floor. "You're sisters? Why didn't we hear about this earlier?"

"Oops. Did I say that? Oh well, we trust you guys enough. Yes we are. We actually got this game so we could be more connected. Lali lives on the east coast and I live on the west." Wow. That meant no matter where the others are from, our guild stretches across the entire country.

"That's so cute! I don't want to refer to you two as 'the sisters' though… that would be too 'friendship is magic' for me." Selene said, her volume trailing off as she spoke.

Rampi gave us an order to go explore, and we scoured every room in the hall. Selene and I went up a steep stairwell to the second floor, and began checking the rooms. One had a library, another a kitchen, and the rest were bedrooms. We went back downstairs, and checked behind the stairs. Another hallway housed five bedrooms, two lining each wall, and one at the end. Each of us claimed one, which had no real in-game purpose, but provided us all with a sense of community.

Rampi called us all back to the long table in the foyer, and set down plates for everyone. We all took our seats. "I know it's dumb, but I am so glad we bought this space. It's nice to have a home to return to while we are here, and I hope you all feel the same." An affirmative murmur echoed across the table, and we all consumed the meat pies laid out for us.

After saying our thank yous, the group followed Rampi out of the guild hall. We retraced our footsteps back to the bridge and made our way back to the forest. After passing through the whimsical collection of gnomes and faeries, we reached the purple tinted Amethyst Woods. We passed the entrance, and to our relief, the metal gap had been replaced by lush grass and moss. Carefully, we all crossed a small river, using a brittle log as a bridge, and found the town. It was surrounded by not only the amethyst blossoms, but also other stunning pastel flowers. We crossed a dirt path, and headed to the market. Kiri hustled through the streets, formed a crowd around a well, and manned shops.

Rampi led us through the town before stopping at a potion shop. "Do they have it? I hope they have it." She was scanning through a list of potions from the merchant. "Yes! Everyone, come here!" We all crowded around her, looking at her with confused expressions.

Apha was the first to question her stop. "Gonna let us know why we are here?"

"Okay, so you know how if we die, we can lose our items?"

"WHAT?" Worried yells unanimously flooded from the group.

"Okay, well yes we can. The more you know. So, if we are ever in a dungeon, if we use an escape potion, we can avoid that. I was reading up on it, and if you drink it before you die, you can be teleported back to the entrance."

I was the first to find an issue with this statement. "Are you sure they aren't a scam? I mean, we haven't been to a real dungeon this whole time. The closest thing was that temple where we fought Ralios."

"Yes, and we could've used the potions there. However, you are right. These don't help us in the overworld. There are only three eligible dungeons I know of. The first is Sonique's

Temple, which we have already cleared. The next is the Sapphire Palace, and the last is Syphon's Lair. I am about ninety-percent sure that the palace is next, so let's be safe and stock up." We couldn't argue with that. While only two of us had legendary weapons so far, we couldn't risk losing anything. We all bought a potion, and headed out of the town.

After a few minutes of travel, we reached the far left end of the forest. Despite the last building leaving our view, we still had more forest on our journey. After clearings, ponds, and some mushrooms, we crossed a small stone bridge, and entered an area with fewer trees. As we ventured further, the trees became even more sparse. We stumbled across a steep hill, and once we crossed it, we were met with a stunning sight.

Far in the distance stood a giant palace. Just as Rampi had mentioned, it was a deep sapphire blue. It was hard to make out the details, but the structure was clear: three floors, an archway in front, and several towers spiraling from its base. Once we crossed the hill, the atmosphere immediately shifted. The clouds churned, turning the field from sun-kissed to dreary. We were surrounded by floating crystals, all blue. Sapphire. They trailed down from the clouds like stagnant tears. Walking through them did no damage, but their presence made the air feel heavy, haunted.

The hill flattened out, revealing a path. A line of darkened gems amongst the sapphires paved the way to the Palace. We followed the path, watching as the clouds roiled and the air thickened. After a short walk across the shining path, we reached a drawbridge. Its silver finish stuck out against the dark blue palace. It felt sharp, cutting, and uninviting. I looked around for a button, a lever, really anything that could help us get in.

"Hello?" Sylvia yelled up to the towers. "Gonna let us in?" On cue, the chains holding up the bridge loosened, creating a deathly rattle as the bridge fell into place. As the walkway descended, a rough figure facing away from us was revealed. It was a deep blue, just like the Palace. It had muscular arms, toned abs, and stubby legs. There was no hair on its diamond shaped head. The creature spun around, grunted at us, and began charging. It let out a yell, shaking the bridge as the sound echoed through the moat. Rampi tried to electrocute it, but the lightning just bounced off of its crystal body.

"Damn. It must be made out of sapphire." Within seconds of the words exiting Rampi's mouth, the creature jumped at her. It leaped fists first towards Rampi's face. Lali jumped in front of her, blocking the attack with her sword.

The counterattack shattered the assailant's fists, but also broke Lali's sword into two pieces. "No! That was my good sword!" I could hear the mixture of sadness and anger in her voice. As Lali got a weaker sword from her inventory, Apha and Rufus were left with the sapphire monster. They pounded it with their fists, taking turns. Apha used all of her force, sending the monster spinning towards Rufus. He sent it back; ping-ponging the creature between them. In seconds, the creature crumbled, leaving behind a pile of crushed gems. A chime sounded, and one of the palace doors creaked open. With one door ajar, a shimmering line of blue light beamed onto the silver bridge.

We were about to enter when Selene stopped us. "Wait. I am not dealing with that wolf shit again." She stomped on the crushed gems, turning them to dust, and pushed the pile into the moat.

I put one hand inside of the large oblong door, and pulled. Both doors came swinging out, revealing a walkway. The hall was lined with candles, each dripping wax onto the crystal floor. Past the hallway was a large square room. The room stretched for at least a few hundred feet, with four rooms lining the walls. There was a door on each side wall, and two on the back wall. We approached the middle of the room, and headed first for the door to the left. As a group, we elected to send Selene in, as she could take an attack if an ambush were to occur.

"Nothing." Selene walked back to the center of the room, surveying the other doors. Apha and Rufus checked the two doors at the end of the room, but they were locked.

I was selected to check the last door. "I don't see anything." My words immediately made me look like a fool. I tripped over a spike in the floor and landed on a pressure plate. A chime sounded in the main room, and three of the crystal monsters fell from the ceiling. They hit the ground with a loud thud, and began chasing us around the room.

"Ew! What am I supposed to do?" Selene shrieked, running away from the group as they followed her.

They made two laps around the room before one of them trailed off and jumped at Lali. "Not again!" Rufus came to her rescue, grabbing it by the head and throwing it to the ground. It lost its limbs, sending them flying into the walls. Despite this brutal attack, the limbs did not shatter. Instead, they came flying back to the beast, reassuming their places on its body.

"Well shit." Rufus went back to fighting the creature, pounding its limbs into dust one by one. I turned my attention to Selene, who was still running around the room, two crystal monsters in tow.

The sight of her brand new staff reminded me of the power of its purple flowers. "Selene! Maybe you can use your staff's special attack. It could infect the crystals, I guess?" I wasn't sure of it, but I was hopeful. I watched as Selene sent vines lined with purple petals crawling towards the monsters. The vines wrapped around their bodies, squeezing them tight before vanishing. I ran up to the creatures, and saw a faint purple glow inside their crystal lattice. "I think it worked!" Their legs went first, slowly turning to dust and producing a purple fizz. The rest of the limbs followed, and the monsters were soon in piles of azure powder.

With a chime, the two end doors flung open. We took a moment to breathe. I hadn't needed to open my journal for monster information since the scalosos, but I wanted to see what information I'd gotten on the crystal creatures. Given that the tutorial was over, I hadn't gotten t a notification, but there was a new entry past entries of the wolves, scalosos, and trolls:

GEMINOID
Average Height: five feet, eleven inches
Area Found: Sapphire Palace, ???
Form: Sapphire, ???, ???, ???
Origin: Natural

I closed the journal, and caught up with the others. They were all staring at a giant chest in the first room. One benefit of clearing an area as a group is not having to open every chest individually. If one person in the party opens a chest or even just gets a mob drop, it gets granted to everyone. The only exception to this rule was with legendary items, making my floral sword even more unique.

Apha walked up to the glowing container, flipped the lock, and lifted its heavy lid. Gold light poured out, and some items were sent to our inventories. We all got some gems, a few coins, and a new outfit. It was a light blue set with dark blue compliments. The knight and brawler outfits had dark boots that led up to light blue tights. The top had a metal chestplate lined with dark toned fiber netting. The shoulders were covered by small puffs of blue, and light colored sleeves trailed the arms down into a fingerless glove. The only difference between the two was a sword hoop on the knight's version.

The mage outfit consisted of a light blue undersuit covered by a baggy dark blue cloak. The sleeves shot out into low hanging circles, and the shoes were small platforms with silver buckles. Rampi jumped with excitement. "I love these! Everyone put them on! Our guild color is now light blue. It's decided. I will pay you to upgrade these as we go, I *need* these to be our staple." I thought they were kind of tacky, but I also liked the uniformity they provided us with. We all obliged, equipping our new uniforms.

We exited the chest room, and headed for the next door. It revealed a large spiral staircase. We ascended the steps, taking in the beautiful architecture of the Palace. The stairway was lined with ornate arched windows. The stained glass of each reflected a different part of the moon cycle. We walked the spiral stairway, watching as the moons went from a crescent to full. The center was supported by high pillars, accentuating the regality of the stairway. After the full moon, there was a large door. It had carvings detailing an eclipsed sun surrounded by a swarm of moths.

I pushed open the door, and we were met with a quaint terrace. We all lined up on the edge of the strip, staring out into the darkened courtyard. There were bushes organized into three humps. The middle was circular, surrounded by two large arches. Inside the circle was a fountain, but no water appeared to be spouting from it. We kept walking along the terrace, but a notification stopped me. The words "**INVESTIGATE THE PALACE**" appeared before me. "So only now the quest begins? What have we been doing?" I asked, slightly irritated.

"I guess it only gets harder from here. Can't wait." Sylvia sighed, virtually dragging her feet as we headed towards an opening to the side of the terrace. We entered through a high arch, finding ourselves in a circular chamber. Candles lined the walls and a large chandelier hung from the ceiling. We went further into the room, using caution. As we approached the center, a small object came into view.

Sylvia inched closer to get a better look. "Oh. My. God. It's so cute!"

"What is it? Is it gonna hurt us?" I was terrified, this area hadn't been very forgiving up until this point.

"No way. It's just a cute little teddy bear!" She said it with a baby voice, picking up the animal and bringing it towards us. She held it out like it was Simba. "Look at it! Isn't it cute?" It was, for about a second. After its short moment of charm, the bear's eyes turned a deep red, and it bit Sylvia on the arm.

"Nevermind." She shook her arm, sending it flying across the room. It barreled towards us, growing with each step. Within seconds, it went from an adorable little bear to a menacing beast. Its arms grew unnaturally large muscles, and its legs were enhanced with a similar look. Its teeth grew long and curved and wicked claws had sprouted. The deformed creature lunged at Sylvia, and she slid under it. She started running around the room, screaming at any chance she got. "Why do you hate me, Teddy? All I wanted was to love you!" She yelled through fake tears. It was nice to see that she had given the beast a name, even if it wanted to kill her.

Given it wasn't made of crystal, it was pretty easy to take down. With a few hits from Rampi, it was paralyzed, allowing the rest of us to take its health down. Sylvia refused to hurt her "little teddy bear," and turned her back as we reduced its health to zero. When the bar dropped down, the bear didn't disappear. Instead, it shrunk back down to its normal size, and rolled over to Sylvia. It went in between her legs and presented itself in front of her. The cub waved its tiny arms around, grasping the air like a baby. "Aw!" Sylvia reached down and picked it up again. She held it like a baby, cradling it in her arms. This time, it did not turn into a devilish monster. Sylvia now had a pet. She wasted no time officially naming it Teddy. She placed it on her head and waved her staff around, ready for the next room.

"Okay, it's cute, but what the hell is a bear doing in here?" Selene sounded so confused, obviously tired from the fights.

"What do you mean? It was obviously here so I could find it. You have your little rat, why can't I have a real pet?" The tension was unbearable.

"Okay! Let's go!" I interjected, not wishing to risk a fight so far into the dungeon. We found a door opposite from where we had entered, and opened it. The door led to another staircase exactly like the previous one. We climbed the steps, and reached a set of double doors. It had carvings, but in place of the eclipse was now only one big moth. Selene and I pushed open the doors, reading each other's minds and acting like butlers. Our idiocy allowed everyone to enter the eerie sanctum beyond the two doors.

The circular floor was lined with archways, all featuring windows and a stage of the lunar cycle. Two staircases led up to a small balcony, and another row of arches lived above it. The arches formed a star shape in the ceiling. Inside the star was an opening, which allowed the moon to shine freely into the sanctum. The door shuttered behind us, and a loud rumbling sound came from outside. A large moth flew in from outside, using the star as an entryway.

It flapped its wings, their deep blue markings shining in the moonlight. The moth's effort sent a gust towards us, knocking us all down. It flew towards Lali, grabbing her with its legs and taking her to the sky. Rampi sent a lightning strike its way, hitting its right wing and knocking it out of the way. The bug quickly recovered and spun around, grabbing Selene and throwing her towards a window.

Rampi aimed another strike at the moth, making it pause. It again recovered with haste, and made more attacks on all of us. Its ability to fly left the mages as the only ones who could land their attacks. Sylvia, Selene, and Rampi all used their respective spells, causing the moth to drop to the floor under a combination of light, blood, and lightning spells. It came crashing down, sending a shock through the whole palace. When I walked over to it, attempting to get a hit on it, I saw its name, Vulnira.

Just as we thought we had a chance, a rumble filled the building. Through the star, thousands of crystals came flying down to the moth. They wrapped its wings, providing Vulnira with a coat of armor. The creature rose, flapping its wings with a new ferocity. The gusts through us all back, each of us landing against a different arch. We got up, and gave it every-thing we could. Slashes, spells, and bashes. We tried everything to weaken it. I remembered Selene's effect on the geminoids. "Selene! Can you use your special attack?"

"Good call, let me get ready. Cover me!" I created a healing circle around Selene, and she prepared for her assault. Her flowery vines passed through my own blossoms, and reached the moth. They restrained the beast, holding it down for a few seconds.

A dark figure suddenly covered the star-shaped aperture. I looked up, and gasped. It was another player, obviously a man, on a white and pink dragon. He leapt off of his winged steed, and drove his sword into the head of the moth. As he pierced its eye, blue flowers bloomed all over its body, taking it down in a floral frenzy. The moth burst into light, and in its place stood a silhouette of the man. Beneath his feet, light and dark blue lilies bloomed.

It was like a dream: the dragon, the man, the flowers, the castle. He was about to get back on his dragon and leave. I couldn't let him get away. "Hello! My name is Mirage! What's yours?" Before he could answer, he was gone. He flew back out through the star, leaving all of us in awe.

I stared at the flowers in disbelief of what just happened. The man from my dreams was real, and he saved us all. I had forgotten about the escape potions, but we were about to need them. Our tanks rested on ten percent health, and the rest of us even less. If he hadn't helped us, we wouldn't have made it out.

A new notification appeared: **"QUEST COMPLETED: INVESTIGATE THE PALACE."** A loud scream came from Lali. "Yes! Guys, I got a new sword!" We all crowded around her as she pulled out the new blade. It was impressive in size, being at least twice as wide as my sword. It was entirely made of sapphire. Its deep blue handle glistened under the moonlight as Lali swung it in circles. The blade was made of two curving lines, dancing around each other to form a double helix shape. Everyone congratulated her but me. I was still staring at the sky, lost in wonder. Who was he?

CHAPTER TEN

The events of last night haunted me. The man from my dreams had saved me, but he left me with a bruise. A bruise of rejection and ignorance, disinterest and avoidance. I was probably overthinking it. Just because him and his dragon had been in my nighttime visions did not mean the same could be said for him. There was also the possibility he hadn't heard me. That he had just leeched off of our hard work and feared an argument. No matter the reason, he was gone.

There was the possibility we would see him again but it was unlikely. He could come back to finish off a boss and avoid the dangers of a dungeon again or we could run into him on the road or see him in another area. We could. But with the capacity of the servers, it would be almost impossible to find him in the open world. Maybe it was for the best. Maybe my dreams of his dragon were warnings, not fate. Or, I really am just overthinking it.

With these burning questions still on my mind, I rolled out of bed. I got dressed and headed downstairs for breakfast. I had a test in AP Lang, so I couldn't risk being hungry. Nothing at home sounded pleasant or filling, so I headed to Starbucks. Our "local" Starbucks was on the outskirts of our neighboring town. It lived in a shopping center, nestled between a Macy's and an old arcade. I drove past the school, Maia's house, and several small banks before reaching the connecting back roads. Quintessential midwest: pass through farmland to reach the most popular shopping center across two towns. I drove past fields of cows, horses, and donkeys, before turning back onto a main road that led right to the shopping center.

I pulled into the drive-thru behind an army green Jeep, and waited for my turn. I had mobile ordered to try and save time but it still took about ten minutes before I reached the speaker. "Welcome to Starbucks, how may I help you?"

"I have a mobile order for Zack." I replied, a little put off by the angry tone of the worker.

"Okay, pull around." Their voice shifted from anger to exhaustion. I couldn't pull around, since the Jeep was right in front of me, so I just closed my window and waited. Someone honked but there was nowhere for anyone to go. After another fifteen minutes, I made it to the window and was finally able to get my food. My sandwich was handed to me with no problems. The same could not be said for my coffee.

The worker dropped it, spilling some on the side of my car. "Shit. Do you want me to make you another? Or do you want a refund?" The worker looked on the edge of a breakdown.

I thought about it for a second, but I really didn't have time to wait any longer. "No. Thanks, I guess?" I left the drive-thru disappointed and slightly irritated, and made my way back to the school. I found my spot, parked, and opened my trunk to grab the towel I kept in the back for emergencies. I knelt next to my car and tried to get as much of the coffee off as I could. As I scrubbed, I heard a voice behind me. "Need some help?"

It was Alex. "Uh, sure. I don't know what you can do, but go ahead." He joined me on the asphalt, and took the towel from me. There was still a little bit of stickiness so I poured some of my water on the car, hoping it would help. The mark was gone after a few minutes and I threw the towel back in my trunk. Alex lingered next to my car and then started to walk me to class.

"So how did that happen?" He gestured behind him vaguely.

"Oh, the person at Starbucks dropped my coffee. An accident, obviously, but still shitty. They were slammed this morning and you could *tell*."

Alex nodded, understanding. "What was it? Like what kind of coffee?"

"An iced caramel macchiato, so nothing too crazy. At least I don't have chocolate sauce all over my car." He chuckled at my comment and we settled into silence. We made it to class and barely sat down before the bell rang.

The test was easy for me. It was just a review on our vocabulary lists and grammar practices. We had to provide definitions for words like "abhor" and "countenance." I always liked vocab because I could come up with sentences to help me study, such as: I abhor Connor's horrific countenance. It was true, and I almost wrote it in the margins of the test. There was a section where we had to make a sentence using specific grammar rules and two vocabulary words. Unfortunately, I couldn't make my slanderous message fit the requirements. We left the class, and I found Maia stressing out by the door.

"What's going on?"

"I'll tell you during lunch. I want to die." Well, that was.

Something. History was boring as ever, and Bostyn didn't have much to talk about. The whole class I just stared at the board, barely taking in anything said by Ms. Tati. After an hour of Woodrow Wilson, it was time to head to lunch. I told Ms. Tati to have a good weekend, and headed to the art room. On my way, I passed several couples making out, the beginnings of a fight, and food already discarded on the floors near the trash cans before reaching the room.

"Hey Ms. Bash."

"Hey Zack! Both of your pieces are looking splendid so far!" She exclaimed and went back to watching something on her computer. I found Maia pouting in the corner, and sat down next to her.

"So... Do you want to talk about it?"

"No, but I will." I prepared myself for her rant. "In English today. I made a big mistake. Sierra and I were talking about our plans to hangout tomorrow, and I almost called it a date." She looked down and looked close to tears.

"Well, did you call it a date? You said you almost did, what happened?"

"I said 'our da-' and stopped. She obviously realized what I almost said, and made a terrified face."

I tapped her shoulder. "Hey, maybe she's just nervous. See if she shows up, and if she does, try not to make it awkward."

Maia pulled me in for a hug, and after a few seconds let go. "So, are you excited for *your* date tonight?" She smirked and a tear rolled down her cheek.

"It is not a date! He just needs help with vocab... or something." Honestly, I didn't really care what he needed my help with. I just wanted to spend time with him.

"Sure... I saw you two this morning. Real buddy buddy. He was literally on his knees." Maia scrubbed her cheeks before bumping into my arm.

"He was helping me clean my car, there is no other way to comfortably do that. Stop being weird." I punched her arm lightly, then took a sip of my Dr. Pepper. "How do you feel about that knight?"

She looked at me confused. "What knight?"

"The one from last night. The guy who flew in and killed Vulnira."

"Oh yeah! Loved him. We were getting our asses handed to us. I would've lost my precious staff if it weren't for him. Why do you ask?"

"Oh, no reason." There was a reason, but I knew Maia would laugh if I said I was having dreams of him. I tried to think of something to shift the conversation and then, I remembered my piece on Holly. "Wait! I have something to show you." I went to a back table where I kept all of my pieces and pulled it out.

"Oh my god, Zack! This is incredible!" She looked stunned, and tried to touch the paper.

I smacked her hand. "Thanks. Don't touch it though, I'm scared of smudges. I still need to shade some of it, and then I'll be done."

"Can I have it? I'll take it home right now. I am not joking. You don't even need to finish it."

"Are you dumb? Sorry, that was rude. But no, I have to submit it for my AP portfolio. After everything is done, sure, I don't care."

She made a face and returned to our corner. I put the paper back on the table, and sat back on the floor. We sat in silence for the remainder of lunch. I watched *Dance Moms* again while finishing off my Dr. Pepper. Maia and I still didn't say anything as lunch ended and I left for biology.

As soon as I entered the classroom, I was instantly met with a concerning slideshow. It was titled "Snail Reproduction," and showcased two snails stuck to each other. For the entire hour and twenty-five minutes, Mr. Ralph went into gory details about snail sex. How they were gender neutral and attracted each other with darts. How they stuck to each other to reproduce. He ignored a student when asked if this was in the curriculum, and continued on with his powerpoint.

He finished the class with a monologue on his fascination with snails, and unveiled a glass cage on his desk. He informed us that he'd begged the principal for a class pet and was finally able to bring in a large African snail. He also told us that the species was illegal in the U.S. but only the school would be held liable if anyone found out. Probably.

After that horror, I was ready to hide in the art room. I beat Alex to the classroom and brought our pieces to the table. I had finally finished the blade of my sword, and was ready to make the flowers. I cut off a few pieces of clay and rolled them thin, then shaped them into petals and began layering, forming a rose shape. As I was working on my second rose, Alex stumbled into the classroom. "Ms. Bash, I am so sorry I'm late! I had a presentation and Mr. Hill made me stay to finish it!" He was panting with a worried look on his face.

"It's okay, I believe you. Just try not to be late again. I won't count you tardy today. Please find your seat." She updated her attendance, and went back to what she was doing.

"That is so... pretty." Alex said, looking at my sword with a puzzled look. While he was stressing out over attendance, I had finished my roses and was placing them on the sword.

"Thanks. I'll feel lost when I'm done painting it though, I've spent so much time on this sword." I laughed, expecting him to as well.

He just kept staring. "What color are you going to paint the roses?"

"I'm going to paint some pink and some white."

"I'd go with blue, but it's your piece."

His comment confused me. I was glad he was making conversation, but his input was off-putting. "So, how is your tree going?"

"Oh... I scrapped that." I looked over and saw a squished pile of clay. "It was too confusing, I think I'm just going to make a cat or something.

I smiled at him. He was so charming even when he was defeated. "Hey, if you can find the symbolism in a cat statue, knock yourself out." The rest of class went on like that, small talk about our pieces followed by awkward silence. Before he left, I made sure to give him my address. I watched as he left, excited to see him later.

For the last class of the day, I finished the Holly piece. I painted shadows and highlights, defining the transition from reality to fiction. By the time class was over, I was ready to put the painting on the drying rack.

Almost right after the bell sounded, I went straight to my car, and scurried home. I needed to prepare for Alex.

I tried to quickly clean up my room. I swept empty cans from my shelves and vacuumed the floor. I made my bed, and pulled an extra chair up to my desk. Nervously, I waited for the next hour, checking the window every few minutes. Finally, I saw his car in the driveway. I raced downstairs to greet him, and introduced him to my mom. "Hello Alex! It is so lovely to meet you. It's so nice to see Zack's making some friends."

I had to stop it there. "Okay! Let's head upstairs." I led Alex to the stairwell. "I am so sorry about her."

"Don't be! She seems great. Really different from my parents." I took Alex past rows of baby pictures, which got some laughs out of him. We finally made it to my room, and he let out a gasp. "Wow! It is so nice! I love the posters, and it's just so big." He stared at my walls and stopped in front of my *Ultraviolence* poster and pointed at it, smiling stupidly.

"You like Lana Del Rey?" I questioned.

"Of course, and Beyonce is my shit." Maybe he wasn't straight after all.

"Cool, me too. Obviously." I felt my face get warm as I sat down at my desk and pointed to his seat. He took a seat and scooted the chair closer to the desk. Closer to me.

I took a deep breath. "What is it that you need help with?"

He pulled out a binder. "Here is my last full length essay. I am so bad at writing my body paragraphs." I decided not to bring up the last paper I saw. He had gotten an A on only body paragraphs, so his desperation seemed unwarranted. I scanned the paper and it was the one he had gotten a 65 on. I scoured the paragraphs until I found the issues. He wasn't finding a theme that his evidence supported.

"Okay I see it. You need to have a theme for your literary elements. For example, you could talk about some type of syntax for a body paragraph, but the evidence needs to support a theme. I pulled examples of a short syntax as evidence of a theme of desperation and limited time." He stared at me, barely looking down at his paper as I critiqued his work. I went over various strategies he could use, always referencing his paper. He never looked down to see where I was pointing. Every time I looked up to make sure he was following along, he was still staring at me. "I think that's all I can-" Before I could finish, he kissed me.

I didn't respond to the kiss. There was no way this was real. There was a boy in my room kissing me. There was a boy in my room kissing *me.* There was *this boy* in my room kissing me. I couldn't believe it. I was having my first kiss, and not even reciprocating. He pulled away. "I'm so sorry!" He started tearing up and buried his face in his palms. Through his hands he choked out, "That was wrong, *this* is wrong. You should be a girl I-" His actions caught me off guard, but nothing felt wrong about them. Everything felt right. I wouldn't allow him to feel bad for what he did. I pulled his hands away from his face and held them with one hand. I reached out again, this time touching his face turning his chin towards me., I pressed my lips to his. His lips were soft and tasted like mint. I didn't want to stop, but I had to. I slowly pulled away, not wanting to worry him even more. I used one hand to wipe a tear from his face. "Don't ever apologize for that. There's nothing wrong with it. Or you. I won't tell anyone, but I am *so* glad you kissed me." I hugged him tight. "I like you, Alex."

It took him a few moments to respond. He hugged me back and moved his lips closer to my ear. I could feel his breath on my neck. "I like you too, Mirage."

Everything stopped. How did he know that name? Was he messing with me? Did someone put him up to this? Did Connor get him to fuck with me? That absolute motherfucker. I let go of him. "How do you-"

"How do I know that name? Zack, I could never forget your voice. You're the only thing I listen to in English. I knew it was you from the first word last night. When I heard your voice, I got scared and ran. I didn't want to leave you, but I knew it was too risky to talk to you there. Knowing you also played *Echoes* only made me like you more. I probably would have confessed right there, in my own house. " It was him. Our rescuer last night was him. My first boyfriend - *boyfriend? Were we boyfriends now?* - played video games just like me. He was perfect. I kissed him again, gripping his shoulders as our lips collided.

Once we broke apart, I grabbed his hands again. "I think I love being a tutor."

His expression of joy returned to its earlier darkness and he let go of my hands. "I shouldn't have kissed you. My parents are going to kill me."

"Hey, we don't have to tell anyone. This can be our secret until you're ready. Hell, I'm not even out yet." I didn't want to make him come out, but it had always been my plan. I wanted to officially come out when I had a boyfriend. That way, if it went south, I would have a loving shoulder to cry on. However, for someone as amazing as Alex, I would hide forever. Even from Maia.

Alex cried in my arms for at least ten minutes. I felt so bad for him. He shouldn't hate himself for liking me, but it was obvious he did. I could only imagine how his parents were. He wiped his tears and we waited for the red in his eyes to disappear. We made plans to meet again later tonight in *Echoes*. I didn't want him to go, but I couldn't wait to see him again. I walked him to his car, and got ready for our rendezvous.

A few hours passed, and it was time to meet him in *Echoes*. My heart racing, I put on my headset. I loaded into the game, and waited in Wysteria. After a few minutes, a dark figure approached me. It was Alex, in deep black armor. He had a silver chestplate that had carved abs towards the bottom.

His pants were baggy, with straps hanging off and swaying as he walked. His sword swung from his side, its blue-toned flowers shining in the sun. He removed his hood, revealing an avatar that looked just like him. From his tan skin to dark curly hair, it was Alex striding towards me. He didn't say anything, but grabbed my hand and pulled me past the crowds in the plaza.

We reached the bridge, and he whistled for his dragon. The creature came flying down towards us and landed next to Alex.

Its white scales refracted the moonlight into a beautiful shine, complemented by the coral undertones of its body. Alex climbed up and extended a hand towards me. I got on behind him and we soared into the sky, riding above the clouds. We hovered above the plains, looking down on the mesmerizing fields of blossoms.

I finally found the confidence to speak. "What doI call you?"

He responded in his comforting voice. "Here, I go by Somnus."

CHAPTER ELEVEN

Monday, January 21st

School wasn't the same with a boyfriend. It was better. AP Lang was filled with glances and grins. I didn't pay attention to Mr. Wills' lesson - I think it was only a review. Even though I had barely paid him any attention before now, I couldn't take my eyes off of Alex's beautiful hair. By the end of class, I would have been able to draw a portrait of the back of his head from memory, with every curly nuance and bit of frizz. I shot up when the class was done, and collected my blank papers.

Once everything was shoved in my bag, I looked up to see Alex smiling at me. He waited for me to sling the bag over my shoulder, and walked me out of the room. We found Maia waiting outside, and he handed me off to her. "See you later." He grinned, and waved goodbye.

"Now what was that? Don't tell me you got together. If a twink like you found love before me I swear to god-"

"No Maia, we are not together." I laughed it off, hoping

Maia wouldn't spot my lie. I walked with Maia until we reached my history class. I stopped her as I entered the door. "Tell me all about Saturday during lunch."

She smiled, a good sign given her anxiety going into the meetup. "You've got it."

~

Lunch rolled around, and I raced to the art room. "So, how was it?" I took a seat with Maia, this time at a table.

She looked up from her phone with a smirk. "It went well."

"That's all? Really?"

"Yes. It's not like we made out or anything." She paused. "Is that what you and Alex did?"

I tried to hide my blush. "What? No! We went over sentence structure and stuff." I whipped my phone out to hide my reddening face.

"Sure... whore. Anyway, it wasn't awkward at all. We talked about our interests, and she even held my hand to pull me into a store."

"That is amazing Maia! I am so glad it went well!" She rolled her eyes. It was scary how suspicious she already was of Alex. It was going to be hard to introduce him to the guild on Thursday, but I would find a way.

Even though Maia was my best friend, and gay, there was no way I could violate Alex's trust and tell her. No matter how much I wanted to scream from the rooftops that I had a boyfriend, I wouldn't allow that to happen. I had to protect him, which was ironic given he was the one who had saved me last week.

Art finally arrived, and I was greeted with Alex beaming at me. "Are you going to glaze Spring's Vigor today?"

His words made me smile. I had forgotten he also had one

of the legendary swords in *Echoes*. "Damn, I forgot you have one of these."

He laughed, and pulled my seat out for me. "Yep! And I would argue that mine is cooler than yours."

"Sure, but is yours as pretty as mine?" I hit his arm playfully. I got up and searched the back for the colors I needed, then started glazing the piece. Alex continued working on his sad looking tree. "So, do you normally steal kills from hard working players?"

"What? No! I just saw some action happening and decided to stop by! I swear I wasn't trying to take anything from you guys!" He started blushing and waving his hands frantically. "If I stumble across anything of value in the next area, I'll give it to you! Hell, I'll even farm for stuff. I'm so sorry!"

I felt like I was in a movie. I was sitting with a boy, making art, while he delightedly talked about VR games. "You're okay, I believe you. Also, it's not that serious. It's literally just a game." That seemed to calm him down. "So, my guild meets every Thursday to clear a new area, would you like to join this week? I'm hoping you haven't cleared the next area yet. I don't even know what it is."

He looked bewildered. "You have a guild? Those exist? I've just been wandering around by myself since the tutorial. I would love to join you. I haven't cleared the new area yet. I did check it out though, it's called 'Sunrise Lake.'"

His comment about soloing bosses overshadowed my thoughts of how stupid he was for not knowing about guilds. "You have been beating all of those bosses as a solo player? Do you know how hard we had to work for each of them? You must be stronger than all of us combined."

He let out a lighthearted chuckle. "I am far from stronger than you guys. I doubt I am even near your level. The bosses scale their power to the amount of players attacking it. So if there's one player it's weaker than if there were seven. I would be nowhere if they had fixed amounts of health."

Humble, funny, artistic, and cute? I really struck gold with Alex.

CHAPTER TWELVE

Thursday, January 24th

The time had come to introduce Somnus to the guild. During art, I told him to find me in the tavern. I waited on a splintered stool and ordered some food. As the NPC handed me my plate, Somnus stumbled through the doors. "Za- Mirage!" He walked up to the bar, and sat on a stool next to me.

"Hey, Somnus." I said, trying to sound flirty.

"Are you ready to go? I can't wait to meet everyone." I smiled, and got up from the stool. We walked out of the tavern and down to the guild hall. Rampi had given me a key, so I slammed it into the door and walked in. Somnus followed closely behind me.

"Hey everyone! I have a friend I would like you all to meet." Luckily, everyone was already sitting at the table. I sat down, watching Somnus nervously scramble for a chair.

Once he sat, he made his own introduction. "Hi. This is awkward. I'm Somnus, and some of you may recognize me."

Apha was the first to make the connection. Angrily, she said, "You're that knight who stole our kill."

To my surprise, Rampi came to Sommus' rescue. "Not exactly, he kind of saved us. But yeah, I agree. I wish you had to deal with the entire dungeon like we did."

"Well, I was wondering if Somnus could join us, and become a Sleepless Knight." I said hopefully.

Lali thought about it for a few moments, and made her decision. "He can come clear the next area with us. If we work well together, he can join. I don't want to disrupt what we have."

"Thank you so much, I won't let you down." Somnus did a cheesy salute, and almost bowed before I stopped him. We all filed out of the hall, and headed back to the palace. Apha caught a ride on Somnus' dragon, Swift, to test his skills.

As we flew, Selene found a place next to me. "Is that…"

"Yes. I am as surprised as you are. I can't believe *he* was the one who saved us last week."

"Well go you, slut! You got yourself a man who even plays this nerdy ass game!"

"We aren't dating!" I protested, Selene flying further ahead to drown me out. I raced to catch up, and we were soon back at the Palace. The skies had cleared and the grass glowed a lively green. The blue gems were still there, but now they caught the light beautifully, casting a rainbow shine around them. I pet Jinkx on the nose, and dismissed her. She flew into the sky, doing a flip before joining the others.

We walked down the same path that connected every area of the land. Near the Sapphire Palace, the path was lined with fruit trees and bushes, ferns, and even some beehives. Something about the path brought me comfort. I liked the uniformity and structure it provided us with. I *hate* going off route in anything I do. Sometimes, it's okay. Most times, however, it makes my skin crawl.

On the horizon, we could see the lake. It stretched so far that the end wouldn't even load in. Across the body of water, there was a large bridge with stone spires on each end. A small town nestled against the right bank of the lake, and hills surrounded it. We could see a stone staircase on the side of a hill. It seemed to lead down to the lake. We were almost to the stairs when Rampi put up an arm, signaling us to stop. "Wait. Did you hear that?"

"Hear what?" Even Lali was confused.

"Some rustling, I think it came from that bush."

"Probably a beehive, I don't hear anything." Lali shrugged it off. Suddenly, a small goblin leaped from the bush and grabbed Lali's sword from her side. "No! Not again!" She started chasing it around the hills, crashing into trees and bushes alike.

She drove it back towards us, allowing Somnus to grab the goblin by its ears. He held it out towards Lali and let her grab her sword. That was a good start to his first adventure with the guild. I flashed him a small thumbs up and watched as Lali went crazy.

She ripped the thief out of Somnus' hands. "You little bitch. This sword, while amazing, is already a replacement!" She spun in three graceful circles, and launched the goblin into the air. It flew out over the lake and landed in the water with a splash. "That'll do, let's move on." Lali wiped her hands, and glared at us.

"What the hell?" Rampi was stunned.

"Have you got a problem? Because I did, and I disposed of it." Lali snarled. I could understand why she was mad. In one week, her sword had been taken away twice. Still, it was a game. No matter how real it felt at times.

The rest of us kept quiet and followed Lali to the staircase. We hustled down the steps, skipping past mystifying vines, bushes, and flowers. After reaching the last step we officially entered the new area. Sunrise Lake was surrounded by lush banks of flower spotted grass. The lake itself was even more impressive up close.

We decided to head towards the tiny village on the outskirts of the lake. As we entered the town, we noticed a lack of life. The buildings were in perfect condition, but there was no one around. Lights were off, crops were left unattended, and chimneys were clear. The only house emitting any sign of life was at the far end of the village. Its chimney was slowly piping out smoke, and candles dimly shone in the windows. We went up to the small red door and knocked. An old man opened the door and smiled. "Hello there, travelers! Come in, come in!" He motioned to the inside, holding the door open for us as we crammed into the small stone house. "I would offer you kids some food, but ever since *it* showed up, we haven't been able to find many fish. Honestly, I am not sure what 'we' means anymore. Most of the villagers fled to the Plains."

That explained the emptiness, but also created another question: who, or what, was "it?"

After a deep breath, the fisherman continued. "You know what? If you kids can find me some trout, I'll cook you a meal you will never forget." A new quest appeared: **"SIDE QUEST: A GILL-FULL PROPOSITION."** The man handed each of us a cheap looking fishing rod, and opened the door. We rushed out of the door, tired of the cramped feeling of the room.

"So... we have to fish?" I said, disappointed. "I'm gay. These aren't the kind of rods I touch." I put a hand over my mouth. "Oops. Guess cat's out of the bag, totally forgot I didn't tell any of you."

"We don't care, I'm pretty sure most of us are gay anyway. I mean, we all play a game like this..." Sylvia said, trying to reassure me. Rufus and Apha confirmed; Rufus was pan and Apha was bi.

"Well, both Rampi and I have husbands, but I love drag queens." Lali was trying her best to be supportive. It was sweet, but I still laughed that she used drag queens as her evidence.

"You already know me bitch, and I already basically called Sonique hot. So you all know." Selene tried to pat me on the back.

"Well, I'm straight, but I don't have an issue with it," Somnus said. Ow. I knew his parents could probably hear him, so I didn't judge him. It still hurt to hear though. Especially after all we had done together. I tried not to let it remind me of Connor.

"Okay, let's move on. Please. This was sufficiently *My Little Pony*-esque for me." I grimaced. It was nice to have their support, but that little confessional was embarrassing. Both for me and everyone else. I shook it off, and headed to a part of the lake to cast my line. We paired up: Lali with Rampi, Apha with Rufus, Selene with Sylvia, and me with Somnus.

Somnus threw in his line. "I'm sorry."

It was obvious what he was talking about. "It's okay, I know you can't... you know." I didn't want to say it bluntly, I feared his parents may be listening. We stood in silence for five minutes before I felt a tug. I tried to reel it in, pulling back with all of my strength while spinning my handle. I was being pulled towards the water. Somnus grabbed onto my rod with one hand, and helped me haul the fish out of the water. "That is just sad." The fish was smaller than my sword. I could swing that sword with ease, but I couldn't reel in a fish?

Somnus quickly reeled in his own fish with ease. We met

up with Rufus and Apha who seemed to be struggling. Not with the catching, but actually finding the fish.

"Hey, why don't you guys go check out where we were fishing? We got our fish pretty quickly." Somnus' kindness only added to his charm.

"Thanks!" Rufus and Apha traveled further down the bank, and cast their lines. As they searched for their scaly bounties, I saw Selene pulling her fish out of the water.

We ran up to Selene and Sylvia. "Yes! It's huge! Wow, Mirage, yours is tiny." Selene jeered.

"Thanks." I replied dryly. Sylvia soon followed in Selene's footsteps, reeling in a fish of a similar size. Apha and Rufus caught up to us, and we headed to Rampi and Lali. They were sitting on a porch in the village, their prizes next to them.

"Are you slowpokes ready?" Rampi snarked.

We all followed her into the old man's house, and watched as he jumped in glee. "Yipee! I haven't seen fish like these in ages! One moment please, and I'll have your meals ready." We waited as the old man turned on his stove, got out some pots, and threw in the fish. He reached into a cabinet and dumped in a mix of spices, stirring the pot as each was added. Steam floated up from the bubbling concoction, disappearing as it reached the ceiling. With one final churn, the old man poured the contents over eight plates, and took trips handing them to us. As we accepted our plates, the completion notification appeared for the quest. In quick succession, a new quest was presented. The real quest: **"CLEANSE THE LAKE."** Before digging in, I checked the meal's description. All I could find was: *GRANTS WATER BREATHING FOR 30 MIN.*

"Guys! Don't eat it yet!" I was given confused looks, and some plates were already cleaned off. "Nevermind." I ate mine quickly. "We have to act fast now, we have thirty minutes to find the boss. He said 'it' was killing the fish, I can only assume he means the boss of this area. If it's killing the fish, it must be in that lake."

"Oh shit. Let's go." Selene was the first through the door, dropping her plate as she ran. The mages sent balls of light into the lake, then we all dove in. The swimming was surprisingly lifelike. We scoured as much of the lake as we could. It was too deep, and we didn't have time. The mages got in a circle, and started shooting energy balls in all directions. After a couple minutes, a loud roar echoed from the bottom of the lake.

A force shifted the waters, sending an invisible wave in all directions, shooting us all back. Once we stopped spinning, we went back under. Before us was a giant fish. It was the same brown color as the others, but it had large black spikes protruding from its back. An unnatural looking lantern dangled from its head, and its teeth jutted out, displaying an uneven bite; an angry fantasy anglerfish. It charged towards us, its torn fins moving furiously in the dark water.

With a groan, the fish swam towards us, chomping down rapidly as it charged the group. Lali swam past us, sword in hand. She stabbed it in the side, then swam away from it. It roared in pain, and took a right. The force of the movement threw Lali off course, sending her deeper into the ocean.

Sylvia raced towards her, sending healing beams as she swam. I watched as the fish charged at Somnus, following him as he took the beast in circles. So, he's a tank. Cute.

Rampi couldn't do much for this fight. She had maxed out her lightning skills, but electricity in water was not a good combo. As I checked the fish's name - Itaina - Sylvia flew by me. She had trapped Lali in a healing bubble. It was a form of magic I had never seen before. A few seconds later, Lali was back in the fight. I watched as Apha and Rufus charged Itaina. They approached from opposite sides, hitting its jaw and driving it downwards. Somnus sliced the creature's eye. Itaina blindly jerked its head around, moving wildly until it found Somnus again. It grabbed him with its giant teeth and started to swim down.

I screamed and swam down to help him. I waved my sword, hoping he wasn't too far down for my flowers to reach him. A lily bud grazed his shoulder, latched on, and bloomed. His health was filled back to half, and he broke free from his captor.

He swam up to me. "Thanks." He mimicked a kiss to the cheek, and went back down to help Apha. I blushed, even in a fake world he made my knees weak. I snapped back to the action when I saw a fin about to smack me across the face. I sped to safety and watched as Sylvia swam around, furiously healing anyone she could.

With a final jab from Lali and her brand new weapon, the fish reared back. It burst into a cloud of silt, and sank to the bottom of the lake. The water instantly cleared, going from a sickly brown to a beautiful aqua. New inhabitants of the lake appeared. Fish of many different colors and tiny tadpoles swam by gracefully.

We got back to shore, and saw an illuminated village. Candles were lit in the windows of every building and chimneys merrily puffed out smoke. People bustled through the streets.. The quest was over: **"QUEST COMPLETED: CLEANSE THE LAKE."**

"It's so cute!" We all turned to Sylvia who was waving a brand new staff around. It was the same shape as her basic staff, but made of freshwater pearls. The off-white spheres glowed iridescent in the sun as she spun her staff.

"That is so pretty, Sylvia!" Selene high fived her, and they clicked staffs.

"Now, onto business," Rampi turned to Somnus. "You did great out there, and we would love to have you."

My boyfriend was great, and everyone agreed.

CHAPTER THIRTEEN

Tuesday, January 29th

From now on, Alex and I would be almost inseparable.

I got out of my car, and found a smiling Alex waiting for me. He was holding something in his right hand. "I know you got scammed the other day, and I really wanted to make you happy." He got me an iced macchiato. He remembered my order from the day we kissed.

I felt my eyes grow hot. No boy had ever shown me this affection before. I was always the one chasing them. "Thank you so much. You have no idea how much this means to me." I mumbled. He winked in response. It wasn't a good wink. Both eyes almost closed and he looked like he was straining, but the effort was applaudable.

Before I could take a drink, Alex took a sip. "I paid for it. Now I'm wondering why. That was nasty." He smiled that charming smile he always hit me with, and handed the drink to me.

"Not a coffee drinker?" I took a sip, pressing my lips to where his just were.

"No, my parents have always preached its negative side effects. Specifically stunted growth, which obviously didn't affect you." He very obviously looked me up and down. I was tall - just over six feet. Still, it felt like Alex loomed over me even though he couldn't have been more than six-foot-three.

Art class had finally rolled around and I couldn't wait to see that captivating grin. There it was, as soon as I walked in. I saw him waiting for me, smile and all. I took my seat, and got out a new block of clay. My model of Spring's Vigor was done, and I was ready to move on.

I racked my brain for more ideas that fit my intended subject. I tried to consider that a large part of AP Art was the essays. If I could skillfully craft an art piece, and have sufficient writings to go with them, I could probably get a high score. I decided I would do something for each of my virtual friends. I had four pieces decided. I would make another sword like mine, but with blue flowers; it would pair with Spring's Vigor. The piece would show my relationship with Alex, and how we were connected through both flesh and pixels. A little much for never having been on a real date? Maybe. Too much for my desperate ass? Never.

The other three would be detailed sculptures of the other legendary weapons in the guild. The pearl staff for Sylvia, sapphire blade for Lali, and mushroom staff for Selene. I could only hope that everyone would have a Legendary weapon in time for portfolio submissions, or at least a signature motif.

As I sketched my next design - the pearl staff - Alex kept

staring at me. "Don't you have work to be doing?" I said play-fully, slightly concerned he would get behind.

"What could be more important than watching you do what you love?" His stupid lines worked on me. However, I found it odd he was so open with me here. I mean, anywhere in the school is risky. Rumors fly faster than jets and anyone would start them. Nevertheless, his words made me blush. I tried to hide behind the sleeve of my beige sweater. It smelled like laundry detergent, which brought me back to a normal state.

For the rest of the school day, I worked on my sketches. It was convenient that I was using a similar theme for both port-folios. If a sketch for a model was good enough, I could turn it into a real drawing. I sketched out all three items, and rummaged through my bag to find my old sword sketch. I would need it to complete the second floral blade.

I found Alex waiting by my car, a soccer ball in hand. He looked at me with a pleading look. "Would you come play soccer with me?"

Ew. No. That sport is horrible, and it is January, in Missouri. Did I look like a fool? Even with my hatred for soccer, I couldn't make him sad. "Sure." We walked along the cracked sidewalk to the nearby soccer fields. Once we arrived, I followed him to the middle of the field, and waited. He set the ball down on the ground. It was like he expected me to do something. "Oh, am I supposed to kick it?" I pointed to myself, disbelieving.

He laughed, "Yes, dummy." That was something else perfect about him: he was always sweet. Never rude, just playful. He could have easily called me a dumbass, but he chose the cuter, more playful word.

I took a step back, raised my leg, and swung. The ball shot to the left, and rolled into the gutter. "Oops. I'll go get it." I jogged out to the road and waited for a break in traffic. I quickly grabbed the ball and trotted back to Alex. I pondered kicking it back but didn't want to kick it wildly astray again. I set the ball down delicately and used my hand to slowly roll it towards Alex.

"I'll kick it, and you kick it back." He smirked." Try not to aim for the road this time." He gracefully passed the ball to me. I successfully sent it back this time, with no accidents. We kept this up for a few minutes, and I got cocky. When he sent the ball my way, I kicked it harder, sending it past him. I began running towards the goal, catching up with the ball. I managed to keep the ball between my feet and almost made it to the goal. I was about to take my final kick when I felt warm arms grab my waist. Alex hugged my stomach and lifted me off the ground. His embrace was shocking but comfortable in the January cold.

"Hey! Penalty! Foul? Whatever it is! You aren't allowed to use your hands in soccer!" I slapped his hands pitifully, wishing he'd never stop.

He put me down and let me go, then flopped down in the grass. "Sorry. I can't let my rookie boyfriend beat me." He smiled at me, and got up. He held a hand out to me, and pulled me down to his level. I could feel him breathing on my neck. I saw his hazel eyes scanning me, pupils wide.

I reached up to his hair, pulling out a blade of grass stuck in a curl of almost-black hair. "You forgot this." He grabbed the piece of grass from my hand and tucked it behind my ear.

∾

I was back in the lake. Alex was holding my waist as we floated in circles. I looked up, Jinkx and Swift were flying above, dancing just like we were. I knew it was a dream, but I didn't care. I wished this could be real. That we could escape to a new world, and still be together. That we could always be together, without the worries of the real world. That I could love my boyfriend in a world where no one could share their harmful opinions. A world made for us.

CHAPTER FOURTEEN

"Can I see it?"

"No! It's a surprise." Alex was carving away at a large piece of clay, hiding the front at all costs.

"That's fine, but you don't get to watch me sketch anymore."

I thought he would be sad, but he just looked at me and smiled. "That's okay, I can last a few days. Especially for how good this is going to be." That was worrisome. What could he possibly be working on?

I threw the question away and focused on the pearl staff. It wasn't until I was working on the staff that I realized how dumb this idea was. I had to make dozens of pearls, then paint each one. Despite its slimmer body, the staff would take longer to finish than my blade.

"So... I was wondering if you'd like to come over today?" I asked, scared he would shoot me down.

"Of course! I need to know more about your interests, and

what better way to learn than by snooping around your room some more?" He squeezed my hand, leaving pieces of wet clay all over it.

"Well thanks for that." I had just washed my hands.

He shot me a worried look. "I'm so sorry!" He started trying to scrape the clay off of my hand, just adding more.

I started laughing. "I was joking! I'll just go wash my hands again." I got up, and tried to walk to where I could see the front of his piece.

As I walked, he turned the clay in the opposite direction. "I'm not letting you see it that easily."

I surrendered, throwing my messy hands up in defeat. I washed my hands and returned to my seat, this time not trying to sneak a peek.

Alex found me in the art room after the last class of the day and walked me to my car. He sent me off and ran to his car. As I left the parking lot, I could see his Honda trailing behind me. I reached the house and parked in the driveway. Alex parked by the curb but stayed in his car. I walked to his car and knocked on the window. "You can get out now."

He was staring at nothing, and snapped back to reality after a few seconds. "Sorry." He got out and followed me to the front door. I entered the code: 0319, my birthday. I opened the door and let Alex in first.

"Hey Ma! Alex is here!"

My mom rushed to the front door. "Hi Alex, so nice to see you! How long are you staying? I planned on getting Panda Express tonight, so just let me know if you need to eat!" She patted him on the back and brought us into the living room.

He looked so happy. "Thanks, that sounds amazing. Let

me ask my mom first." He got out his phone and sent a text. The response was almost instantaneous and he initially looked excited. As he read the full message, his face dimmed. He shook himself and went back to his usual grinning self. "She said yes! I'll have whatever Zack is getting."

"Good choice, he is boring. You won't be trying anything adventurous with orange chicken and white rice. Now, you boys go upstairs and gossip. After dinner, though, I need to see Alex's Mario Kart skills."

Alex gasped comedically. "Is that a challenge?"

My mom grinned like a villain. "Why yes it is, and you're going down."

Alex inched closer to me. "I'm scared." I grinned at him and then pulled him up the stairs and straight to my room. I sat down on the bed, and turned on my TV. He stood in the doorway, not following me in.

"Are you okay?" I asked.

"More than okay. I mean I'm here, in your room." He looked clueless. If he didn't want to talk about his mom's message, I wasn't going to push him.

I scrolled to *RuPaul's Drag Race*, and hit play. "If you want to get to know me, you have to watch *Drag Race*." He got next to me, and stared at the TV. I chose season five, hoping to stun him with the wild dramatics of the season.

Almost immediately, he started commenting on the show. "She looks amazing!" He was referring to Jinkx Monsoon, the drag queen I had fondly named my dragon after. I chose not to spoil the ending for him, but said I agreed. "Wait! Coco and Alyssa already have drama? This is episode one!"

I grabbed his hand. "You won't believe this, but they both competed in a pageant a while back. It's so messy to explain." Every time something I thought was funny happened, he laughed before I got a chance to.

I stared at him for most of the episode, watching as his beautiful face shifted from confusion to glee to even sadness when Penny Tration was eliminated. "But it's the first episode, she didn't even get a chance!"

"That is just how it works, it's brutal." I got up and walked to my desk. I got out my drawing of the many iterations of Holly and motioned for Alex to come over. He hopped off of the bed, and practically skipped to me.

"What am I looking at? I mean, it's great, and I know *that* is a qorlin, but why is there a cat?"

I laughed, I forgot he hadn't really met Maia. "So Selene is actually my friend Maia, and she has a pet cat named Holly. She also got a pet qorlin from a quest and named it after her cat. This painting shows how our world and the virtual can be bridged through personal emotion."

He looked at it in awe. "That is so beautiful, I love it." His admiration dissolved into confusion. "Since when did Selene have a qorlin? I have never seen it, did she kill it already?"

I tried to hold back my laugh. It wasn't at his words, but what Maia had done with her virtual pet. "No, it isn't dead. She didn't want to put it in danger, so she left it at the guild hall. She literally figured out how to make it a kitty city. It's in her room, we can check it out tomorrow."

"That's so ridiculous, but also admirable? She doesn't strike me as the compassionate type, she seems pretty rash." He was right, both in *Echoes* and real life Maia was bad at showing her deep empathy, but she truly felt a lot of emotion for others.

"Yeah, that's Maia for you. She has been my best friend since I can remember." He went back to my bed and laid down. I sat next to him, about to start another episode when he pulled me down. I was now laying down, my head on his chest. "Well, hello."

He didn't kiss me, just kept his arms around my body. "Can I talk to you about something?"

I looked up at him and saw the sorrow in his eyes. "Of course, what is it?"

He was already choking up. "It's about my parents. Zack, I really like you, but they would never let me be with you. In front of them at least. My dad is a pastor, and I mean an old school pastor. The amount of times I've heard the word 'fa-' sorry, I can't say it. It hurts too much." Tears were streaming down his face.

I grabbed his face, wiping the tears from his cheek. "Alex, you shouldn't have to feel that way, it's not okay. I understand though, there are still stuck up people out there. I'm still scared to tell my mom. I mean, she's the nicest person ever, but you never know." I realized that wasn't helping. "I'm so sorry Alex. Do we need to stop?" As I said the words my stomach dropped and my heart felt like it had been stabbed. Only now, I was the one holding the knife.

My words tore him to pieces as well, I could see it in his eyes. "What? No! I really want to be with you. Just talking about it helps. I don't want to lose you. Please don't leave me alone."

I didn't mean for it to come off the way it must have. I didn't want to lose him either, but I guess that wasn't apparent. I wrapped my arms around him, and laid on top of his chest. We hugged like that for what felt like ages, then my mom yelled up at us from the foyer, "Hey! I'm back with the food, you guys can come eat!"

Before we headed downstairs, I used some tissues to dry Alex's tears. Once his eyes returned to normal, we went to the kitchen. My mom passed out our bowls, and we all ate together at our tiny table. The table had four chairs, one for me, one for my mom, one for a guest, and one for my dad. The last chair was never filled. He had died before I was old enough to remember it.

"This is really good! Amazing choice, Zack!" Alex said through bites, being careful not to chew while speaking. "My mom never lets us eat out, so thank you so much."

My mom laughed. "Good for her! We barely eat around here, it's usually take out." We ate our meals with haste, and sat around the TV. Ma had gotten very good at setting up Mario Kart. She grabbed the switch and shoved it into the dock. She fished around in a bin for all of our controllers, then laid them out on the coffee table. There were pro controllers, fake wheels, joycons, and even tennis racket attachments. "Take your pick!"

Alex settled on a pro controller, just like me. We all sat down and selected our characters. "Which would you say I should choose?"

"Whichever one you like, we won't judge." While I said it truthfully, if Maia were here, she would definitely make a quip about his selection. He chose Morton - which Maia definitely would have said something about. I obviously chose Daisy, and my mom chose Rosalina. With our characters selected, it was time to pick our vehicles. I chose my favorite, a car with two horses at the end, and my mom chose her signature purple motorcycle. After much deliberation, Alex settled on the basic bike. After some debate, we settled on the Flower Cup. It didn't take long for the racing to get heated.

"Which one of you bitches threw a shell at me?" My mom screamed, falling back into third place.

"Sorry Ms. Catrone! I want to win!" Alex shot a guilty glance at my mom. I hope he could tell she really didn't care, and was just having fun. The playful banter continued through the rest of the matches. Alex finally stepped into it by the final map, Shy Guy Falls. "Looks like you're lagging behind, Ms. Catrone!"

"Oh I'll get you!" She did. With a final red shell, she knocked Alex out of first place at the last second. "Yes! Undefeated!" She did a little dance, and sat back down. She turned to Alex. "Good job though! You almost beat me!"

He shrugged good naturedly and flashed a smile. "This has been amazing. I mean it, thank you so much, Ms. Catrone. I have to go now, but I'll definitely be back for some takeout!" My mom hugged him, and I walked him to the door.

"Thank you for coming over, I had so much fun." I closed the door behind me.

"No, thank *you*." He looked around, then kissed me.

My face went red. "I'm still not used to that, but I love it." He started walking backwards to his car. He pressed his hand to his lips and blew a kiss. Lovestruck, I watched him get in his car and drive away.

I went back into the house, and before I could head to my room, I heard my mom. "He's a sweet boy."

"Yes, he really is."

CHAPTER FIFTEEN

Thursday, January 31th

We were all finally level 56, which meant it was time for the beach. We started at the guild hall for convenience. We could have headed to the beach from the lake, but it would be easier to cut through the Plains. I found the dusty alley where the hall laid, and saw Somnus waiting by the door. He must have been scared to go in without me. "Hey! How long have you been waiting?"

He became animated in an instant. "Not that long! Just like twenty minutes." He sounded sincere.

"Twenty minutes? You should have texted me, I would've hurried up." I got out my key and unlocked the door. No one was in the foyer, so I headed to Selene's room. With a gloved hand, I mimicked knocking. "Knock, knock. Let us in Selene!" The door cracked open, but she wasn't standing behind it. "Okay! Come through with the magic!"

"Hey guys." She was sitting on her fake bed, staring at

Holly. The qorlin ran around the room in circles. Starting on the makeshift tower, it jumped down, circled the bed, and ran back to the top of its habitat.

"So how are you?" Somnus asked while watching the little creature run.

"I'm fine, how are you two?" She said, an obvious tone of mockery in her voice.

"I'm great, I can't speak for Somnus though."

Somnus stuttered over his words. "Yeah, same for me."

"Well! This has been awkward enough, let's head out to the table..." I pulled Somnus with me and headed down the hallway.

"You weren't lying about the virtual kitty city. I swear I have seen that at PetSmart." After Selene came stumbling to the entrance behind us, we were ready to go. We exited the guild hall, twisting through the bustling streets of Wysteria before finding the bridge.

I was about to call on Jinkx when Rampi stopped me. "No dragons today. I want to see the Plains up close again. And even if it's fake, we should take a walk on the beach." To my surprise, no one argued. We walked the whole way down the giant bridge, and entered the Plains. I hadn't seen them before, but hidden in the tall blades of grass were tiny green snakes.

I was not fond of snakes, but these little reptiles were so cute and looked pretty harmless. "Aw!" I picked one up. "Look at it! I don't remember seeing these before." The snake slid around my arm and rested on my shoulder.

"Really? They've been here since we cleared the Plains. You probably didn't see them due to their size. Unlike Ralios, these guys are so tiny." Apha resolved my confusion. "Oh, and don't try to tame them. They are such sweet creatures but for some reason, they aren't tamable. Speaking from experience..."

"That's too bad." I scooped the snake off of my shoulder

and lowered it to the ground. It squeezed my hand then slithered away, disappearing into the grass. I secretly wanted to keep it. If Selene could have a pet, why couldn't we? Then I saw it. Holly was on Selene's shoulder. "Woah! Selene, you brought Holly with you?"

"Yeah." Selene petted the animal. "She seemed so full of energy, I couldn't leave her again. Especially for the beach. She took Holly off of her shoulder, and set her on my head. "Her Guncle can take care of her before we get to the beach."

"Thanks..." We passed the village, which was still thriving. The expansive plains stayed vibrant. Ever since we defeated Ralios, the flowers never wilted and the animals were always lively. Where Selene and I had once fought our first few scalosos was now a well. Its bright stone shone in the sun, and it held plenty of water for the village.

As we passed the village, going in a new direction, we saw a small cave. The entrance was hung with thick vines and covered in shells and barnacles. It emitted dim, natural light. We reached the cave, which was more of a tunnel for a small wooden bridge. It opened from each end, allowing the sun to hit different parts of the bridge. The bridge itself consisted of several wooden planks held up by old rope. The ropes connected to posts, making the bridge wobbly and creaky. Below the passage was a pool of aquamarine water populated by small crabs. We carefully crossed the old bridge, going in spaced out pairs.

Once we were all on the other side, we exited the cave, stepping onto a stunning shore. The beach was filled with pure white sand, littered with shimmering seashells. Unlike the other areas, the beach appeared unaffected. Its shores practically glowed, the sand was pure, and NPCs walked the sands with carefree strides.

Just as we thought we were safe, a shark jumped at us. It

walked on two legs, had a coat on, and a pirate hat. Above it read "LVL 56." It looked like an enemy, so we were all on guard. In a raspy voice, it spoke. "Ahoy! Are you here to challenge us?" An option menu appeared, and we all chose the safest choice: **"NO."** The shark stepped back, sheathing its curved sword. "Good to hear! Welcome to Tacean Sands! You are free to explore our many relaxation options, but if you want a real quest, come back to me when you're ready, argg!" The shark spun around, finding a wooden post to stand against.

"I'm not opposed to exploring before taking on something serious." Rampi said contently, leading us to the beach. We walked across the sandy shores, looking out into the shining ocean.

Somnus bent down and grabbed a small seashell. "Isn't this pretty?"

It was pretty. With its scallop shape, pure white color, and perfectly creased edges, it was stunning. "That is so cute. It would be great on a necklace." I watched as Somnus added it to his inventory, then kept walking.

We eventually reached a bustling oceanside town. The houses and shops were made out of small boats, and the paths were lined with seashells. We passed elves, sylphs, shark-people, orcs, humans, anyone who could live here, did. The diversity stunned me. The most diverse place we had been to yet was the United Forest, and even that area started out lacking in diversity. It was nice to see a friendly and peaceful area for once. It still left me uneasy, wondering what we would have to do to clear the area.

After passing bars, beach houses, cabanas, and even a gazebo, we reached a restaurant. Rampi stood on the steps, waiting for us. "We have to check it out, come on! It's on me." We followed her in, looking around the giant space. There were dozens of tables and unique seating options. From a bar to booths to standard tables, the restaurant had it all. A shark-man took us to a long table in the back, and handed us our menus. I wondered what the point of being here was, we couldn't even truly eat.

Rampi soon answered that question. "We have to get this one! This lobster plate gives you a permanent shield boost!" The meal wasn't cheap, but Rampi offered to pay for us all.

Ever since founding the guild, Rampi had slowly made her leadership more motherly. She was acting like a caregiver more than a leader. The question was burning a hole in my mind. "Rampi, do you have kids?"

"Why do you ask? But yes, I have two kids. A boy and girl, they are my world." I nodded, the information not surprising. "Before you start wondering where they are, their dad is watching them. I work from home, so he gets to give me a break in the afternoons."

Lali raised her glass. "I know that's right. Kids are lovely but sometimes I just need a break."

Selene laughed. "Thank god I'll never have kids. The closest thing I want to a kid is a pet. Give me a cat or chihuahua and I'm good." She finally took Holly from my shoulder, and started petting her while eating her lobster.

We finished the meals quickly. All we had to do was raise the plate near our mouth, so it didn't take long. We headed back out through the door and headed back to the shore.

Rampi stared out into the ocean. "Let's just hang out here for a little bit. The quest can wait, we haven't gotten to enjoy these areas at all." No one was going to object to that. Somnus and I found a spot on the sand and sat down.

I watched as a small pink crab waddled over to him. "I think someone wants to be your friend."

He looked down and saw the little creature. "Aw! It's so

cute. Don't tell Selene I said this, but I think it's cuter than Holly. The qorlin, not the cat."

I laughed at the fact he had to clarify which Holly he was referring to. Before I could respond, Selene came barrelling down the beach. "I heard that. Do you want to apologize to Holly or deal with me?" She held out the qorlin by its arms, shoving it into Somnus' face.

He laughed dryly. "I'm sorry Holly. Maybe you two can be friends?" He picked up the crab and held it level to Holly. Selene set her pet down and Somnus followed. What I saw confused me. The two animals circled each other, then started playing in the sand. These were just NPCs, pixels, but they had so much life. I was torn. Part of me wanted to silently cheer for the developers, the other part was saddened by what this meant for all of the other animals in-game. If Syphon was taking these animals from their homes, doing *something* to them, and using them for his own game, players were being denied this happiness. Were the pets in this game as rare as legendary items?

An even more troubling question emerged in my mind: why did I care? This wasn't real. The noises, the plants, the enemies, the animals, the NPCs. It was all fake. However, the players were very real and their joy was real and I would protect it as best I could.

Somnus took me out of my depressingly pointless thoughts. "Mirage! I got to name the crab!" He came flying down the beach, Holly and Selene following behind. I hadn't realized how far the animals had roamed as they played. He held out the little crab to me. "I named it Jessie. Not sure why, but it seemed to fit."

I had no clue what part of "Jessie the crab" was "fitting," but his evident joy was hard to crush. "You're right, she really does look like a Jessie! Great choice!" I scratched its head, or back, whatever it was on a crab, and let Somnus play with his new pet.

The others ran over to see what the fuss was about. Sylvia was obviously saddened by the new find. "I forgot to bring Teddy on this adventure. Just like the last one. Dammit!"

I tried to cheer her up. "It's probably for the best, we are on a beach. Last time was at a lake. I don't think those are optimal places for a bear."

That didn't seem to work. "No, I can't abandon him like Selene does."

"Hey! We have left our pets at the same amount of places bitch! Don't try me!" Selene protested. Watching them fight over fake animals ironically warmed my heart. Maybe this felt real to them too.

Sylvia called her dragon down, sending sand flying. "I'm going back to Wysteria, back in a flash." With that, her large silver dragon took off, and she headed to the city.

I looked around for something to do to pass the time. I saw a volleyball court further down the beach. They even had volleyball here. It felt like the developers had thought of everything."Guys! Let's go play volleyball!"

"That sounds great! We aren't going to have evenly matched teams though..." Rufus' voice went from excitement to defeat.

Rampi was there to save the day. "Don't worry, I can referee." We split into teams of three. Lali, Apha, and Rufus on one side; Somnus, Selene, and I on the other. We ran back and forth on the court for around five minutes, hitting a monochromatic green ball back and forth, not paying attention to the rules of volleyball.

We decided to call it quits when Somnus tripped trying to avoid stepping on his virtual crab. "I know it's fake but I can't step on an animal. I did that to my cat once, I was never the same." The match ended with a score of 5:4, in favor of Apha's team. They were happy to let us end it, especially because we were gaining on them.

Quickly after finishing our game, Sylvia came flying in. She tapped her dragon. "Thank you, Bianca, you can go now." The dragon flew away, and Selene walked towards us, her bear on her back. "Hey, did I miss anything?"

"Just a sad game of volleyball." Selene responded, running up to pet Teddy. Their feud over whose pet was better had ended. They now let Holly and Teddy share the spotlight.

Rampi stepped down from a rock she had used to "referee." Her refereeing included scrolling through her spellbook, checking the map, and studying her logged enemies. Not much of a referee. "So, are we ready to head out?"

Everyone agreed, and we headed back to the pirate. On the way, Rufus voiced his concern. "Does no one find it odd that we are helping a pirate? I mean, he started as an enemy."

"I actually thought about it." Lali spoke up. "I don't think he was truly an enemy. I mean, you can access the beach from the first area, they needed a preventative measure to keep new players out. I think it was just a reason to keep people on track. Look around, the pirates are obviously doing something right." She was right. It wasn't uncommon for open-world games to scare away players with the visage of a dangerous area.

As soon as we reached the shark, he got up from his post and swaggered over to us. "Hey there! Are you ready to accept my mission?" This time we all chose "**YES**."

He instantly went into story mode. "The sea is not how it used to be. Our shores are still lovely, but far out there, it's no man's land. No man's water. Before, we used to explore the farthest reaches of that shimmering blue. Now, we aren't sure what has taken place in that once tranquil basin."

He took a seat on a nearby rock. "My finest sailors have

been disappearing. We sent out search parties for each disappearance, and search parties for the search parties. Every time, no one returns. It is up to you to find the cause of these vanishings, and return the sea to how it once was. To our second home. Only if you think you can handle it." He ended his emotional monologue with a condescending smirk. The quest now appeared for all of us: "**NEW QUEST: WHAT LURKS BENEATH?**"

He hopped off of his rock, nodded, and shook our hands. He continued in a more upbeat tone, "If you follow me this way, I have a boat for you." He showed us past a large rock formation, passing abandoned pieces of rope and life preservers. We entered a cove, and saw a large ship facing the open sea. It was complete with a hull, stern, rudder, and three black flags. The middle flag protruded from a small crow's nest. We all climbed aboard the ship, and watched as the pirate used a sword to cut the rope binding us to the cove. "Good luck! And don't get eaten!" He waved goodbye, and we were all left confused.

"So... I'm guessing a giant man-eating monster is what 'lurks beneath.' Probably one of Syphon's minions." Selene said, climbing up to the crow's nest.

"Well that is lovely, but who is gonna steer this thing?" I asked, watching as our new boat sailed aimlessly into the open ocean.

Somnus stepped up to the wheel. "I've got this! I took a boating class once. Didn't really pay attention but I got that license!" His chipper attitude did not rub off on everyone else.

"The boating portion of Driver's Ed doesn't count!" Selene called down from the crow's nest.

"We're definitely screwed." Rufus complained.

"Well, does anyone else have any experience with boats?" I questioned, trying to defend Somnus.

"I watched *Titanic*." Apha tried to lighten the mood, but everyone seemed tired. "Eh, nevermind. Have at it kid." I joined Somnus on the deck, and watched as he sailed us around aimlessly.

"You don't know where you're going, do you?"

"Not really, but at least I have my crab. Oh, and you."

A yell broke us from our flirting. "Guys! I think I know where we are supposed to go!" Selene shouted from the crow's nest. "Look there!" She was pointing at a large rock in the middle of the ocean. As we neared the rock, it appeared to have an opening.

Somnus stopped steering the boat, and Rampi threw down the anchor. "Sorry Jessie, I think you should stay here." Somnus, Sylvia, and Selene all put their pets in the captain's quarters, and came back out. We used a ladder to get off of the boat, swimming a few feet before making it to the cave. As we entered the small cave, we saw a flight of steps. The steps were very rough, more like ridges of old rock than actual steps, but they at least led down.

"Well this is shitty." Selene spoke up, saying what we were all thinking of the misshapen steps. We finally reached the end of the raggedy stairs, and found ourselves in a cave system. Water dripped in from tiny holes, dead coral lined the floors, and seaweed caught on the walls. We walked past an empty room and found ourselves in an even larger cave. All around us, there were piles of bones. Skulls, legs, pelvises, arms, tailboncs, everything. Sitting around those bones were pirate hats. These were the sailors. "Maybe we should leave now!" Selene exclaimed.

"Be quiet Selene! You never know what could be around." Just as I suspected, the far wall of the cave came crashing down. From the new opening crawled a giant crab. Its long pincers smashed down onto the rocky floor. Its back was lined with purple rocks, and its eyes shone a bright red.

The fight was one of our easiest. The crab moved slowly, as if it was tired. Its lazy swings allowed for fast action on our end. We all swung, cast, and smashed rapidly, bringing the crab to its last leg in less than ten minutes. Apha took the last hit, crushing its hardened back in one blow, and sending it through the ceiling in a flash of yellow light. The notification appeared: **QUEST COMPLETE: WHAT LURKS BENEATH?"**

"That was way too easy..." Rampi said with an edge of fear in her voice. I could tell we were all wondering what made this a level 56 quest. We all waited around, but nothing else happened. The shark made it seem like they had stopped sending out search parties a while back. Without sailors to eat, the crab was about to die anyway, and we just had to put it out of its misery. That was my conclusion, anyway.

We got back into the ship, and sailed back to the shore. The sun had set, but the town was as lively as ever. Torches were lit, casting everything in a warm orange. Dancers spun sticks of fire on the shore. Every house had lights on.

When we reached shore, most of the group said their good-byes. Soon, only Selene, Somnus, and I were left online. "Mirage! I need to show you something." Selene pulled me to a far end of the shore, away from all of the village dramatics. She set Holly in front of her, and motioned with her hand. The qorlin did a flip, ran down the beach, then did a somersault.

"Wow! That is really impressive! I really need to get a pet some day."

"You don't think three is enough?" We started laughing, then Somnus rejoined us, his crab on his head.

"What's so funny?" As Somnus started talking, Selene motioned that she was going to leave. It was just us.

"Oh, we were talking about how many pets the guild has now." I answered.

"Yeah, I didn't realize Sylvia had one. Where did she even find a bear?"

"It was so dumb, it was just some monster in the palace that she tamed."

"That is insane!" He sounded so shocked, just like we all were when she decided to keep it. "I really enjoyed this area. It was a nice change of pace, you know? Instead of slashing and running, we got to relax and explore."

I knew what he meant, and just nodded. I enjoyed getting to spend time with him on a beach, but that wasn't going to happen in real life. We lived in basically the center of the United States. "I have a surprise for you." He said, reaching into his inventory and grabbing the shell, only this time it was attached to a string. "I found an artisan in the village, turns out you can turn any shell you find into jewelry."

I grabbed the necklace from him with haste. It was just pixels, but it meant everything to me. He had remembered what I said, and actually chose to make me something from that memory. "If this were real life, we would be making out in the ocean right now."

CHAPTER SIXTEEN

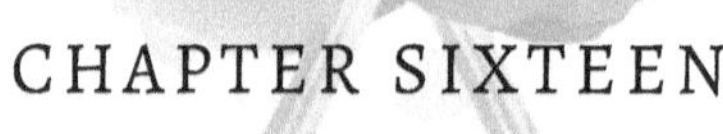

lex had decided he wanted to tell Maia. A risky decision, but one he was insistent on making. To start his day, he was going to pick me up. For the first time in my life, I was getting to use a boy as a personal chauffeur.

My excitement was stunted by fear. I had never been in his car, what if it wasn't clean? He did play soccer, what if I would get in and be met with a horrid stench? I brushed it off when I saw his car in front of the house. I threw my bag over my shoulder and jogged out to his car.

His white Honda glimmered in the sun as I opened the door. "Hey!" I sat down, and it did not smell bad. In fact, I immediately recognized the scent as Rose Water, one of Maia's favorite scents. "Smells good in here."

"Thanks! I just got this air freshener from the mall. I love it." His ability to foster love for anything, no matter how miniscule, always made me swoon. "Are you ready for the essay today?"

I definitely was, and I hoped after our "study sessions," Alex was too. "I think so, how about you?"

"Oh yeah. Your 'wisdom' has made me so much better with my writing." He winked, and shifted his car into drive. We reached the school, and I told Alex to park in my usual spot. As we pulled in, Maia was waiting in her car.

I got out and knocked on her window. Today's serenade was *Twice* by Charli XCX. This time, she quickly snapped to attention after my first knock. "Hey!"

We all walked to class together, Maia throwing me weird glances the whole trip. "Have fun in English, say 'hi' to Sierra for me!" She stuck her tongue out and left Alex and I standing alone.

"Who is Sierra?" Alex questioned, scratching his head.

"Oh, I've never met her, but Maia is head over heels for her."

"Huh, reminds me of someone." I immediately started blushing, and raced to my seat to avoid more hazardous flirting.

The essay flew by. In no time we were all done, or at least cut off. The bell sounded, and we all got up. As I was packing I felt a tap on my shoulder. Obviously, I thought it would be Alex. A smile formed on my lips, and I turned around. That smile instantly turned to an annoyed frown when I saw Connor standing before me. "Did you write about how desperate you are?"

I composed myself. "No, I wrote about Gatsby. Did you write about chronic acne?"

His expression darkened and he scowled viciously.. "My face is not that bad. Take a look at yourself before commenting on my flawless appearance. Let us not forget you used to want *this* so bad you even started cutting-"

Alex stepped up next to me and cut him off. "Hey! Be nice. There is no need to bring up the past. Do you know how hurtful you're being?" I winced internally, that cringey shit was not going to stop Connor.

"Oh, let me guess, you wrote your essay on how in love you are with this little bitch?" Connor scoffed.

"If that's how you want to play it, okay.. Then no, I actually pay attention in class, so my essay was on Gatsby. However, I also pay attention to petty little bitches and can see through that fugly visage of yours. Let's not deny it, your face is a wreck and your legs are as tiny as those of that chair. Your hair looks like it hasn't been washed in days, and you smell like the local dump. I would not be surprised if you had lice, and I mean *everywhere* on your body. While we're at it, it's obvious you're the one in love with Zack here, and you just can't accept that, can you?" Connor shut up and left the room. I had no idea that Alex - athletic, quiet, sweet, thoughtful Alex could read a bitch like that. It only made me like him even more. Hell, a read like that was good enough to get on *Drag Race*.

I practically skipped to history, which was instantly noticed by Bostyn. "What has made you so happy?"

With a large grin I shared the events from English. "My boy- my friend read Connor for filth. You had to be there, Connor couldn't even respond. It was amazing." Having to catch myself would become a dangerous little chore.

"Dammit! I wish I saw that!" All these years later, and her feelings for Connor had never changed. I applauded that dedication, especially when it was harbored for someone so awful.

I joined up with Alex after class and headed to the art room.

Maia was in a corner, watching something on her phone. "I see you brought a friend today."

Alex and I joined her on the floor. "Hey Se- Maia. Sorry I haven't really talked to you in real life." Alex started sweating. "Um. Sorry."

"What he means to say-" I interjected.

He cut me off. "No, I've got this. Maia, I really like your best friend. He is the best thing to happen to me." He grabbed her hand dramatically. "Please don't tell anyone, but I wanted you to know. He lights up my life in a way no one else has. He lifts me up in both of our worlds. He is everything to me. I just want your blessing, as I know you two have been through a lot together."

Maia laughed. "What do I look like? The lesbian fairy godmother? No, but for real, that is amazing. I mean, it was really obvious, but I am so happy for you two. Now, if you could let go of me..." She forced his hand off of hers. "Ah! I just realized you're his first boyfriend! Aw! That is so cute. I'm gonna take a picture to commemorate this moment." We tried to protest, but she pulled out her phone and took a picture. "So cute!" She turned the screen to us. What we saw as a blurry image of both of us looking horrified.

"Sure... cute!" I looked at Alex, and gave him a short hug. "Why are you crying?"

He had tears streaming down his eyes, falling onto my shirt. "Sorry, it's just so nice to say that you're my boyfriend. Like, being able to tell someone, and not just repeat it over and over in my head makes it feel real. You're my boyfriend."

Maia wasn't having it. "Pack it up, twinks. I've had enough of this cheesy ass coming out. Let's watch some Abby Lee Miller." I pulled out my phone and opened up *Dance Moms*. Here we were, sitting in the art room, watching our favorite show with a third person. Not just any person, but my boyfriend. My perfect, amazing, *real* boyfriend.

That very gay lunch was followed up by a very homophobic lecture. In biology, it was time for human reproduction. After discussing everything, Mr. Ralph switched gears. He turned off his powerpoint, and went into a rant about the horrors of gay relationships. The phrases "it's not natural" and "God didn't want this" were thrown around quite often. By the end of his speech, I wondered how he was still able to teach at the school. Right before a rant on transgender issues, the bell saved us. Even the most conservative students were upset, and everyone left holding their breath.

I decided to grill Ms. Bash when I entered art. "Do you know what the hell is going on with Mr. Ralph? He randomly went into this homophobic rant, and a while ago he made us learn the gory details of snail sex."

"Oh yeah. He is a mess, but he is tenured. So many complaints against him, but no action. I guess that's what happens when you've been teaching for thirty years." She rolled her eyes, obviously not surprised by my complaint, and started scrolling on her computer. I took my seat next to Alex, and wasn't surprised to find him with a large grin on his face.

"What's that smile for?"

"Usually for you, but I'm ready to unveil my project." He winked, and raced to a back table that housed his piece. He walked back carefully, watching as he took each step. "Close your eyes!" I obliged, but wondered why I needed to close my eyes for a block of clay. "And... Open!"

I opened my eyes, and I almost started crying, but somehow held back my tears. Before me was a bust of myself. From the shoulders to the head, its proportions were exact. The lips curved just as mine did. The eyes were filled with life, and there were even indents below to depict my slight eye bags.

The eyebrows were full and the hair curly. It looked exactly like me, no mistakes. "How?" I repeated that word through sniffles. "It's amazing, but you couldn't even make a tree, how did you make *me*?" I was so happy it hurt. He did so much for me, and what did I do in return? Make a sword?

His next words hit me with the force of ten diesel trucks. "I find it easier to capture your essence than that of the most natural creations. To me, you are natural. You are my fuel, my anchor to this world." No one had ever spoken to me so poetically. And without Maia here, I could bask in his poetic nonsense with idiotic glee.

"I don't know what to say..." I started.

"Sorry, you're crying now and I feel bad. That romantic stuff was a joke." He shrugged helplessly. "I've actually always been good with clay. I just wanted you to talk to me on the first day..."

There was certainly no chance of me spilling tears now. "You bitch!" I threw a piece of clay at his face. "Are you insane? I'm not even that mad about that fake romantic stuff. But have you really been wasting weeks worth of time just to make me think you didn't know what you were doing?"

He peeled a piece of clay off of his eyebrow. "Ow. Sorry, what I said is true though! And I've been coming in for help from Ms. Bash during my health class anyway, so I'm not *that* behind."

"Sure..." I laughed. My boyfriend was talented and thoughtful and even if it was a joke, his romantic ramblings made me feel like I was in a dream.

"Zack! Time for dinner!" My mom yelled from downstairs. We were having Cheesecake Factory, one of our favorites. We always split the sliders. I grabbed plates, napkins, and silver-ware, and set the table. It was an old table and takeout, but we tried to keep it classy. Ma brought over the food and evenly separated the four sliders onto our plates. She poured out the fries after, keeping more for herself. I had no issue with this, the fries from The Cheesecake Factory were mediocre at best. "So, how was school?"

I put down my little burger. "It was okay. I didn't get a lot of work done on my portfolio, the essay was boring, and my biology teacher stayed weird as ever." There was truth to what I said. Mr. Ralph was weird, and I hadn't done much for my portfolio. However, the essay ended in a bang, and I had a whole art piece created in my honor. I wouldn't say that was just "okay." Maybe magnificent, or fantastic, or lovely.

"I'm sorry to hear that. I got this done today!" She pulled out a giant blanket. She somehow had the skills to crochet and read at the same time. A truly deadly combo I could never figure out. I could do both, just not at the same time like the master that sat before me. Her expertise yielded many baby blankets and even some full sized ones, like this one. The blanket featured a blue ombre effect that led to a contrasting tan color. "It's a beach! I haven't been to one in years but you never forget that feeling." She was the type of middle aged woman to live thousands of miles away from a beach but still have a beach themed bathroom. Her admiration of the shore was, well, admirable.

The blanket struck me with a new idea. A way to pay back all of Alex's loving gifts. I had learned to crochet with Ma, but hadn't used my skills in a few years. I would sometimes go back to it just to see if I remembered how, and it was like riding a bike. There was no way I wouldn't be able to conjure some-thing up for Alex. I finished my plate and put it in the dishwasher. "Hey Ma? Do you think I could run to Walmart really quickly?"

She looked up from her plate. "Yeah sure, no problem. Just get me some milk while you're out." I nodded, and headed to my car. On my way out, I heard her yell. "Also get me some M&Ms! You know what kind!" I did, she loved peanut M&Ms even though I never got the appeal. I drove to the nearest Walmart, which happened to be next to the Starbucks, and found a spot near the front.

I grabbed a handheld basket and made my way to the crafts section.. Navigating past fabrics and jewelry making supplies, I finally reached the yarn aisle, and spotted the perfect yarn for my project. I grabbed two pale pinks and a white, then threw them into the basket. I circled through the food sections to grab the milk and M&Ms and rushed to the self checkouts.

Self checkouts were my first true love. I despised having to make small talk about my purchases and self checkouts were an easy way out. I never used cash so they always accepted my payment method. I was also usually much faster at scanning and bagging my items than another person. It was only in the most dire of circumstances that I wouldn't use a self checkout.

I quickly paid for the items and raced to my car. I didn't want to stay up too late, so I needed to be home quickly. I dropped off the groceries with Ma, and headed upstairs. I found my old hook and stitch markers, grabbed a pattern book, and flipped until I found an amigurumi crab. It was perfect. Its measurements seemed to fit how big Jessie seemed in-game, and it looked just like her. I spent the whole night slaving away over small pieces of the crab, making legs, claws, and two body halves. I got out my yarn needle and attached each part, watching Jessie come to life before me. It was 2:00am by the time I finished, but I was left with the perfect Valentine's present for Alex.

CHAPTER SEVENTEEN

Thursday, February 7th

"Who am I looking at?" Somnus was holding out Jessie, except this time she had something on her head.

"It's a bow! Isn't it cute? I found a boutique in the woods. I think purple looks nice, don't you?" He shoved her closer to my face.

"Yeah..." I struggled to see a bow, it really just looked like a poorly drawn star. "Are you sure you bought the right thing? It looks like it's slipping off."

"Oh shit it is. Wait... I think I bought a star fragment by accident. I don't think that was a boutique..." He ripped the star off of the crab and pocketed it. We'd decided to stay on the beach instead of returning to the guild hall. Everyone who had a pet, had it out.

Teddy, Jessie, and Holly played as we discussed our next plan. "If we head north past the restaurants, we should make it to the next area." Rampi explained, pointing north for clarity. "I'm not sure what we are looking for, but it is the only way we haven't been." We headed past the restaurant, and into a small valley lined with palm trees. Large rocks created a forced pathway and led out to nothing.

"Huh? There's just a giant hole in the ground." Sylvia bent down, staring into the abyss. "I'm not jumping down there! Someone else go!" We all stared blankly at each other, lost.

I threw my head up in confusion, and finally saw it. "We are so dumb. Look up." Above us were three flying islands. One huge island in the center and two connected to the larger one with bridges. Rocks jutted out from the islands, trailing down through the sky like stalactites. It was hard to make out what rested atop the islands, but one thing was apparent: a temple. From one of the smaller islands trailed a thin line. It reached a point on a mountain at the beach, and attached to a post. "I think we need to go to that peak, that could be a zipline."

Selene was confused. "Why not just ride our dragons?"

I was prepared for this question. "I thought about it too, but if you look right there at that red line, that is the flight limit." Above the clouds, a faint red line was marked across the islands. "We could get about half way there, but not much further. It's best to just take the normal route."

"I'm with Mirage on this one, let's go." Lali confirmed my plan, and we went back to the beach. After reaching the far edge of the beach, we climbed up the small mountain. The air was clear and no trees sprouted from the tan rock. The zipline only took one person at a time, and I volunteered to go first. I grabbed the blue handle and hung as the electronic block moved me up the line. I watched as my friends faded out of view, and the islands became more clear.

The two that connected to the main island had heart

shaped ponds, and nothing else. Each island had a white stone bridge that led to their mother island. All in all, the two baby islands were bleak and simple. The large island however, was home to a giant tower. Its golden material shone brightly in the sun, its proximity to the glowing ball making it evermore lustrous. The base tower had two smaller watchtowers jutting from the sides, their bases curving out to form a pitchfork shape. The roofs of each tower spiraled to a single point, almost scratching the sun.

The zipline stopped, and I jumped off. The device that brought me up to the islands shot back down, reaching the peak in no time. I took in the environment as I waited for everyone to arrive. White birds flew in circles around the islands, some even rested atop the heart shaped ponds. Qorlins, now a gliding variation, chased each other around the ponds, rolling into bright pink flowers. Soon enough, Lali, Rampi, and Apha landed on the island. After a few moments, the others trickled in. Somnus was last, and zoomed straight to me once he was on the island. "This is so romantic." He mimicked grabbing my waist, and brought me to the pond. "Look!" A little carefree, but I didn't mind. Even if it was risky, I just wanted to be with him.

He threw in his star fragment. I watched as the misshapen star met the floor of the pond, shot up, and released three heart shaped clouds. "Woah. That is so cute!" I was about to faint from excitement. Had he gotten that star by accident, or was it just to impress me? Either way, his charm was never brought into question. We passed the pond, walking across the small bridge to get to the main island. The pathway to the tower was lit up with golden lamp posts. The lamp posts spiraled up from a thick base, then shot out into golden branches that held an orb of light.

Before we could get to the tower, a flurry of light raced

towards us. The light bent until it took a form. It was Illia, and she had tears streaming down her face. "Warriors, you have come so far in liberating Velouria, but there is still much work to be done. What you see before you is my tower. I have done what I can to protect the animals of this area, but Syphon has placed one of his... experiments into my tower. It is unsafe for me to battle the beast, and if I tried, I would put all of these beautiful beings in jeopardy." She waved her hand, gesturing at every bird, bug, and mammal in the area. "While I do my work out here, please free my tower. You are almost at the end of your journey, do not give up hope now." She placed a hand to her heart, wiped her tears, and fluttered away into a million stars. As she drifted away, our new quest appeared: **"NEW QUEST: RELIGHT THE TOWER OF THE PRIESTESS."**

As we walked down the pathway, the lights went out one by one. Once we reached the door, all of the lights had dissipated, and the sun had been replaced by a full moon. The golden tower lost its shine, transforming it into a dark and daunting structure. The door swung open unprompted, eliciting a reaction from Selene. "Now what the hell was that?" I took the first step in, and blue ghost lights lit up the first circular room.

The floor was checkered, appearing black and blue. Given the outside of the tower, I assumed it was actually gold and white. The room was bare except for a podium in the middle. It reminded me of how the cathedral was set up, just scarier. We reached the podium, and found a large button. Selene decided to press it, triggering the appearance of seven bird statues. The statues shot up from trapdoors in the floor, and turned to face different directions. The bird at the far end of the room emitted a bright blue light and the rest held mirrors.

"Look up there." Apha pointed to a large closed eye above

a new door. "We probably need to get the light to hit that eye." Everyone but Apha took a statue. We turned the statues according to her directions. "No! Your other right!" "Up!" "Down a little?" and many more directions were heard from the druid. We eventually got the light to angle up and straight, hitting the eye. The eye shot open, and as its iris was revealed, it sent out waves of rainbow light. The light filled the room, restoring the color to it. The floors were now gold and white, the lights were bright orange, and the podium was revealed to be marble. We pressed the now gold button, and the door opened. "Yipee! I was right about something!" Apha cheered, an odd reaction for someone who usually brought logic to the group.

We walked through the door, up some stairs, and into another dreary and open room. In the middle of this room was an obscured creature. We inched closer, trying to make out the animal in the dimly lit space. It growled, then jumped at me. "Oh shit!" The blue lights lit up as I was chased around the room. A large rodent came into view, revealing an even more concerning name: "**MINI BOSS: QORLIN GUARD**." This thing was related to Holly? No way.

"What am I supposed to do here? I can't in good conscience hurt it." Selene mused, staring at the malicious squirrel. She quickly changed her mind when it bit her leg. "Holly run to the other room! I need to take down your bitch of a family member!" Selene sent the qorlin to the ceiling of the room with a single hit. However, this qorlin - like the smaller ones outside - could glide. It stretched its long tan arms and flew around the room. It took down lights and wall decor, making the whole room a safety hazard. Apha used Rufus' back to launch into the air, taking down the flying squirrel with another hit. Something was different in her punch. Her gloves used to be black with silver spikes, but now they were tan with sharp shells jutting from the knuckles.

With the qorlin down to our level again, we quickly defeated it. I felt a twinge of pain as it dissolved into the ground. Seeing a qorlin in that shape only made me want to fight more. It was obviously not its normal state, something made it that way. Large and furious was not how I was used to seeing qorlins. I was used to the cheerful, pocket sized, squirrel creatures like Holly. I threw away these thoughts to bother Apha. "Apha, when did you get new fists? Did you get the legendary drop from the beach? Sure looks like one to me…"

"Uh, yeah. I did. Sorry, I just didn't want to make a big deal out of it." She said quietly. She had her loud moments, but Apha generally blended into the background.

"This is amazing! If we all get legendary weapons, which is still possible, we could be the most powerful guild ever!" Lali yelled, looking up at the newly colorful ceiling. Defeating the mini boss had restored the room to its original colors, making it much more welcoming. At the end of the room, a large door clicked open. It was surrounded by carvings of doves, each flying towards the top of the door. The wall was covered in the delicate birds, displaying a tent shape as they flew in formation.

We all stepped through the new door, watching as a giant staircase unfolded before us. Above the steps was a large golden throne. The staircase and third floor both retained their golden hue. The walls were lined with gold torches and a large red rug contrasted with the metallic feel of the rest of the room.

As we stepped onto the red carpet, the room completely changed. Everything shifted to that terrifying black and blue. The lights went out and a screech was heard around the room. A blue light erupted in the chamber, and a giant raven, or so I thought, appeared. It alighted on the throne for a few seconds;

a dominating presence. It let out another screech and flew back towards the ceiling. It circled above us then dove down, straight into Lali. She dodged, clipping one of its claws.

The bird flew back up and circled around to attack Somnus. He stabbed the checkered floor with his blade, producing blue flowers. The buds latched on to the raven's wings, pausing its movement for a moment. I took this window to study the beast. Its name was "Davenine," a regal name for a false king, or queen. The bird broke free of the grasping blossoms. It screeched again, piercing my ears. I looked at the health bar. No damage had been done.

I saw Sylvia struggling in the top right of the room. "Hey! Are you okay?"

"Yeah, I'm just trying to heal. It barely hit me, but I almost died." Sylvia produced orb after orb, working to mend her cuts and get back into the fight. I hadn't been hit yet, so I stabbed the floor and drowned her in healing flowers. After a few seconds, Sylvia was ready to get back into the action. She ran back in, Teddy following close behind.

I watched the bird do another arc around the room. It hovered right above Selene, and dropped a giant fork. I heard a scream from her. "Is that a fucking fork?" She ran away, barely missing the fork.

I realized why it had happened, and made sure to calm Selene down. "I think it's because it's a raven, or crow, or whatever. Don't they like shiny objects? Or is that a myth?"

She caught her breath. "Girl, I have no clue. Cool mechanic though. If that's the case." She ran back in.

"Crows like shiny things, that thing is a crow!" Lali yelled as she was smacked out of the air. She had tried to get on the bird, but was hit by a wing in the process.

I found Somnus and decided to make small talk. "So... how is the bird treating you?"

He laughed through deep breaths. "It's such a good host. So kind, such great manners, screech like a lullaby. What else could you want?" Just as he finished his joke, a pocket watch came flying at us. His comedic timing was always impeccable. I too had an object to dodge, a giant spoon came barreling at me. I swiftly dodged, and went to heal Rufus. He was also caught by the edge of a fork, and was very low on health.

Once a silver plate came flying at us, everything went to hell. It rolled and rolled before eventually falling flat on Lali. She survived by a hair, and beckoned me to come heal her. I found Somnus on the way to Lali and grabbed him. "Hey, do you have an escape potion?"

He looked in his inventory, switching his gaze from his menu to the crow. "Yes, I got one from a monster."

"Good. Keep it handy." I let go of him and raced to Lali. I created another healing pool. "What are we going to do, everyone is dying. I think we need to leave, Somnus has a potion too. We could save ourselves and come back again. I'm pretty sure the rest of our progress saves. Selene was looking through forums and said something about that. Either way, it's a risk we need to take."

Lali thought it over for a few seconds then yelled. "Everyone! Drink an escape potion!" Everyone kept running, but pulled out their potions. We all took a drink at the same time. With a swirl of purple in my vision, I was back on the front lawn of the tower. I looked around at my guildmates. Everyone was almost dead. I threw my sword down again, doing what I could. After a few minutes, Sylvia and I had everyone healed.

We took the zipline back down to the beach and stopped at the restaurant. "I'll pay for the meals again, we need more shield points so badly." Rampi treated us again, this time ordering seconds. We ate quickly, and ran out to the beach. Once we were in an open area, we summoned our dragons.

Apha caught a ride on Rufus' red and green dragon, Noel, whom he'd named for its holiday color scheme. We raced back to the Lavender Woods, crossing over the Plains and the rest of the unified forest. We finally reached the purple topped region and landed.

I bought two more escape potions. If we needed another one later on, I didn't want to fly back here to get it. As I mounted Jinkx, I saw the new improvements in the forest. Buildings were all over, moths fluttered freely, and kiri walked the streets without fear. It was nice to see our work triggering such an effect, and it made me want to defeat Syphon even more.

As we flew back to the beach, Somnus and I silently raced. We pushed our dragons to go faster, trying to beat each other every second. Once we realized our dragons had the same maximum speed, we settled into a sort of dance. Above the clouds, Somnus and I wove around each other. Flipping around and circling one another as we passed the regions in a sweet tango.

We reached the zipline again. We shot back up to the islands and raced to the door. The first two rooms still glowed a pristine gold. We rushed up the stairs to see Davenine tearing apart the room.

This time, we were ready. Selene ran around, pulling the bird's attention and calling out every time a new object came into play. In the woods, Rufus and I had constructed a plan. If I could stab an object as it rained down, I could heal him as he jumped on it, allowing him to get closer to the beast. When a teapot came flying towards us, I threw my sword into the spout. It started glowing a faint pink color, and vines billowed out from its openings. I helped propel Rufus to the pot, sending him flying to the silver kettle. He landed, took three strides, and jumped on the raven. He punched it five times in the face, and jumped off.

The crow burst into a bright golden light, color washing the room of its past grime. The crow transformed in the light. Its black feathers faded to white. Its body shrank and the talons turned into small orange toes. A golden crown fell upon its head, and it floated softly to the ground. The notification appeared: **"QUEST COMPLETED: RELIGHT THE TOWER OF THE PRIEST."**

In a flash, a cluster of stars appeared next to the dove. "Thank you, warriors. You have freed my Lily, and restored Dove Skies to its former peace." Illia threw her hands up, and Lily fluttered into her arms. She brought her arms into a cradle, holding the dove like a baby. "When Syphon took my sweet girl I was lost." She stopped for a second, as if her words had a deeper meaning. "When I saw what she had turned into, I couldn't just turn my back on her. For a while, I didn't even believe it to be her. Despite my denial, here she was, trapped in a darkness none of us will ever know. However, there are many other animals out there who do understand. Free them, my warriors." Illia took a seat on her throne and stroked her pet.

I rushed to Rufus, he had barely survived his attack. As I threw my sword down, his black gloves grew soft white feathers. His spikes turned gold, and his fingers grew sharp golden talons. "Woah." He stared at his fists as they transformed. "Sick."

I wanted to cheer for Rufus, but terrifying questions burned in my mind: what did Illia mean? She said other animals were feeling an overwhelming darkness. Could she be talking about the other bosses? Of course she was. We fought a snake, wolves, a moth, a fish, a crab, and a bird. All animals native to their respective regions. Somehow, Syphon was exploiting the amethyst flowers, and transforming innocent animals into malicious monsters.

Even as I was having these thoughts, I was struck by how pointless they were. There was no reason other than fear for me to care so much about this world. Fear of the real world. Fear I could lose Alex. That I could lose Somnus. If finishing this quest could keep him near me, safe from the prejudices of the real world, I would fight corrupted animals forever.

CHAPTER EIGHTEEN

"Good morning sweetie, got any exciting plans today?" My mom ruffled my hair and grabbed a bowl of *Froot Loops*. If she could eat cereal for every meal, she would.

"I know I usually answer with no, but yes I do. Actually, I am going to the arcade with Alex." I tried to act normal, but it was hard.

"Well, I can tell you're excited." Great. "Is Maia coming along?"

It was a date, so no. I hadn't even thought of asking. "Oh, she said she couldn't make it. We really wanted her to come."

"That's too bad." She took a bite of her rainbow cereal. "I'm glad you're all getting along. You know, it was only you and Maia for the longest time. It's nice to see you making some friends."

"Yeah, I'm surprised they get along so well. Maia doesn't

usually take kindly to outsiders. It's funny watching them accidentally call each other Selene and Somnus though." I laughed, but my mom just looked confused. "Sorry, those are their in-game names."

"Ah. You kids are so weird these days. Just call each other by your real names." She rolled her eyes and went back to eating her cereal.

"Sure." I rolled my eyes right back. "I'm going to go get ready. Love you."

"Love you too." She said with food in her mouth. I blew her a kiss and went upstairs. I got the water running and stripped down, my *Hello Kitty* pajama pants falling to the tile floor. I ran my hand under the water until it was warm enough then pulled the valve to switch the water to the showerhead. I climbed in, and completed my basic shower ritual. Separate, high quality shampoo and conditioner, none of that sixty-eight-in-one straight people shit. I used my newly purchased rose water scented soap -a sad attempt to make Alex like me more - and applied some curl cream to my hair.

Even after finishing my routine, I stayed there, staring at the wall. I was going on a real date today. Not just kissing and crying in my room after watching *Drag Race*. A *real* date. It was no surprise that Alex and I shared a love for arcades; gaming tied us together. The endless opportunities of virtual experiences solidified our relationships' validity in an unlimited amount of worlds. Whether we were in the world of Mario, Velouria, or even in the world of competitive *Fruit Ninja*, we were always together.

My alarm broke me from my love-driven thoughts. I had thirty more minutes to get ready. I jumped out of the shower, slipping and banging my head on my towel rack. "Are you okay?" Ma's voice echoed from downstairs.

"Yeah! Just slipped!" I got up, grabbed my towel, and dried

myself off. By the time I was done in the bathroom, the pain in my head was gone. I got dressed quickly, trying to make up the time I'd lost by staring at the shower wall. I took the stairs slowly, not wanting to slip again. I safely made it down the stairs and headed for my car.

My mom called out to me as I left. "I put $40 in your account for food, don't cheap out." She winked at me. Did she know? I nodded and left for the garage. Before starting up my car, I put his address into my GPS. My Australian Siri came to life, directing me to a small neighborhood, with petite but luxurious houses. Each house had stunning cobblestone paths leading up to the front door, blooming gardens, and large driveways. I stopped in front of a gray brick house, with blue and pink flowers blooming in the yard.

Alex soon came tumbling out of the front door, his phone in hand. I looked him up and down. His outfit screamed 2016, but it was still cute. He seemed upset, but his expression cleared as he jogged to my car. A small smile curled onto his lips and his eyes brightened. "Hey." His smile turned to an all out grin as he opened the car door.

"Hi, you look cute," I said, trying to hide my embarrassment as the words left my mouth.

"Uh, thanks. You look cute today as well. Wait! You always look cute, it's just this outfit is-" He started blushing.

I cut him off, laughing, "It's okay, I knew what you meant." He ducked his head, his blush fading.. "So, what are you looking forward to playing today?"

He looked back up and his cheeks returned to their normal tan coloring. "I love *Dance Dance Revolution*. You have no clue what you're in for. I am so good."

I kept my eyes on the road and responded. "Yeah, I suck at that, but I'm good at *Just Dance*?"

That got a laugh out of him. "Definitely not the same

thing. I can't wait to beat you. What are you looking forward to?"

I thought about it for a little bit. Maia and I had gone to Dave & Buster's almost everyday over summer break. "I am really good at axe throwing, surprisingly."

"What?" He practically screamed it. "They have axe throwing at Dave & Buster's?" He was dumbfounded. I looked over to see his incredulous expression.

"Yes," I said. "It's all made of plastic but the axes actually stick into the targets and stuff. It's great."

"I can't wait to try it with you," he said quietly. He started scrolling on his phone. "Can I play some music?"

"Yeah sure, do you already have a playlist in my honor?" I joked, hoping he actually did. He didn't respond. "It's okay, I made one after you kissed me the first time." What started as reassurance turned to embarrassment.

He smirked, "Well in that case, yes I do." He connected his phone to my cord and pressed play. The first song was perfect. He chose one of my absolute favorites, *Snow on the Beach* by my two favorite artists: Taylor Swift and Lana Del Rey. He was even smart enough to choose the "more Lana" version.

We sat without talking for the rest of the ride. Listening to all of our favorite songs. Not a single song played that one of us didn't like. From Björk to Beyonce, we were always on the same page. We pulled into the parking lot and I turned off the car. I ended up cutting off Rina Sawayama in the middle of *Paradisin'* but we knew she would be there when we came back.

The time came to purchase our Power Cards, and before my turn in line, Alex had paid for both of us. "Here!" He presented the card with glee.

"You didn't have to pay for it, I had money." I was happy to accept it, but he had been so giving since we got together. It made me feel like I wasn't doing enough to make him feel appreciated. Like if I kept letting him do things for me, it would end our picture-perfect romance.

I reluctantly took the card, and led him to axe throwing. We passed flashing neon lights and air hockey tables and eventually reached the booth. There were two separate games, but we could compete. I chose Player Two, and hit the challenge button.

"Okay..." He grabbed a foam axe and threw it at the spiky target. It hit the edge, rewarding him with zero points. "Damn." He threw his last two axes, gaining another zero points for the second and fifteen for the third.

"Cute, now watch how it's done." I threw my three axes, gaining one hundred, fifty, and fifty. I did a little bow and collected my card.

"How? You aren't exactly muscular." He reached out to grab my bicep lightly.

"Watch it," I snapped. I pretended not to relish his touch on my arm. "It's not all about muscle anyway. Those axes are super light, and you just have to be able to aim."

"Whatever, I think you just have some freaky axe throwing genes or something." He shrugged, and headed to the claw machine. "If you're so good at aiming, try and get me that seal."

I looked at the blue seal at the back of the box. "You know there are other factors, right? Like how much money has been spent already, how far the claw-"

He cut me off, "Yes, but I think you're good enough. At least from what I've heard." He raised an eyebrow, "It's on me." He swiped his card, not realizing the irony of his statement. Whether he used his card or mine, it would still be his money being used.

I moved the joystick, pushing the claw as far back as I could. I centered it above the seal, then checked from the side, and saw that I needed to move it slightly to the right. I adjusted the claw, and double tapped the button. It was some technique I saw on YouTube when I was ten. I don't know if it works every time but it seemed like I was in luck today. The claw contorted, grabbing the animal at an angle. I thought it wasn't going to be able to pick it up, but it did. It shot up and wiggled concerningly. Miraculously, the seal stayed in its grasp. The claw deposited its captive into the chute and I bent down to grab it. "Here you go, sir," I dropped the seal into his hands with a grin.

He was stunned. "Okay, I thought that was gonna be impossible. Go you, Zack!" He looked around for something new, "After that humbling experience, I need something easier." We walked over to the Big Bass Wheels, and each spun one as a deep-voiced fish hurled angler lingo at us.

"Damn," I only got twenty-five tickets, and Alex got forty. "What about these?" I pointed at the booths to the side. One required you to knock down clowns with red balls, the other was ring toss. "We can take turns."

"Great, I hate clowns so this should be fun." I learned something new about him every day. I took on the ring toss, only making two of fifteen throws. "How'd you do? Oh!" He saw my awful score.

"Yeah... How did you do?"

"Great! I hit every one of them, well, except for the red ones! I guess I can aim too." He grinned at me, then grabbed my hand. In public. We were holding hands in public, in the middle of Nowhere, Missouri. Not that it mattered, we went early enough to avoid the rush of teens. Still, it felt liberating.

He pulled me to the basketball hoops. "Well, I'm screwed,"

I said. We swiped our cards and watched as our balls rolled down. The timer started and we threw in as many balls as we could. I tried hitting the backboard but only got four shots in. Luckily, he only got in three. "Yes! I beat you in a sports thing!"

"Sure, a 'sports thing'," he said, looking into my eyes as he laughed.

I grabbed his soft hand and dragged him away from the hoops. "Let's eat!" I pushed past the chiming machines and circular tables. We found the restaurant inside the arcade and sat down. "It's on me, so get whatever you would like!" I smiled at him, trying to ignore that he wasn't looking at his menu, just me.

"Whatever you say, Zack." My heart fluttered as he threw in my name.

"So, what are you getting?"

"I'll probably get a cheeseburger, how about you?"

"Uh, can I just steal some of your fries? I'm not super hungry, I ate at home." I didn't eat at home, but I wasn't about to deal with the whole "are you okay?" issue. I was fine, more than fine because I was here with him. Sometimes I could go a whole day without eating and not even realize it. It wasn't on purpose, so why did everyone act like something was wrong with me?

"Yeah sure, you're paying for it anyway!" He was so cheerful, it snapped me out of my infuriating thoughts.

The waitress came up to our little booth. "Can I get you any drinks to start? ? If you're ready to order, you can go ahead with that as well."

Alex spoke up. "Hi! We'll share a cheeseburger with fries. I'll have water and he would like Dr. Pepper."

"Okay! That'll be out shortly." The waitress closed her notepad and headed to the kitchen.

"You remembered."

"Yeah, I mean, Dr. Pepper is really all that you drink..." He laughed, then grabbed my hand across the table. "Thanks for asking me to come here with you. I've had a blast."

"Are you kidding? Thanks for agreeing to come. I've never been on a real date."

"There was no scenario where I would've said no." This made me cry. God, how embarrassing could I be in a single day? "Oh no, what did I say?" Alex's loving expression faded to fear.

"Nothing." I said through tears of idiocy, "I just never thought I would have a boyfriend. One who actually wanted to be with me, I mean. Ever since the whole Connor situation..."

"Hey, I am nothing like him. He's rude, manipulative, and even worse, ugly. I could never be like him, or do to you what he did to you."

"Woah, do we need napkins?" The waitress was back, holding our drinks.

She handed me some napkins from the table next to us. "Thanks, sorry about this."

"You're all good, I was just crying in the kitchen. This job is horrible." With that bombshell, she slowly headed back to the kitchen she was recently bawling in. I wiped my tears and laughed. Alex grabbed my hand again, and just stared at me until the waitress came back. "Yass queens! I have a gay brother, slay!" She set down the plate and flicked her wrist.

I took a sip of my Dr. Pepper. "Oh!"

"That was interesting..." Alex didn't look mad, just happy. "That was a horrible way to talk to customers, but it was nice to not be called a slur."

I had forgotten how often he heard awful words at home. "I'm gonna take a fry." I reached over, grabbing one from the side of the plate. We ate in silence - well, Alex ate and I had a couple more fries - and I paid the bill.

After he finished, Alex tapped his hands on the table eagerly. "It's time for my favorite game."

"Really? *Dance Dance Revolution* on a full stomach?"

"Oh shit. Actually, I don't care." He gave up his concern, probably because I hadn't eaten. I followed him to the machine, and watched as the pink and blue arrows lit up when he slid his card in the reader. I stepped onto the right platform and grabbed the bars. "Your pick."

I scanned the song choices and settled on *...Baby One More Time* by Britney Spears. "Good luck?" I said, knowing I would need it more.

We danced across the illuminated arrows, hitting each step as the beat demanded. By the end of our run, I garnered a total of 1,809 points. "You beat me?" Alex sounded offended. "How?"

"Your buff soccer legs can't save you every time." I smirked, knowing I only beat him by a few points. "Let's go to the prize counter, I want a stuffed animal."

"Bet." We walked over to the dimly lit room, passing a few toddlers on the way. The room housed walls lined with stuffed animals, candy, toys, and even gaming consoles. "Okay, just so you know, I cannot afford an Xbox."

I laughed, "I didn't expect you to, I can't either." We walked past rows of familiar faces: Sanrio characters, Nintendo characters, and even Barbies stuffed the clear baskets.

"How about this one? It is in my budget." Alex held up a pink Yoshi.

"It's great." We walked up to the counter, and awkwardly checked out. The worker did not say a word, just scanned the plush, ripped the card out of Alex's hand, and shooed us away.

"Well, he was nice." Alex walked me out to my car, opening

the driver's side door for me. Once he was in, I started the car. He plugged in his phone, and Rina Sawayama's melody filled the car. He looked at me and grabbed my face. He stroked my cheek with his thumb then kissed me. His lips pressed against mine in a flurry of passion. He kissed me for a few seconds, then pulled away. His lips tasted like ketchup. "I want to take you out on Wednesday. It's a surprise."

CHAPTER NINETEEN

Today was the day Alex was taking me on a surprise date. I checked the weather app on my phone, noticing the chilling thirty degrees today would bring. With wind chill, it would feel like twenty. I pulled on my warmest clothes. I buttoned my coat up to the top, and headed downstairs. "Hey Ma!"

"Why aren't you at school today? It's 12:00 pm!"

"It's a teacher workday today. I have no clue why they always have these days in the middle of the week. Like, just let us get out for Friday!"

"I know that's right. I would rather you get a half day on Friday. Remember those in elementary? You were so cute then, what happened?"

"Thanks."

"You know I'm just messing with you. Why do you care about Valentine's Day though, haven't you been single since you left my womb?" She laughed dryly, probably unsure if this was a sore spot or not.

I lied through my teeth. "Yes, I'm the single king of Hill Crest, but I just hate seeing *those* couples in the hallway. I saw two people nuzzling last year. Like animals…"

She mimicked a vomiting action. "Absolutely not. I believe you now, I would rather get hit by the school bus on the way in than have to see that."

"You don't know the half of it. People also like to have sex in the bathrooms, like every day. People don't get freaky just for Valentine's Day!"

"Okay, I am never stepping foot in that school ever again." We shared a laugh, but it got broken up by the doorbell.

I raced to the door, ripping it open to find Alex grinning at me. "Hi."

"Hey! Hi Ms. Catrone!"

"Hello Alex, where are you two headed?" My mom got up from the couch and stood by the door.

"It's a surprise, but don't worry, I am not killing your son."

She lifted an eyebrow and crossed her arms. "Didn't think of it until you said it…"

His face instantly went a deep fuschia color, like he was about to run out of air. "I'm sorry! It was a joke, I didn't mean to scare you!" He was slurring his words, almost spitting them out.

She tapped Alex on the shoulder. "You're okay Alex, I know it was a joke. I'm not that dense, you're a good kid." She winked, then headed back to the living room.

"Are you ready?" Alex hit me with another stunning smile.

"Can I be? I don't even know where I'm going." I smiled back, following him out to his car. He opened the door for me yet again. It made me feel so important that he was always there to open the door for me. He had opened so many doors for me already, even if only a few were literal doors.

Alex looped around to climb into the driver's seat and started the car. "Just sit back and enjoy the ride."

"Oddly sexual but okay." I strapped in and got a playlist ready.

"Not like that. Just get comfortable, it's not that close." He didn't seem embarrassed this time, just entertained. I started the playlist I had made for Alex, causing *Arcadia* by Lana Del Rey to start blasting. "Sorry, my music is usually really loud."

"I can tell, but it's okay if you want to leave it that way." Not only was the volume high, but the bass was strong. I could feel the music all over me; the vibrations rattled through my body. Part of me cringed at the volume, another part admired his love for music. We exited the neighborhood, and began heading for the interstate. "Oh, the highway!" I said, startled.

"Yep! But first we are stopping to get food." The entrance to the interstate was a few blocks down, but he turned right into a McDonald's. "I know it's not high class, but I don't want to be gone for too long. Sit-down restaurants take so long around here."

"Yeah, definitely."

"Wait. Let me guess what you want to eat. So a Dr. Pepper... and a nugget Happy Meal?" He was spot on.

"Yes, how did you know that?" I was dumbfounded.

"Well, you like Dr. Pepper, like, a lot. You also don't eat too much, and you didn't want any of my cheeseburger. But you were eyeing the chicken tenders on the menu from Saturday."

"Okay, nice detective skills. What sauce do I want though?"

"Oh no. I think I may lose my streak. Barbeque?"

I made a buzzer noise. "Wrong! I like ranch."

"Well, still, I got most of it right."

I did a little golf clap. "Congratulations, psychic Alex. You have figured me out."

"I feel like I did that a while ago, but I'll take it." He drove up to the order window, and placed our order. To my surprise, he also knew to get extra fries instead of apple slices.

We were told to move ahead, giving us a few minutes alone. "How did you know I'd want extra fries?"

"I would really like to say I got it from our date, but let's be honest. Who eats the apple slices here? I just assumed you were normal. They taste like battery acid."

We paid, collected our food, and got back on the road. We drove for a while, passing several exits but Alex made no move to get off the interstate. We drove by a sign for nearby attractions, which only featured a logo for Smithville Lake. Shortly after, Alex got off of the interstate.

We passed a couple of churches, gas stations, and restaurants before turning onto a smaller road. The road wound through the forest and the sound of the tires was muffled by the fallen leaves. As we ventured further into the forest, our destination became more apparent. He was taking me to the lake.

We drove until the road ended in a small gravel parking lot near the bank. Alex parked the car and turned to me with a massive smile. "Ta-da! We're here! What do you think?"

It was everything I wanted, sitting right before me. I wanted to grab Alex, and drag him into the lake. Clothed or stripped down, I wanted to dance with him in the blue waters. That was until it hit me, and my excitement died down. "It's so beautiful, but you know it's below freezing, right?" We wouldn't be swimming, we wouldn't even be getting out of the car if we wanted to stay healthy.

"Now I'm realizing that, yes..." His smile faded.

"It's okay, we can sit here and just be together. Just like at

Sunrise Lake. We watched from afar, not being able to actually experience the beauty of the lake, but we were together." His childish grin reappeared, and he unbuckled his seat belt. "You aren't jumping in, right?"

"No, silly." To my surprise, he turned around, and threw his legs over the console. After almost knocking my Dr. Pepper out of its cupholder, he crawled into the back. Did he want to have sex at a lake, in freezing weather? "Come on!"

"Okay..." I was not about to crawl into the back. There were doors for a reason, and doing it any other way made me want to vomit. I got out of the car, opened the back door, and got in the backseat, sitting rigidly in the middle. He motioned for me to come closer, and I relaxed into him, resting my head on his chest. I had never felt so relaxed. With his soft muscles, Alex became better than any pillow, any mattress, I had ever laid on. He fished around in his pocket with one hand, holding my back with the other. After a few seconds, he pulled out his phone. He swiped until he found the app he was looking for. He opened it, and pressed a big play button. It was *Drag Race*. He had taken me to a lake to watch my favorite show.

Before we could even get past the recap, I started crying. Dumb, pointless, but very real tears. Alex pulled back from me slightly, trying to see my face. "Woah, I'm sorry, did I do something wrong?"

Through tears, I formed my reply. "No, that's just it. I feel like you do so much for me, and I do nothing for you. The bust, the Power Cards, this, what have I given you? You even stood up to Connor for me, and I never repaid you. I am a horrible boyfriend, and you're just... perfect." I kept crying, burying my face into his chest. Again, I used him for comfort, even when I was being awful.

He started crying too, and I couldn't tell if he was sympathetic, or if he'd realized how much of a scam our relationship had been. "What are you talking about?" He lifted my face from his chest so I could look him in the eye. "You have given me more than you can even begin to understand. You are my rock, my confidant, and the first person to ever accept me. You have given me space, understanding, and love when I wanted it all to end."

That last part made me push away from him. "What are you talking about?"

He looked past me, trying to speak through his tears. "I realized I was gay a year ago, and I've wanted to exit this world ever since. Somehow, someway, I just wanted to get out. I first believed if I did, I would go straight to hell, and that stopped me from doing it. Then, I started having worse thoughts. I thought that was what I deserved, that I should burn forever and ever, never feeling a true connection with a man. I mean, if I couldn't please my family, why would I want to stay around for them to hate me?" He wiped his tears. "That was before you, and before *Echoes*. You see, I got a headset for Christmas, and pre-ordered the game as soon as I could. It made me feel like there was another world out there, just for me. One where I wouldn't be judged by the confines of religion, one where I could be myself. A way to escape this world without going straight to hell. The game saved me from myself, but when I heard your voice at the palace, you brought me back to life."

He paused, clutching me even closer to his chest. "I knew I had to try, just try to be with you. After leaving you there, I beat myself up. I left you all alone, in the world where we could have been together. That's what made me make a move on you during our study time. I originally just wanted to be near you, but my dumb mistake pushed me to bring my feelings for you into reality." He took a deep breath, more tears forming as he exhaled. "You gave me a connection that surpassed reality, surpassed Earth. I have a perfect boyfriend here, and there.

Who can say that, but someone like me, who was blessed by your presence?"

I was speechless. I had no clue he felt that way. That the ever positive Alex even could feel that way. I pulled him close by his now damp shirt, into a deep kiss. As our lips touched, I was reminded of our twofold connection. I could feel us in the flesh, with the memories of the imaginary. I could grab him, feel him, but sense his emotions that were amplified through the virtual world. I pulled back, using my thumb to wipe his tears. "Let's watch some Jinkx."

"Actually, I kind of went ahead. I'm on season eleven now..."

"That's okay with me, let's enjoy some Vanjie." He really was perfect. We sat there watching *Drag Race* for hours, only stopping to watch the sky fade from blue to orange. We had first adventured together at Sunrise Lake, and now, here we were, watching the sun set over a real lake. It made me sentimental, and provoked a dangerous question. "I know it's scary, but would you like to tell my mom? I'm not out to her yet, but together, I think I can do it."

He paused the show. "Do you think she would tell my parents?"

"Honestly, I don't know. She has never been big on religion, so I know she wouldn't agree with them. Still, I can't be sure she'll even accept me. It's a risk I'm willing to take, if you are."

He thought about it for a while, scanning my face for certainty. "Sure. If she threatens to tell my parents though, we are telling her it was a prank." He laughed, for the first time since our talk, and smiled at me.

"How about Friday? After Valentine's Day?"

He kissed my forehead. "That sounds perfect." I crawled back into his arms, resting on his chest as we finished our episode. I heard his heart beating a rhythmic tune. The music of him. I pushed up, resting my head on his shoulder. I wanted to stop everything here, never move forward. No more school, no more fear, just us. However, there was still one more thing on my mind..

"Hey Alex?"

"Yes?" He said sweetly, holding my hand.

"It's really stupid, but answer me honestly. Do you feel a commitment to save Velouria? I know it's all fake, but-"

He interrupted me with a kiss. "Yes, yes I do. How could I not? Velouria is the world where I realized I could be with you. Where I learned how to express my feelings for you through both what's real and what's not. Even if it wasn't the world that truly tied us together, that story is sad as hell. All of those animals getting experimented on and shit? Yeah, we need to finish it."

I kissed him again, this time on the cheek. "I think we need to go home."

"Which one?"

...

CHAPTER TWENTY

School was over, and it was time to give Alex his present. He had driven me to school, so I had the perfect window of time to give him the gift. I kept the crab tucked away in my bag, hidden so he wouldn't see it during the school day. As I got into his passenger seat, I rummaged around in my bag, shoving aside loose papers to find the gift box. I finally found it, and shoved the box in his face. "Here."

"What's this?" He joked, obviously knowing it was for Valentine's Day.

"Oh, my bad. Will you be my Valentine?"

He grinned, "Anyday." He pulled the pink ribbon off of the sparkly silver box.. He lifted the lid and tore away the tissue paper to reveal the crab. "It's Jessie! Zack, oh my god! I love it! Thank you so much!" He leaned over and hugged me, crab in hand. He set it on his dash, and felt around in his pocket.

"Close your eyes." I obliged and waited as he opened the small box he had pulled out. I felt his hands graze the sides and back of my neck, sending a shiver through my body. "Okay, open them!"

I opened my eyes, looking down to see a shell necklace. A small white scallop hung from a beautiful golden chain. My hand flew to my mouth, "it's amazing! You're amazing!" I looked around, saw no one near, and kissed him. "Happy Valentine's Day. Now let's get home, we have a much more exciting date to attend to."

We stayed on the islands after the boss fight last week, mainly because Sylvia wanted to try something. Before we dealt with Sylvia's idea, Rampi called us to a meeting. "Hello everyone, happy Thursday. As you know, this is our last area before the boss, but it is also Valentine's Day. I know we have some love birds here, so let's give them our full attention." I turned to Alex, stunned. Had he told Rampi? I turned back to Rampi, but she wasn't looking at the two of us, she was looking at Apha and Rufus.

Apha moved closer to Rufus, and put her arm around his neck. "Yep! It's only been a couple weeks but we're going strong!"

Everyone was shocked to their cores. A screaming chorus of confusion echoed through the group. Rufus spoke up, "It's true, we started dating around the time we cleared the beach. Actually, we stayed a little after you guys at the lake, and found out we lived ten minutes away from each other. We set up a date for the next Thursday, and we've been seeing each other daily since!"

"Well I think that is great," I said. "Let's give them a round of applause." A comical clap sounded from the group, and we all went back to normal.

"Great for you guys, but I want to try out my theory. So, if we could end this annoying ass show-and-tell, that would be great!" Sylvia paced towards the edge of the island. "I am going to jump off of this island, call for Bianca, and if it works, I'll send a flare." She threw a peace sign, and fell off. After a few seconds of fearful waiting, a bright yellow orb came flying up at us.

"Well, she was actually right for once." Selene laughed.

"Selene, that's so rude. But you aren't wrong." I scolded through muffled laughter. Selene and I waited as the others jumped down. We watched as everyone else took turns jumping from the ledge. Apha and Rufus jumped together, which surprised no one. "So, with this whole Rufus and Apha thing, do you think you have a chance?"

"What?"

"You know, is Sylvia actually Sierra?"

"Absolutely not, I would know Sierra's voice if I heard it, and I already asked."

"You asked if she was Sylvia?"

"No, but I asked if she played VR. She wasn't rude about it, but she said no."

"That's too bad, at least you guys are still doing well."

"For sure." She jumped off of the edge, screaming as she fell. I followed shortly after her, slipping off of the earthy edge and watching as the island passed above me. I waited for the flight limit to pass my body, then called for Jinkx. In a flash, Jinkx's mint body was under me, carrying me towards the others. They waited close by the islands in a giant circle.

It was now that I could see their dragons in better detail. Rampi sat upon her sleek lavender dragon, Raja. Lali was atop her golden ride, Syd. I had seen the others before, but still, Somnus' pink and white dragon always made my heart skip. I had known that creature longer than I had known Somnus, even longer than I had known Alex.

"Okay, so I heard from someone in the village that we should head towards the palace. Apparently, there are caves back there that lead to Syphon's Lair." Rampi sounded so professional, like being our leader had become her true job. She pushed ahead, crossing the large lake below and lowering down into palace territory. We landed in the courtyard, passing large bushes and the fountain. Aimlessly, we circled around the palace, watching as it shimmered in the daylight. As we rounded the large blue castle, we stumbled upon a rocky cave. The hole laid agape on the side of a tall hill. The sun hit the opening in a way that made it bounce back as a patterned, colorful light.

A mixed rainbow of light poured out of the cave, prompting Selene to punch me and say, "Look, it's you!"

"It's all fun and games until you realize that's you too." We laughed on the way in, but got instantly shut up by the beauty before us. The entrance opened up to a massive cave system, with crystals covering every wall. Crystals of all color, shape, and size glowed from the rocky space, creating a chilling and bright atmosphere. Purple, yellow, green, blue, orange, pink. Every shade imaginable was reflected by these shimmering spikes of color. As for the cave itself, its gray walls stretched for what seemed like miles. Arches and pillars of rough stone broke up steep hills of the same material. Stalactites hung from the ceilings, and bats flew by in small swarms. As we were all standing there stunned, something jumped at us from the side of the wall.

Selene let out a yell of anger when she saw what it was. "Not these bitches again!" A scalosos with dark purple scales lunged at her, knocking her over with one hit. As she fought off her attacker, more lizards appeared. They swarmed into our space, backing us up in different directions. I was standing back to back with Lali, waiting for one of them to attack. As they jumped at us, the ceiling caved in, splitting the group up. Lali and I got locked away with two of the nasty lizards.

"I've got this one, you get that one." Lali spun towards her scalosos, bending down and knocking it to its feet. I watched in awe as she moved like an acrobat, perhaps a reflection of her real life athleticism, and destroyed the creature with a few swings. I hadn't even touched my lizard. "Just gonna stand there?"

"No ma'am." I jumped at the lizard, hitting it twice in the head before wrapping it in flowers. Once it was stuck in a tangle of blossoms, I stabbed it in the chest and watched it sink into the ground. My flowers fell down with it, sinking into the ground and releasing a healing spore. "Okay, let's try to find the others." We went through a large arch, opening into a small part of the cave. In the middle of the clearing were three purple rocks.

"These could be worth something, let's try to harvest them." Lali bent down to get a better look at the gems, but reeled back as they started vibrating. "Nevermind! Run!" The purple crystals rose from the ground, revealing a new variation of the geminoids. "We can't do shit to those things, hurry it up Mirage!" We ran out of the enclave, passing small arches and similar colored gems. We pushed past small mounds, spiky rocks, and even fallen stalactites before entering a large open area, similar to the one near the entrance. The geminoids followed closely behind us, spilling into the cleaning as we tried to catch our breath. From another entrance to the space, Selene, Somnus, and Sylvia all poured in, green geminoids in tow.

The purple and green crystals meshed together, creating an

angry mob of color. "Where are the brawlers when you need them?" Selene sounded like she was about to cry.

"Probably making out or something."

"Good try Sylvia, but I don't think they can do that in VR." Selene high-fived her for effort. As we finished making fun of them, they zipped into the clearing, Rampi and some pink geminoids close behind.

"Sorry for the late arrival guys!" Rufus yelled, fists clenched.

"We were not making out, and yes, we heard that!" Apha punched two pink gems as she snapped back at Sylvia. The rest of us worked to stall the gems. From knocking them down to getting chased in circles, we did a fantastic job as distractions. In a few minutes, the power couple had the crystal men down.

"Guess you two are making good use of those legendary weapons." Selene said, high fiving their large fists.

Apha let out a light chuckle, "Oh yeah, they are great."

"Speak for yourself," Rampi said. "I still don't have one." She sounded so defeated.

Lali stepped in, "We still have this cave to get you one, don't give up!"

"Oh I won't, because if I don't get one from the boss, I'm crushing up all of these little rock bitches and smelting my own staff."

"Well, that's a positive view on things!" Lali said sarcastically. Their spontaneous aggression definitely proved that they were related.

Rampi shrugged and walked out of the clearing. We all followed, passing crushed gems and fully formed crystals. Rampi jumped over a small stream of water, leaving us all on the other side. Lali and Apha made the jump, sending a vibration through the cave. A quiet rustling sound echoed from the walls, and dozens of giant stalactites fell from the ceiling. The spikes flew down towards us, forcing us to duck and dodge, separating the group once again. Somnus and I were separated from the rest of the group, which seemed like fate.

"Well, it's just us I guess," Somnus said, obviously not too mad with the arrangement.

"Guess so." We shared a smile.

"Look at this!" He pulled Jessie out of his sleeve, an odd hiding spot, and presented her before me. "I finally got her that bow!"

"Aww! That is so cute, it looks like the one I had on your present."

"It does, and speaking of, I taped crochet Jessie to my shoulder!"

"Why would you do that?"

"Because you made her for me, and I don't want to lose something you made. I also thought it would be cool."

I laughed, "Okay, then. I can't tell if that's romantic or dumb."

"Yeah," he said quietly, as if he didn't want to confirm or deny one of the options I gave him. He set Jessie on his shoulder and headed further into the cave. "Let's find the others now, they definitely miss us."

"Oh yeah, what would they do without the real 'lovebirds' of the group?" I said flirtatiously. He laughed dryly, obviously uncomfortable by what I said. "Sorry."

"For what?" He acted dumb.

"Never mind, let's just go find them." Given his mono-logue yesterday, I assumed he did love me. It was a little soon, but I knew how I felt. It's not as if we had other queer teenage relationships in real life to look to as examples. I was addicted to his touch, and obsessed with his smile, but would he be able to say "I love you" back if I mustered up the courage to say it first? I shook myself, discarding the poisonous thoughts of unrequited love and followed him deeper into the cave.

We entered a cave filled with pink crystals. From the floor to the ceiling, rose quartz covered the cave. "Isn't this pretty?" He asked, trying to switch gears. I had hoped he would call it romantic, but he obviously wasn't feeling it.

In a monotone voice, I said, "Sure is."

"Here." He got out his sword, and sliced a crystal in two. The crystal split down the middle, and fell to the floor. He picked up the pieces, handed me one, and pocketed the other. "Happy Valentine's Day."

"Thanks, it's really cute."

"Not as cute as you." So confusing. Had he picked up on my saddened tone and faked a romantic encounter? He was jumping all over the place with his emotions. From passive-aggressive to flirty to dismissive, I couldn't figure out how he felt. We searched around the pink enclave for ten minutes before hearing a loud, excited scream.

"Yes! Finally! Out of my way bitches!" It sounded like Rampi. We raced in the direction of the shout, walking into a huge open room with everyone in it. Rampi was standing on a giant rock, attempting to pull a large staff shaped crystal out of the stone. The crystal bent like a staff and was made purely of a bright yellow crystal. It flickered, emitting tiny bolts of lightning and throwing Rampi off of the rock.

The floor shook violently, and the giant rock started moving. The big gray boulder grew arms, anchored them on the ground, and pushed itself out of its earthy home. It leapt over our heads, spinning in the air and landing behind us. It had stacked rocks for legs, each rock getting slightly smaller as it reached the body. Its arms were similar, with large boulders for hands. It had no face, just a giant scuffed stone with no expression. Everywhere on the rock that was once below ground had a faint yellow glow, small holes littering its rocky build.

Lali stepped back, its shadow covering her entire body. "Well, shit. You better kill this thing and get that staff…"

"I know, I know! Sorry guys!" Rampi pushed past the monster, distancing herself to formulate a plan. "That staff does seem perfect for me," she said in a singsong voice.

Rampi was renewed, optimism took over her formerly downbeat attitude. She sprung back into the fight, switching out her signature lightning for fireballs. She ran around the room, sending flaming rocks at the creature, knocking it down again and again.

I checked the health bar, her attack had only done a miniscule amount of damage to the "Stone Golem." This was the boss of the area, but it had such a boring name. The giant boulder spun on its legs, discharging the rocks that made up its remaining arm into the room. One almost hit me, and I could hear it whizz past my ear. The rock smashed into a million pieces as it hit the wall, some even ricocheting and hitting me.

I surveyed the room. Rampi was still doing better than ever; Lali and Sylvia were keeping their distance; Rufus and Apha were gearing up to charge the monster from opposite sides. Somnus and Selene stood out to me amongst the group. Two out of our three tanks were far away from the boss, talking.

I ran up to them. "What are you two doing? You need to be in there, you are our tanks!" I sounded more upset than I really was.

"I'm sorry," Somnus said, sounding hurt. "We were just talking about real life stuff."

I immediately thought they were talking about me. How I threw out the word "love" without warning. How I must be obsessive, weird, and annoying. It was like Connor all over again. I must have screwed it up. "Well, get in there," I barked back, running away after I said it.

Selene chased after me, casting spells as she ran. "Are you okay?"

I spun around to face her, the tears rolling down my cheeks invisible to her. "No? I probably ruined everything with Somnus, and now he's making you tell me to leave him alone."

"What? No. Why would you think that?"

"I threw out the term 'lovebirds' earlier. He didn't seem to like it."

"Okay, well I have no clue why that would make him mad. We were talking about you, but it was all positive. He was talking about how lucky he is to have someone like you. Someone who will play stupid games like this, someone who is understanding and can listen to his problems. Hey, I don't know why he told me, but I'm glad he did. You didn't ruin anything, so don't make an ass out of yourself now." Selene dashed away, leaving me alone with my thoughts.

So I really was just rude as hell. He was just caught off guard, not mad. He wasn't like Connor, so why did I constantly compare us to that toxicity? Would I ever get over what he did to me? I knew I was over him romantically, but did I ever heal from the pain he caused? These questions burned through my mind, stabbing little holes into my already sunken heart. It felt as if the holes were filling with blood and inflating my heart's weight. I began hyperventilating, standing in the corner I stared at my fake hands as I tried to breathe normally. I tried counting, looking around, narrowing my lips, everything. Nothing helped.

I couldn't tell who it was, but a figure flashed in front of me. "Zack? Are you okay?" It was Somnus. *Alex*. Using my real name snapped me back to reality. I was at home, not a cave. I was with Alex, not Connor. There was no reason to be passing out over petty memories.

"Yeah, I am now, thanks." I got back up, pushing my shaking hands to my waist and grabbing my sword.

"Anytime, lovebird." He said it. No, it wasn't the same as confessing his love, but it was enough for me. Enough for the moment. "We're almost done with the boss, if you would like to finish it off."

"I'd like that, but how long have I been over here?"

He laughed, "Not long, like five minutes. Rampi's just going crazy right now, you need to see it." He led me back to the boss fight.

I tried to jump in, but Rampi zipped in front of me, her breath heavy. "It's mine," She growled. I watched in awe as Rampi jumped into the air, staff in hand. Midair, she released a flurry of five fire balls. She hurled them at the golem, and it fell to the ground. She did a flip, landed on the angry rock, and stabbed her staff straight into its stone body. Her basic staff, made of dark oak wood, stabbed through the now softened stone. The golem cracked into a million pieces, but so did Rampi's wooden staff. She snatched the golden crystal from the pile of ash, and waved it around celebratorily. "Yes! Finally!" She swung it around in an arch, letting off a powerful flash of lightning. "Damn! This is amazing!"

Everyone was silent. "Congratulations?" I said as more of a question.

Somnus corrected me, "Actually, condragulations! You have won this week's challenge and earned the legendary item!"

"Huh?" Rampi obviously did not watch *Drag Race*.

"It's a *RuPaul's Drag Race* reference, Rampi." To my surprise, it was Lali who knew it.

"How can one sister be so cultured, but the other not?"

Somnus jeered, earning him a warning strike from Rampi's new staff.

Behind Rampi, part of the cave dissolved. An arch opened up, revealing a dark and twisted realm. Withered trees lined the deep purple grass. The sky was dark and a broken cobblestone road went before us.

Rampi was ready to give a dramatic speech. "Okay, on a more serious note, this is where we have to go next week. Yes, it looks horrible. So, let's all make sure we are rested, ready, and able to cross into Syphon's territory. I know it's just a game, but it brought me all of you. You have all been vital to getting to this point, especially the three that joined us. If you can even remember this, Selene and Mirage weren't with us at first. However, finding them in the plains made all of this possible, and I cannot thank the two of you enough. And Mirage, thank you for bringing us Somnus, he has been a real asset."

Rampi's pep talk was finished, and most of our guildmates logged off, leaving Somnus and I alone. "Sorry that today has been awkward, I don't know why I was acting like that."

Somnus stepped closer to me. If it were real, I would've felt his breath on my neck. "It's okay, I mean, you have a lot going on tomorrow."

I had completely forgotten. We were coming out to my mom soon. Not just me, but him too. *We* were coming out. Coming out as not only gay, but also as a couple. A singular unit. More than study buddies. "Oh yeah, are you still up to it?"

His previously dismissive attitude had dissolved, and all of his attention was on me. He didn't take any time to think, just stepped away while saying, "I would never change my mind about you, Zack."

CHAPTER TWENTY-ONE

Friday, February 15th

It was happening. After almost seventeen long years, I was coming out to my mom.

I got dressed quickly and rushed downstairs. I grabbed some food, and ran out to where Alex's car was parked in front of my house. I greeted him with a kiss, "Hey."

"Good morning to you too." He never seemed to stop smiling.. "Are you excited for art today?"

"Definitely. My portfolio is finally falling into place. With the others getting their legendary weapons, my ideas are all possible. I can't believe it took Rampi this long to get her staff."

"I know, right? She is literally our leader. It must have taken so long because it was meant to be - like that lightning crazy woman getting a lightning rod as a staff? Come on now."

"So, you believe in fate?" I questioned. Maybe he had dreams of me - or my dragon - before we ever met.

"In some cases, yes. I mean, to find someone as perfect as you - twice - and have two classes with you? It had to be fate."

Okay, so no dragons. Still, that was pretty cute. My fortune-telling dreams were pretty stupid anyway. My subconsciousness just put together the most obvious scenarios when I was asleep. It was stupid to think anymore of it, and it was nice to finally realize that. He pulled the car away from my house and drove to the school. We pulled up next to Maia's Kia Soul, but she was already gone. My guess was that she was hanging out with Sierra.

"Can't wait to see my best friend in English!" I said sarcastically, accidentally bumping into Alex as I laughed.

"Yes! Connor and I are BFFs! You know, I might leave you for him, he's just so…"

"Ew. Please stop, that's not funny even as a joke." I made a fake vomiting noise and opened the car door. We walked to AP Lang, which ended up being as boring as ever. Mr. Wills tried to make it interesting, but nothing woke up our first period class. English Class was finally over, and the next was just as boring. It was hard to focus on history when something I feared for years was happening in a few hours.

The lunch that followed was equally awkward. The three of us sat in complete silence playing on our phones. I only drank half of my Dr. Pepper, and even Alex barely ate. I tried to distract myself by watching *Dance Moms*, but even through the drama, my mind still wandered. Every second a new scenario played out in my head. In one, my mom beat me up until I was unconscious. In another, she accepted us. Then another one would feature her kicking me out, calling Alex's parents, and making sure we never saw each other again.

I almost started hyperventilating again, but Alex placed his hand over mine to calm me down. He didn't say anything this time, just made sure I knew he was there for me. Him comforting me still felt crazy and unbalanced because he had so much more to lose than I did. His parents literally worked at a church, and my mom didn't give a shit about religion. I should have been comforting him instead.

Art class came after an equally boring biology class, and our silence ended. "What are you making next?" I asked.

"That is a really good question, I have no clue. I don't know why, but I haven't felt the need to make anything. It's like the time crunch has dissolved, and I have no reason to be rushing."

"As nice as that sounds, we only have a few months left, so I would hurry up."

"It's hard to create art when the best art piece is in front of me."

Normally, I would blush and be unable to respond, but this was serious. "As sweet as that is, I'm being serious. I don't want to be the reason you get a bad score."

"Fine, fine. I'll make our dragons I guess." We spent the rest of the class working together. Planning, sketching, sculpting. Everything to help Alex create his next piece; a symbol of our time together. It was truly a testament to how our relationship functioned. From the classroom to the battlefield, we were inseparable.

After another mind-numbing session of Mr. Ralph's ramblings in Biology, I made it to 2D art. I touched up some drawings, adding some more creatures from the world of Velouria to my artistic collection. Jessie was my most recent subject, evoking a baseless sense of nostalgia. Our time on the beach was barely more than a week before, and I was already missing it.

I left 2D art and headed for his car. I was instantly met with the sound of *I'm Coming Out* by Diana Ross. "Are you serious?"

"Sorry, I thought it would lighten the mood."

"Hey, I love queen Diana as much as the next guy, but now is not the time." I felt like I was going to throw up.

He switched it to another Rina Sawayama song, and we were off. My nerves picked up as we neared my house. With every turn, my heartbeat increased, my mind raced, and my breathing got heavier. "It's going to be okay." Alex was so calm. I had no idea how *he* could be so calm. *He* was the one with the proudly homophobic parents. There was no way I could even compare to the pressure he must have been feeling. My mom never used slurs, but his parents did. My mom didn't care for religion, but his parents prioritized it over him. He had real reasons to be scared, and I was just weak. I swallowed the lump in my throat, pushing down my fear.

We walked up to the door, put in the code, and entered. "Hey Ma," I yelled into the house.

"Hey guys, I'm going to get dinner, you two hold down the fort." She yelled back, not waiting for a response. I heard the garage door close, and knew she had left.

"What are we eating?" Alex asked, excited for the take-out.

"Cheesecake Factory, I ordered you the same chicken that I get."

"Sounds great," Alex said, a smile beaming from his soft lips. He took my hand and led me up the stairs. He opened my door and started kissing me. His lips smashed into mine with a surprising haste. I jumped as he grabbed my waist, his warm hands transferring energy to my chilly body. He kept his hands on my waist, and started backing up towards my bed. He fell down, "Ow." He rolled to the center of the bed, waiting for me. I sat down next to him, and continued kissing him. His touch soothed my nerves, lowering my heartrate down to his level of consistent calm.

I was practically on top of him when his hand grazed my stomach. My ab-less, boring stomach. Every hair on my body stood up. I wanted him to keep going, but I was too nervous. "Sorry, I'm not ready." I pushed off of him to sit back against my pillow, pulling my knees up to my chest. I rested my head on my knees, trying to hide the way my eyes had started welling up.

"Hey, why are you crying?" He said it with an immense amount of concern in his voice.

"I just, I feel like I don't give you anything. I'm so sorry." Tears began spilling out of my eyes. They rolled down my cheeks, dampening my crossed arms and the front of my shirt.

"We've been through this, you have nothing to feel sorry for. You have given me everything and more. And if you think *that* would change anything, you really need a refresher." He slid his hand along my arm, grabbing one of my hands and placing a kiss on it.

"Sorry."

"I am sorry if you ever felt like I'd be disappointed with you. I've never been intimate with anyone. I don't even know why I did that."

My smile was back. "Because you really like me." I was being so dumb. Why would he be mad about that? I sat back in his arms and stared up at the ceiling. "I really need to fix my eyes before my mom comes home. She'll think you were beating me or something."

"Wow. I agree though, definitely not a great first impression as your boyfriend." He grabbed a box of tissues and handed it to me. I wiped the remaining tears away and closed my eyes. I was so comfortable in his arms. Closing my eyes always felt like I was falling into a deep void, but now I was being held in place, unable to fall into the darkness. I could only fall into his embrace. "Hey."

"Yes?"

"While we are giving apologies, I am so sorry for how I acted yesterday."

"What are you talking about?" I knew exactly what he was talking about.

"The way I was a little flaky with my emotions. It was dumb, and I am so sorry. The only reason I was trying to avoid romance was my parents."

My heart dropped. "What did they do now?"

"They haven't *done* anything, just said things to me. It's becoming obvious that they are picking up on... well, us. I'm scared, Zack."

I sat up to face him. "Hey, I am here for you. I'm sorry that I'm so emotional and deranged sometimes, but you know I will do anything to help you. Just let me know if you need anything."

Our talk was soon interrupted by my mom. "I'm home!" Before going downstairs, I checked my eyes in the mirror. They were back to normal. I quickly caught up with Alex, and met my mom in the kitchen. "Hey kids, I set out each of your meals, we can eat at the table again." She seemed annoyed.

"Are you okay?" I asked, praying the answer wouldn't compromise the rest of the night.

"Yeah, I just had some stupid people to deal with at the restaurant. Like, how hard is it to get the order right? I placed it online, can you read? It's okay though, they gave me a gift card for the troubles." Deep down, my mom was a very forgiving person. Still, she had her Karen moments, especially at restaurants. "Anyway, once I got the manager involved, you both got your parmesan chicken meals made correctly."

"That's nice?" I said.

"Thank you so much, Ms. Catrone." Alex said, trying to change the subject. "I can't wait to try it."

"Aww, you're welcome. Thanks for keeping Zack company, I know he's really weird."

"Wow. Okay Thanks Ma." I was used to her jokes, but today was not the day to be calling me weird. Might as well replace it with "queer." We sat down at the table, and started eating.

"Good call Zack! This is amazing," Alex said in between bites.

"Well, I do have great taste." I lowered my hand below the table. I swiped my hand around to find his, grabbed it, and gave it a tight squeeze. I nodded at him and turned to my mom. "Ma?"

"Yes?" She put down her fork.

"I think I have something to share with you?" I had no clue how to go about doing this.

Alex interjected, "Well, we do." At least I wasn't alone.

She stared at me with her full attention. "So... what is it?"

"We are dating." Silence.

"Yeah, and I really like your son, so please don't kick him out."

"Alex! Not helping," I snapped.

"Hey, it's okay," my mom finally spoke up. "Gay? That is so crazy!" She didn't sound surprised, or even look surprised.

"You knew, didn't you?" I asked, honestly hoping it was true.

"I mean, yeah. Sorry, but it was kind of obvious. I love you and I wanted to give you time to come out on your own." She reached out to grasp my hand that was still laying on the table. "Even if you didn't dress up like Princess Merida every day when you were three, there were other factors."

"Like what?" I prepared myself for the barrage of gay stereotypes.

"Well, it doesn't really help that I saw you two kiss on the Ring doorbell." She laughed, but we both went red.

"You let me kiss you, knowing there was a camera?" Alex joked, obviously relieved at my mom's response.

"Hey! Don't put that on me, you kissed me without warning," I said, flustered. No way I was talking about kissing my boyfriend with my mom right there.

"You're right, my bad. I'm still gonna do it though," he grinned, squeezing my hand. "Thanks for not freaking out, Ms. Catrone. While your response has been perfect, can you please not tell my parents? They are..."

"Of course," she grabbed Alex's free hand as well. "I know how it is around here. But you two, don't ever feel ashamed or unwelcome in this house. Just don't make out in front of me."

So that was it. I had built up this nightmare in my mind for seventeen years, and she had known pretty much the entire time, and didn't even care. It was perfect. We ate our dinner while my mom rattled off embarrassing gay anecdotes. From my abrupt obsession with Chris Pine at twelve, to my love for *Drag Race*, she detailed how she read me like an open book my whole life. It was comforting to learn that we had been speaking an unheard language of trust this whole time.

After a surprisingly calm dinner, we played Mario Kart. This time, Alex and I tied, leaving Ma in second place. "I let you win, it would be rude to not do so after you two came out tonight." She rolled her eyes, and headed to her room.

"Well, this is goodbye for tonight." Alex exited through the front door, pulling me behind him. He tucked a piece of paper into my pocket, waved at our Ring, and kissed me. He jogged to his car, got in, and drove away, leaving me alone on the porch. In the dim light, I pulled out the piece of paper and read it. "Meet me at the Guild Hall, Room 3, on Sunday at 3:00pm."

CHAPTER TWENTY-TWO

Sunday, February 18th

"Hello, Mirage." Somnus said, sitting on a couch in his virtual room. He beckoned me forward, patting the fake cushion. He tapped on a menu screen that was invisible to me, and a large black rectangle flew to the wall of the room. "Happy one month anniversary, Zack." The dual naming was confusing already, but this shape confused me more. In a flash, the black rectangle began showing *Drag Race*.

"What? How did you get a TV in here? Aren't we in medieval times?" I was stunned, lovestruck, happy, amused, impressed. Any positive emotion I could feel, I felt then and there.

"Don't question my ways." He tried to put his arm around me, remembered it wasn't possible, but still kept it there. We sat on a fake couch, with fake contact, but with real feelings and a real anniversary.

"It's perfect. Happy anniversary Alex-slash-Somnus." In that moment, my love for him blossomed. We had only been together for a month, but it felt more like a year. I loved Somnus, and more importantly, I loved Alex.

I knew it was a dream, but that didn't stop the very real tears. Somnus and I flew above the clouds, but as we flew, a dark storm engulfed us. I lost him, and he lost me. I dove down, hoping to find him safe and sound. Instead, I found him, bloody, bruised, and unconscious. I screamed into the sky, cursing, crying, and asking "why." Over and over again. The only thing that saved me was waking up. I jolted awake and found myself back in my room. I didn't know why my mind had forced me to see this. We had come out to my mom successfully. None of those scenarios I had thought up were true. We were safe. But if it was just a nightmare, why did it feel so real?

CHAPTER TWENTY-THREE

The dream from Sunday night hadn't crossed my mind. Not until we were back in *Echoes*. As I looked at that haunting path, the image of Somnus' bloody body flickered back into my mind. I would pay extra attention to him now. If he got a slight cut, him being a tank didn't matter. I would be there. Even if it was just a game, I wouldn't lose him. I would protect him, no matter what.

"Welcome back everyone! Are we all ready to take on Syphon?" Rampi asked eagerly, stepping out of the cave and into the wasteland before us.

"Sure..." Lali said, probably not too sure.

"Can't wait!" Somnus was the only one excited to take on the final boss.

"That's the spirit!" Rampi said. "If it makes you all excited, I learned a new spell. I can only use it once, so everyone huddle around." She wove her staff in the air, creating a star shape. Tiny blue specks rained down on us, melting into our skin.

"It's a shield boost," Rampi explained. "It should help give us an upper hand."

"Thanks, Rampi," I said. We headed further on the broken path, passing withered trees and streams of purple liquid. Crows sounded around us, and rough winds rustled the already fragile trees. The sky was dark and black clouds loomed above. We could see lightning flashing through them periodically. The atmosphere felt stale and poisonous.

I walked close to Somnus, making sure nothing happened to him. We soon reached an outpost. It was relatively small, with dark purple, almost black walls. From each corner, a watch tower shot up. Big flags stuck out of the towers, featuring black birds set against a purple background. The front of the structure was lit by two tall torches, casting a dim orange light over the walls and path. A small wooden door sat in between the torches, with a tiny lock on its side. I approached the tower entrance, sliced off the lock, and opened the door.

For a few moments, we stood there cloaked in darkness. Soon enough, the room lit up a ghastly red color, and ten goblins jumped from the second floor. They were just like the goblin that stole Lali's sword. "Oh hell no," Lali yelled. She pocketed her legendary sword and pulled out a basic one. "I am not risking it."

The goblins raced towards Rampi, or towards her staff. She threw a beam of lightning at them, sending them flying against one of the dark walls. The thieves slammed against the purple stone and slid to the floor. Rampi put her staff away, exchanging it for another lower level one. "Do they just like crystals or something?"

"No!" Sylvia screamed. "Just anything of value." She was hitting goblins off of her with her pearled staff. As they fell down, they reached up at her weapon, grasping at air. She ran to the other end of the room, switched out her staff, and came back. For safe measure, the rest of us swapped out our weapons. Luckily for us, pretty much every area gives you a basic weapon with a slight level increase.

"Okay, I say we get them in a crowd, and cast spells on them." Rampi always had a plan. We got in a circle around the little monsters, pushed them together, and the mages executed Rampi's plan. Nothing happened. Obviously, our weak weapons were no good, but we couldn't risk using our good ones. Especially when we were outnumbered.

The brawlers and knights tried too, slashing and punching away. Again, no progress was made. I saw the exit behind us, and had to think of something. I backed into a corner and checked my inventory. As I saw a glint of pink, I knew exactly what to do. "I am so sorry, Somnus!"

"What?"

I took out the crystal he had given me, held it above my head, and threw it to the opposite side of the room. "Go get it!" The goblins scurried to the other end of the room with animalistic haste. "Come on!" I opened the door and motioned for everyone to get out. By the time the last person was out, they were done with the gem. "Someone hold the door!" I raced to find one of the withering trees and cut it down. I rolled the tree to the door and used it as a lock. "That should do."

"Wow," Somnus said.

"Again, I am so sorry!" I hoped I didn't make him upset.

"Oh no, that's not it at all. That was so impressive, good job!" He seemed so happy, so excited, so full of life. We continued down the path, which cut through the outpost and further into the forest. We didn't make it very far when the ground began to shake. We turned around, and saw the cause. A huge goblin, ten times as big as the small ones, was barrelling towards us. The green beast was moving on all fours, like a rabid dog. It gained on us with incredible speed, knocking down trees and cracking the dirt beneath it as it stomped.

The goblin got up to stand on two feet, jumped in the air, flipped, and landed in front of us. The trees around us blew down, and an arena was created. We carried out a basic attack plan. The tanks got as close to the beast as they could, moving it as needed. The damage players did most of the damage, and the supports healed from the sidelines. With our better weapons back, the fight was painless. Everyone got in a few slashes, punches, or spells, and the monster was down quickly.

The goblin flopped to the ground, belly up. Its fall caused the ground to crack even more, splintering the stone path and the dry dirt around it. The goblin turned to ash, its dust falling into the cracks in the ground. In its place laid a big key. I picked it up, and stashed it in my inventory. "'Key to Syphon's Gate'," I said, declaring its title to everyone else. "So crazy idea, but we will need this to get into his lair."

"You are so smart, I would have never guessed!" Selene added on to my sarcastic performance. We continued down the path, watching as the forest transitioned into a mountainous region. The dark and twisted trees faded into grassless rocks. The dirt stayed, but began to slope upward. Spiked rocks surrounded us, each spewing some purple liquid from their tips.

"Well, this is delightful," Apha said. "Great place for a picnic."

Rufus was quick to go along with her joke. "Oh yeah, I think we could string some fairy lights from that spike to that one."

"That would be so magical!" Apha did a little spin, then moved her fingers into a camera shape. "What a picture perfect landscape!" It reminded me of my room. Not the death and decay, but Apha's hands. I had taken pictures of Alex and I in real life, as well as Somnus and I in here, and hung them on my walls. It was nice to watch as both of our lives grew and developed, while also intersecting in a synchronous timeline.

I fell back to find Somnus. "How are you feeling today?"

"Great, I got extra sleep last night. I even slept a little in health class, I am so ready to take down Syphon." That's a relief. He would be fine but my anxiety was always out to get me. We carried further on, stumbling across a clearing in the mountain.

"Hey guys, do you remember that time we tried to camp out in the mountains?" Rampi asked.

"No," Somnus said jokingly.

"Well, everyone else does. Anway, we should take a group photo here, it is such a full circle moment!" We all crowded around, used the built-in camera stick from ViLar, and took a group photo. I would definitely be pinning this amongst the photos of Alex and I. We broke apart, all us checking our libraries for the clarity of the image.

"Hey, Zack! Wait up!" It was Sylvia. "I wanted to give you this." I expected her to pull something out of her inventory, but she just opened up a menu. I soon got a private message from her. It was a picture. A picture of Somnus and I. We were walking together, obviously laughing despite our forcibly emotionless faces. "I think you two are just so cute together."

"Aw, thanks Sylvia, that's so sweet. Did he tell you we were dating?" I was so happy.

"He didn't need to, your chemistry is undeniable. Don't worry though, I won't tell anyone." She practically skipped away, staff in hand.

I quickly found Somnus again. "Look what Sylvia just sent me," I sent him the image.

It took him a few moments to open it, but once he did his

good mood was immediately recognizable. "This is amazing, it's so... candid? I think I'm using that correctly."

I laughed, "I think so. No clue really."

Our love fest was interrupted by a warning from Rampi. "Woah! Guys, hold up." She put her hand up, and we all caught up to her. Before us was a large river of purple poison. Logs flowed down the stream, falling off into a lower basin. We walked to the edge of the mountain, and the sight stunned us. A waterfall of purple liquid fell down the mountain, leading to a large castle. It was distant, but its presence was undeniable. A sinister energy echoed from the palace's black spires. On the other side of the river was a staircase, leading down to the lower level of the area. "So, I am just going to slide down the mountain. You guys will too, right?"

I couldn't take my eyes off of the staircase. Again, the "correct" way of doing something was presented. It was like a paved path as opposed to walking in the grass. A crosswalk instead of jaywalking. A staircase instead of cutting through a hill. A car door instead of climbing over the console.

I wanted to abandon the staircase, and just go down the mountain, but I couldn't. It was fake, but it still felt wrong. Everywhere else, a continuous path had given me the support I desired, and where there wasn't a path, a rightful option was presented. Now, I saw a practical alternative, but I had to cross an ocean of trouble to get there. I was at war with my mind, and I couldn't win. "I'm sorry, Rampi, I have to cross the river."

"Eh, you do you. See you there." No one seemed mad, which calmed my nerves.

"Are you okay?" Somnus stayed on the mountain with me.

"I think so, I don't know. I just know the staircase is how I'm supposed to go down. My mind won't let me go the other way. I know, it's dumb."

I expected him to make fun of me, but he just made me feel understood. "I know, you did something similar at the lake."

"What?"

"Not the one here, the real lake. You could've just crawled into the back of the car, but you got out and went back in through the door. You did what you thought was right, it's okay. I'm here to go with you, don't worry." He started to cross the river, jumping from log to log.

I joined him, and landed on the same log he was on. The logs formed a misshapen path, allowing us to hop to the other bank. We hopped from log to log, passing each other every now and then, dancing between the rafts. In a flash, we reached the other side of the river. We raced down the stairs, and saw the others stuck in a fight. "What did we miss?" I asked.

"Oh, just us getting ambushed by some trolls. You know, the usual," Selene responded, waving her staff around. There were five trolls. Just like in the valley, the blundering monsters swung clubs and shot arrows, usually without grace.

An arrow flew straight above my head, prodding me into rushing at the archer. I was a support, but I still had some power. I charged the troll, my blade in my hands. I took a big swing, knocked the bow out of its gangly hands, and tripped up the beast. After landing another slash across its face, it turned to dust.

By the time I had finished with my assailant, the other trolls were down. "Well, that was fast."

"Yeah, but we outnumbered them anyway." Lali explained. I hadn't checked their health, but I assumed they must have had a lot. The dust piled disappeared, and we were free to proceed towards the castle. We passed more cracked dirt, this time with even deeper lines. The cracks were filled with the purple substance, creating a dangerous walkway. There were many trees, but they were all dead, stumps, or fallen over.

We reached the giant black gates. Each gate was five times my height, with tall spikes lining the tops. They were made of black iron, and featured detailing inside. It was hard to make out, but the iron twisted to reveal skulls, and in the middle, a broken heart. The gates were connected to large brick walls made of the same deep purple as the outpost, and each end featured a small watchtower. We were about to open the gates when a loud scream came from the dark skies.

From a large, lightning filled black cloud, a figure began to approach us. It was a dragon. With black scales, pointy features, and a bulky body, it was nothing like our pets. This dragon radiated cruelty and malice. A slight purple aura was emanating from its dark scales as it flew towards us. With a flip, the dragon landed atop the gate. It roared, causing purple saliva to come flying from its maw. It leapt from the pointed gate and landed in front of Rampi.

"Hi." Rampi greeted the monster with a cheerful tone.

"So... what do we do about that?" I asked, taking a few steps back.

"Uh... I guess we wait to see what it does first..." Somnus was unsure, but his answer was the best we would get before being blown away. The beast opened its large mouth and unleashed a torrent of fire. The flames burned bright and swept across our feet. We all jumped back, attempting to evade the fiery assault. The dragon reared back, closed its mouth, and started stomping in our direction.

"Well, that's not good," Selene said. She shot a red orb at it, taking its attention away from the rest of the group. She broke away from the group and led it toward the dry fields.

Once the dragon was further away, we were able to formulate a plan. "So, I think we should treat this like any other boss fight. Tanks, go help Selene, supports, well support. Rufus and Apha, follow me." Rampi led the group out into the barren forest. Lali and Somnus rushed to help out Selene while Sylvia and I held spots towards the rear. I watched, making sure no harm came to anyone, especially Somnus.

The dragon slashed at the tanks, doing some damage. I rushed to the frontlines of the battle. "Are you guys okay?" My question was mainly pointed at Somnus.

"Yeah, we could use some healing though," Selene answered bitterly.

I stabbed my sword into the ground, wrapping everyone in tiny pink and white flowers. In a flash, everyone was back to full health and ready to slay the dragon. On my way back to my original position, I was able to get some hits on the dragon's legs.

Apha and Rufus did another one of their combo attacks, smashing into the dragon's jaw and taking down its health. Rampi was about to send a bolt of lightning at the creature, but it flapped its wings and knocked us down. The beast flew up and receded into the clouds. "So... I guess he gave up?" I said.

"He'll be back. But let's get into the castle while we can." We scrambled back to the gate and I pulled out the key we had gotten earlier. I stabbed the broken heart with the key, twisted, and opened the gate.

As we entered the dark courtyard, the clouds got even thicker. The already storming sky turned pitch black and the lightning became bright red. We passed dead bushes, black flowers, and fountains of purple goo as we approached the castle. Around the castle was a moat of purple poison. Above the toxic stream was an already lowered drawbridge, ready for us to step into the castle.

"Wait," Rampi warned, checking above for any signs of danger. "See those gargoyles? I think they will attack us if we don't do something."

"I got this," Selene said confidently. She brought her staff above her head, formed two dark purple balls, and shot them straight into the mouths of the statues. In an instant, the monsters came to life. They flew straight at us, flashed purple, then turned to dust. "Huh, I guess my deterioration magic even works on Syphon's minions."

We crossed the creaky drawbridge and entered the palace. The entry hall was dimly lit by two orange flames in the center of the room. We walked past the fiery torches and up a tall staircase. The stairs felt endless but as soon as we crossed into the next room, the door behind us slammed closed and a ring of flames sprung up around the edges of the large arena.

Ten doors were spaced evenly along the circular walls of the room.. All but one arched door was bright red with a silver skull in the center; spikes protruded from the top of every door. The red and black floor tiles made the arena feel like the world's most threatening checkerboard. The tenth door was unlike all of the others. It was detailed with a golden skull and seemed to loom larger than the others. Black bars covered the door, making it appear off limits.

BOOM! A loud noise erupted through the chamber and a red door opened. A figure came slithering through the darkened opening. The wreath of orange flames around the room caused its scales to shine a sickening yellow. It was Ralios, the boss of the Plains. Ralios took a deep breath, then lunged at Lali. "Ew, not this again."

Lali dodged the attack, and jumped behind the snake. In a flash, Somnus hopped onto Ralios' head, and stabbed his sword into the reptile. His flowers bloomed, but he also fell off. He thudded to the ground, taking a big hit to his health. Somnus pushed himself to his feet, "I forgot this wouldn't be as easy as last time."

Ralios then turned to Selene, who tried to send a purple

orb into its mouth. The snake seemed to predict this move, and spun around to counter the attack. It smacked the ball right back to Selene using its rattle, causing her to fall to the ground. "Bitch!" She shot back up, used a healing potion, and got back into the fight. I was still healing Somnus when I saw the rattle coming straight for my head. I fell to the floor, and my foot hit my bed in real life. "Ow."

"Wow, you're committed. You know there is a button for that?" Somnus laughed at my accident.

"Yeah, I just forgot. Sorry that I was trying to protect you." I swung my sword in a star shape and finished healing him. He nodded at me, and I could only imagine that he had a big grin on his face. He raced back to where Selene and Lali were, and tried to pull the snake's attention away from its current target: Apha.

Apha used this chance to jump off of Rufus, land on the snake's head, and pound it into dust. Using her shelled fists, she sent a barrage of punches into the beast's eyes and nose, causing it to crumble to dust on the ground.

Ralios was defeated - again - and we were ready for the next challenge. **BOOM!** Metious came crawling out of a second red door. Where its pipes used to be were now long metallic legs. The robot spun towards us, scythes out. In an instant, the metallic beast was on top of me, crushing my leg with its own. I stabbed my sword into the ground beneath to keep myself from dying while screaming for help. Selene came to my rescue, using her magic to send blasts at the monster's head. The robot reared off of me, revealing where its weak spots were. "Guys! Remember Metious' weak spots? Well, they're on its underbelly now."

"Got it, thanks!" Lali yelled from the other side of the room. I turned to find Somnus, but he was being healed by Sylvia.

I rushed to his side. "Are you okay? What happened?"

"Oh, just a slash from one of its sword things," he said calmly. "What about you? I saw it literally on top of you."

"Oh yeah, I think Metious is into me," I joked.

"Well, I can't let him steal you from me." He got back up and slid under the robot. He stabbed his sword straight into its belly, sending flowers onto each of its weak points. The robot spun around, making its head face the ground. The purple circles were now exposed, and we could take Metious down.

Rufus and Apha jumped on top of the monster together, each taking a side of the plated body. As if they were playing whack-a-mole, the couple erratically took punches at the different spots. After a few seconds, the robot regained its strength and flipped them over. Just as it was about to attack, Rampi slid under Metious, and landed a hit on its last weak point. In a flash of purple light, the robot was gone.

BOOM!. The twin wolves from the forest came rushing out of a third door. We split up into groups: Apha, Rufus, Lali, and Sylvia attacked one and Selene, Rampi, Somnus, and I attacked the other. My group took the green wolf. With a few slashes and spells, our wolf fell limp. It took only a few seconds for the other wolf to do the same, causing them to start their dance. They spun around until they reached the ceiling, then fell down in a burst of light. They emerged from the blast as a singular entity, just like in the forest.

"Hey," Somnus said. "I have an idea."

"Shoot."

"I say the two of us jump on its back, like a horse, and just start hitting it." He sounded so sure.

"That is so dumb. I'm down." We waited for the wolf to attack someone, which happened to be Selene, and enacted our plan. We began running from the opposite side of the room, jumped high into the air, and landed on the back of the beast.

We sat down, grabbed onto the beast, and slashed away into its fur. We were able to stay on until it was almost dead, then it shook us off. On the way down, I stabbed my sword into its side and slid down, my blade slicing through its flesh. I managed to slice deep enough that the wolf went down. The noise of another door being opened rang through the room. **BOOM!** This time the blue moth, Vulnira, flew in from the fourth door. Vulnira immediately went to the giant chandelier on the ceiling. Attracted to the flame, the moth hovered there for a few seconds before it started glowing. The crystals from the chandelier flew to the moth and covered its wings. "That's new," Somnus said.

"No, it's not," Selene responded. "You just weren't there when it happened last time."

"My bad." As Selene and Somnus were finishing speaking, the moth flew straight at the pair. Its crystalized wings shimmered in the flickering orange light as it came barreling from the ceiling. It grabbed Selene from the ground, leaving her defenseless as it flew around the room.

"Well, this is just peachy," Selene said with anger in her voice.

"I have an idea!" It was Sylvia. "I'll try to catch you in a bubble. If I miss, don't blame me, I don't do this often." Sylvia raised her staff and produced a large blue bubble. She sent it flying towards Selene. It grazed the moth and overtook Selene. Once Selene was inside of the bubble, Sylvia pulled her staff towards herself, and with it, the bubble. Selene came floating down and landed back with Somnus.

The moth let out an angry squeak, then raced back down to where we stood. Apha and Rufus did their usual attack. From both sides, they came flying at the monster, punched it, then bounced back. The moth reared back in pain as its crystal shell was lost. The moth got up and flapped its wings manically. A large gust of wind took over the group, sending everyone flying against the wall.

Somnus rose from the floor and leapt towards the moth. He ran across the walls, a skill I had never seen, and jumped onto the moth. Just like when I first saw him in game, he stabbed the moth's head. The moth evaporated, and before Somnus could take fall damage, Sylvia caught him in another bubble. "Thanks, Sylvia!"

"You're welcome!"

"Yeah great work," I said. "But you aren't getting away that easily. What was that move?"

"What move?" He said, oblivious.

"You just ran across the wall..."

"Oh? Let me check." He opened up his menu and checked his skills. "I guess I got something from the other bosses. You should check your skills."

This whole time, I didn't even know we had special skills. I thought they all came from our weapons. That explained Sylvia's bubble, she had been using it before getting her pearl staff. Amongst blank spaces, there it was. "'Wall-running: Run across the wall to gain height and evade attacks.' Weird, but I'll take it."

BOOM! "Oh my god, can we stop with the dramatic noises?" Selene was over it. From another door came Itaina, oddly out of water. "Is Syphon dumb? What is this fish gonna do without water." The room began to flood. "Nevermind."

The fish zipped around the chamber, sending us away from the room's center. Luckily, I was far enough away that Itaina focused on the others, which gave me time to think up a plan. We needed to get rid of this water somehow. Suddenly, a plan came to me - not a great one - but *a* plan. If there was another chamber beneath the floor we could flush out the water. I started stabbing the floor, using my healing pool ability then waiting for the cooldown. Once my ability was unable to be used again, I started making holes in the tile. After I had made ten marks, I swung my sword and smacked the tile. The tile fell out, and fell deep in a void. The hole acted like a drain, slowly taking all of the water out of the room. Once some water had escaped, I was able to swim up to the top and get some air. "Guys! Just evade the fish's attacks for now."

Everyone listened, and we all swam around, just trying to dodge Itaina. After a while, all of the water had escaped through the missing tile, and the fish was unable to stay alive. Itaina flopped around on the now dry ground for a few seconds, then turned to dust. "Good call Mirage!" Rampi jumped in excitement. "I didn't want to deal with that ugly ass bitch again."

I laughed, "You're welcome. Where is-" ***BOOM!*** "There it is." The crystal crab from the beach came crawling out of the sixth door. Its purple gems were much brighter and its claws seemed larger. This was not the same weak crab from the cave; it was at its full strength now. The bulked up crustacean charged at me. It smacked me across the face with its large claw and sent me flying into a wall. "Why?" I whined.

"That was petty as hell." Selene was getting chased now. "Is this payback for how easily we killed it last time?" I watched as it sat on Selene. Sat on her. It didn't do any damage. Just sat there. "Oh, come on. Even I'm not this petty." Eventually, it stood up off of Selene. As it got up, all of its crystals flew out of its back and rained down upon us.

Apha tried to punch one as it fell into her, but she just ended up getting hit. "A little help here?"

I rushed to her side and stabbed my blade into a black tile to heal her. "Here you go."

"Thanks, I'll try not to be stupid again." She got up after a few seconds and headed back into the fight. I noticed that the crab never regrew its crystals, and big holes were left on its back. "I think it's like Metious. It has weak spots where its shell used to be."

"You better be right, I am not getting sat on again" Selene said, crawling out from under the crab's bulk.

"You didn't have fun down there?" I asked sarcastically.

"You know, I am starting to miss it. I couldn't see you when I was getting crushed."

"Now, let's not be petty like that big bitch over there." We both laughed, then together, jumped onto the crab's back. As I slashed, Selene cast, and we quickly ended the crab's life once again.

Another noise echoed throughout the room, but it sounded layered this time. Two booms could be heard in perfect harmony. From one door, the stone golem came stumbling in. Surprisingly, Davenine, not Lily, came flying in from the other. "Didn't we cure Illia's bird? Why the hell is it back like *that*?" I asked.

"I don't know, but I guess we have to watch out for silverware now," Rampi said.

"Don't forget the plates, teapots, and other assorted dishes," Somnus added.

"Oh, of course, how could I forget those?" Rampi joked back. It was nice to see everyone accepting Somnus with such ease. It felt like they were starting to see why I loved him, even if I hadn't said it yet.

By some miracle, the crow did not drop any silverware on us. Instead, it burst into golden light, turning back into Lily, and showered us in stars. We instantly got all of our stats boosted and our health refilled. "Thanks!" Selene was ecstatic. "I really needed that after getting sat on for five minutes."

"Girl, get over it. That is literally your job as a tank," I snapped back jokingly.

"Whatever. You should have been doing your job and *supported* me by pulling me out!" Selene added to our fake fight.

It wasn't apparent to everyone that our fight was all in jest. "If you two don't stop, I am making us leave this dungeon. No questions asked. Am I understood?" Rampi pulled out her mom-voice on us.

"Sorry, Rampi. It was a joke," I answered, slightly scared by her tone. The dove suddenly disappeared, leaving us alone with the rocky automaton. The rock stumbled towards us, arms swinging. It threw some rocks at us, but it was too clumsy to make any shots. Unlike the crab, the golem seemed weaker.

"Rampi, what did you do to it last time?" Lali asked.

"Hey, I didn't do anything. But... I will take all of the 'thank you's you want to give me." The creature threw away all of the rocks making up its arms and legs, leaving it as a singular giant rock. The rock tipped over and rolled around the room. It rolled up the walls and across the ceiling, never hitting any of us. Despite its size and constant movement, no one got hurt. Rampi shook her head, "Okay, let's just put it out of its misery."

The golem went down faster than any of the other bosses from the arena. With a few punches, slashes, and magic orbs, the rocky beast was down in a flash. Our easy victory was quickly forgotten.

BOOM! From the last red door, the dragon waddled in. The malicious beast stomped slowly from its enclosure, making the arena shake with every step. Once it got to the center of the room, it let out a loud roar, some flames, and a puff of smoke from its nostrils. The dragon wasted no time grabbing up Selene and taking her to the ceiling. "You have got to be kidding me."

The dragon reached the boundary, dropped Selene, and

came back to fight the rest of us. I dashed to where she was going to fall and started a healing circle before she landed. "Damn, that was just rude."

"Tell me about it. Thanks though." Selene got back up and charged at the winged beast with renewed anger. As Selene ran for the dragon, I saw Somnus get smacked by its tail. He was sent flying against one of the walls, and looked like he was about to run out of health.

I ran to his side and threw my sword next to him. "Are you okay?"

"I am now. You are so kind, Zack." He used my real name. "Can I tell you something?"

That was always a scary statement. "Sure."

"I know it's soon, but-" He took a deep breath. "But, I think I love you, Zack."

It couldn't get any more perfect than this. Alex was proclaiming his love to me, during a dramatic boss fight, in the game that tied us together. It was soon, but I was more than ready to say it back. "I love-" **BOOM!** The noise interrupted my heartfelt confession. I looked back, the dragon was still there, no doors were down. I turned back to Somnus, but his avatar was limp. It was like he had fallen in real life or threw his headset off. I knelt down next to him, and placed my ear to his mouth to try to hear what was happening on his end. What I heard was horrifying.

I could hear skin smacking against skin; too solid of an impact to be a slap. A punch. Over the worst sound I had ever heard, I could hear a deep voice yelling. "I didn't raise a faggot! I knew something was wrong with you!" Another punch. Then another.

"Stop! Richard! That's our son!" A woman's voice cried out.

I started crying. "Alex? Alex? Are you okay?" No response.

The yelling kept going.. I managed to tear myself away from the prone figure and ran to find Selene. "Maia! Help! I think Alex is dying. In real life." I was barely audible through my tears.

"What?" She sounded petrified. She looked over my shoulder at Somnus's limp body. "How can I help?"

"Tell everyone to drink an escape potion. We need to leave!" I ran back to Alex's body. Somnus's body. It didn't matter which. Alex, Somnus: he was my lover. He was getting assaulted. If I couldn't save him in the real world, I would save what was left of him here. I fished out my two escape potions and shoved one into his mouth before drinking my own.

I didn't even wait for the potion to fully work. I threw off my headset and grabbed my phone. I dialed the only number I could think of. "911. What's your emergency?"

"I need an ambulance to 223 Lily Ridge Road. Please, I think my boy-" I stopped myself. I knew how the police were here. Give them a minority and they don't give a shit. "I think my friend is getting assaulted. I was on the phone with him and then I heard - I heard someone start to beat him up."

"Sir, I have dispatched an officer to that location. Please remain calm. Can you give me any more details?" How could I remain calm? I knew it was her job, but her unbothered tone made me furious.

"Thank you, ma'am," I said through tears. "I think it's his dad. I'm going to head over there now." I hung up, ignoring her protests. I needed to try and help Alex. I threw on some shoes and dashed downstairs.

"Where are you going? It is almost 10:00pm!" My mom's face changed from anger to horror as she saw my tears.

"I think Alex might die." I didn't know what my face was doing but she immediately went to grab her coat.

"Oh, sweetie," her voice wavered. "I'm coming with you."

She ushered me out to the car. I didn't know what I'd find at Alex's house but at least I wouldn't be alone.

My mom got in the driver's seat. She wouldn't let me drive in my state. "What happened?"

"I-" I couldn't answer. I didn't know how to answer. I just stared out of the window, watching as cars passed by.

"Zack?" She was trying again.

"His dad attacked him." My voice was thick, still choked with tears.

"Why? That's awful."

"We were in a dungeon," I took a deep breath. "He said he loved me. But I-" The tears kept flowing. It was only now that I realized I wasn't given enough time to reciprocate his confession.

"Baby… did you get to say it back?" It sounded like she was about to start crying right along with me. "Were you ready to say it back?"

"More ready than you know," I hit my head on the door out of anger. "But before I could respond, his dad started punching him. He was saying the most awful things."

"It's going to be okay." I could tell she was having a hard time believing it herself. Still, I appreciated her saying it. We turned a corner and my eyes were immediately drawn to the lights. Red, white, and blue. The rain did nothing to dim the flashing. Cop cars lined the curb in front of his house, policemen milled around outside. An ambulance was parked in the driveway. As soon as we were close, I opened the door and ran; I didn't even wait for Ma to stop the car.

I ran to one of the cops. "Is Alex safe?"

"Who's Alex? You mean the kid?" I nodded in response to the mustached officer. "They've got him loaded into the ambulance."

"Well what are they waiting for? They need to hurry the

fuck up and get him to the hospital!" I yelled, gesturing at the still stationary ambulance.

"Hey," he barked at me. "I know you're upset but don't snap at me, kid."

I stared incredulously at him. An assault had literally just taken place and he wanted to police my tone? Why didn't he do some actual police work? I looked around furiously but couldn't see anyone being put into a cop car. "What is wrong with all of you? Why aren't you arresting that son of a bitch in there who assaulted his own child. Go get him!" I yelled at the cops who were still just standing there. Then I saw Alex's dad. Two more cops were coming out of the front door, and they were holding onto the man. I ran up to him. "You mother-fucker! Why would you do that to your own kid? I heard every-thing, you fucking pig!"

He spat at me. If his hands hadn't been cuffed behind his back, I'm sure he would have tried to take a swing at me. "Oh look it's the other little fag."

I couldn't control my tears. "I may be a 'fag,' but at least I'm not a monster." The cops maneuvered him around me and led him to a police cruiser. I ran over to the ambulance which still hadn't left for the hospital yet. The doors were closed, but a woman was standing in front of the vehicle. "Where is this headed? Which hospital? Why haven't you left yet?"

She looked me up and down. "Are you the one who called? We can't tell you anything yet, but your boyfriend is headed to Saint Luke's Hospital." I flushed at the word; yelling at Alex's father probably wasn't the best way to keep our relationship secret. At least she seemed sympathetic. The responder reached out, patted my arm, then quickly hit the back of the ambu-lance. It finally turned on its siren and sped out of the neigh-borhood.

I raced back to my mom. "We have to go. He's headed to Saint Luke's."

"Okay, let's go." She was white-knuckling the keys in her hand.

"Are you okay?" I was scared. Had she decided she actually was homophobic?

"No, actually. That absolute bitch of a woman decided to come up to me and call my son a sinner. She said the same thing should've happened to you too." She slammed the car door as she got in.

I hurried to get in the passenger seat. "What?" It didn't make any sense. "She was protesting when Alex was getting beaten up. Why the sudden change?"

Ma got on the road again, the same death grip on the steering wheel. "I don't know for sure, but I think she saw you and changed her mind. Maybe she didn't fully believe her son was gay until she saw his boyfriend."

I couldn't believe it. How could these people be so hateful towards their own son? I completely zoned out on the ride to the hospital. The events of the night kept playing in my head. It was all my fault.

I was the reason he could be dying right now. I was the problem. If I had just told him we couldn't be together. If I had stopped playing *Echoes* when he told me his parents were catching on. If I could have just distanced myself for once, instead of clinging onto a boy. This never would have happened. He would still be awake. He would be fine.

I was able to focus as the hospital came into view. I let my mom park this time, but jumped out of the car as soon as she shifted gears. I raced into the ER and bolted to the front desk. "Is this where you take the emergency patients?" That was too vague. "Where the ambulances come in?"

She could see the tears on my face and didn't care to fight

me. "The ambulance bay is down the hall to the right. Be careful and stay out of the way."

With a quick "Thank you," I was off. I rushed toward the ambulance bay. As I reached it, I saw him. Bloody, bruised, and unconscious. They wheeled his stretcher past me and down another hallway. His hair was matted with blood and his lips were an unnatural red. His nose was swollen and crooked. Doctors crowded the stretcher, shouting medical terms I wouldn't have been able to understand even if I was completely calm. It was like a scene from a TV show. It felt like they were moving him too slow, even though they were practically running. They needed to be moving even faster. I tried to chase the stretcher, but my body revolted. My legs gave out and I collapsed to my knees in the middle of the hallway. The cold of the floor seeped through my clothes and I stared, unblinking at my reflection in the polished floor. I was a mess. I had no tears left but there were still visible tear tracks on my cheeks. My eyes were red and puffy. My hair was all over the place. I looked terrible but nowhere close to Alex.

It should have been me. I shouldn't be left with just red eyes and a snotty nose and drying salt on my lips. Not while he was bleeding out and probably concussed. I should be dying, not him. Not Alex.

I don't know how long I was sitting there before my mom finally caught up with me. She reached to help me up. "Hey, let's go sit in the waiting room." I couldn't respond. I just grabbed her outstretched hand and let her guide me to a waiting room. "I saw them take him this way, let's sit here." She sat us down on a two person seat. The powder blue of the seat was almost the exact same shade as the flowers from Somnus's sword. It made me want to throw up.

I sank into the cushion, and just stared at the floor. Eventually, I couldn't take it anymore. "I'm going to try and find his room." I forced myself out of the green chair and started roaming the halls, checking each room. I couldn't find him and then realized that he'd probably be in the ICU. I tried to slip in to find his room but a hand grabbed me. It was a nurse. "Hey kid. Who are you here to see? The ICU has a family only policy. Anyway, it's outside of visiting hours." A doctor passed us, entering into the ICU, and I tried to catch a glimpse of Alex before the doors swung closed again.

"Alex. Alex Greene. Please, you have to let me go in there. I'm the closest thing to family he is going to get." I couldn't believe it. His family didn't even want him, but I still couldn't see him.

"Sorry, hon," she said with no remorse. "Rules are rules." Rules are rules. Hadn't someone noticed that his "family" hadn't come with him? Didn't they understand that it was me or no one?

I scoffed, then formulated a polite answer. "Thanks. Can you at least update me?"

"I'm afraid not. We can't release medical information except to family members." She patted my arm before gently pushing back in the direction I came from.

I found my mom again, she was nervously tapping her feet on the tile. "What did they say?"

"Nothing. I'm not family so they wouldn't let me see him or tell me anything." I couldn't keep the bitterness from my voice. I flopped back on to the chair and rested my head on her shoulder.

"Oh, baby. I'm sorry that you couldn't find out anything." She sighed. "I wish I could stay here with you, but I need to go move the car. I parked in a fire zone." She kissed my forehead and got up.

I grabbed her hand. "I'll be okay, you can go home."

"Are you sure?"

"Yeah, they have vending machines. I'll go get a Dr. Pepper. It'll be fine. I think I am going to stay the night."

Normally, she would've protested. I had school tomorrow. Not like I cared about that now. "If that is what you want to do, please be safe. I love you, here is some cash." she fished around in her pink purse. Its floral detailing only made me think of him, bringing tears to my eyes. Apparently I wasn't entirely cried out. "You don't need to be paying for that, you've been through enough. I'm sure they overcharge anyway."

I accepted the cash, watched as she left the waiting room, then got up and went to find a vending machine. The nearest one was out of Dr. Pepper. Of course. I turned down a hallway, passing even more sick patients as I searched for another vending machine. At the end of the hall was another machine. I tried it, and it had Dr. Pepper. Thank god. I headed back to the waiting room closest to Alex's room, and curled up on one of the bench seats. I didn't care what anyone else thought. If I had to sleep here all night I would.

Soon enough, I did fall asleep.

CHAPTER TWENTY-FOUR

"Hey," a soft voice came from somewhere above me. I got up slowly, still in a drowsy haze. I looked at the giant clock on the wall, it was 3:00am. "Can we talk over here?" It was the nurse from before.

"Yeah, sure." I got up and followed the nurse to a secluded corner of the room.

"There is no easy way to say this," she took a deep breath. "His family isn't here and won't respond to any calls. Someone should know and I guess that's you. Due to the severity of his concussion and the general trauma to his body, it looks like Alex is going into a coma. It's impossible to say for how long. He's otherwise healthy but we have no way of knowing when he'll wake up. I am so sorry." The nurse seemed like she was about to cry. It was only then that I realized I had started to cry again.

I was speechless. A coma was pretty much the same thing as death. There were two ways for the coma to end. He could wake up or he could die. He was still dying in my eyes. I swallowed around the lump in my throat. "Thanks for letting me know." I withdrew into my thoughts, barely noticing as the nurse left.

So. Our dreamlike romance had come to an end. He was thrown into a seemingly endless slumber; I couldn't meet him in any dream he might have as I had been forced to stay awake in the horrors of this world. When you live in a world filled with so much hatred, every fantasy must come to an end. It's a love just like the movies but the end credits have started. You know your dreams can't last forever; you must wake up, even if it means losing the reality you held so closely to your heart.

The nauseous feeling returned and my hand flew to my mouth. I felt cold against my other palm. I was on the ground again. My breaths were coming short and fast. I couldn't breathe. I didn't know what to do.

I heard my phone buzz and I pulled it out, answering the call instinctively. "Zack? What is going on? Are you okay?" Maia sounded as scared as she had back in the dungeon. I couldn't believe that hadn't actually been that long ago. It felt like I'd been in this hospital forever.

"Can you please come get me? I'll explain on the drive home. I'm at St. Luke's in a waiting room near the ICU." I wasn't entirely sure if I would be able to explain, but for Maia, I would try. Sooner than I would have expected, Maia was holding me in the waiting room. She kept speaking in a soft voice, treating me like a wounded animal. With her arms around me, she practically carried me out of the hospital. She lowered me down into her passenger seat and before getting behind the wheel and starting the car.

A couple minutes into the drive, Maia prompted me. "So, can you talk about it?"

"Alex's dad beat him up so bad that now he's in a coma. He's dying." I could barely get the words out. I started crying again, an action I didn't even think to be possible. She seemed to understand that there wasn't anything to be said so she didn't respond, just started sniffling as she drove me home. "Thanks," I managed to say after Maia pulled up outside of my house. I got out of the car okay but before I could reach the door, I collapsed on the lawn. I was too tired, angry, and heartbroken to move. I really was a wounded animal. My wounds just weren't on the surface.

"Let's get you up," Maia helped me up, taking most of my weight again, and brought me inside the house. "Hey, Ms. Catrone." She settled me down on the couch next to my mom, gave her a hug, and headed out. If she said anything else to me, I didn't hear it.

My mom couldn't do much to console me, but she tried. She put on my favorite movie, *Everything Everywhere All at Once*. She brought me a Dr. Pepper and some popcorn. She sat with me, gently carding her fingers through my hair. None of it mattered. I barely registered what I was seeing or tasting or feeling. I remained silent. It was as if the events of the night had served eviction papers to every emotion but sadness and fear. As if everything that made me who I am had been carved out and all I had left was an empty shell made of sorrow and dread.

The end of the movie broke me from my haze, but only furthered my depression. Hearing about familial love and acceptance tore me open, scraped my insides raw. The words on screen were overlaid with what I heard in the castle. The awful, horrible words spoken by Alex's own father. Words that deemed me a poison, a threat to his son's wellbeing. Words that depicted me as an infection of sin that turned his son into a monster. But the only monster was him. Not Alex. Not me. Him.

Alex's father may not love him for who he is but I did. I turned to my mom. "Ma, what do you do when the person you love is dying?"

She had tried to stay strong for me, but that question broke her into a million pieces. She hugged me tightly. "I never wanted you to go through what I did." She tried to stifle her sobs so she could keep speaking. "Losing your father was the worst thing that ever happened to me. It hurt even more that I couldn't see him in the end. When he needed me most. He was taken in a flash, and I didn't even get to say goodbye. I wish I had been there with him. It pains me to know that you were so close to Alex getting hurt, and now you can't even be with him."

I didn't know how to respond to that. Shouldn't she be trying to calm me down? Not reinforcing my morbid thoughts?

She took a deep breath, trying to calm herself. "Sorry, baby I'm getting carried away. Correct me if I'm wrong, because I don't know exactly how your games work, but he got attacked while you were fighting some evil? An evil that could never compare to the one that took Alex away." She was right. It happened to him in the arena, while he was just supposed to be fighting a fake monster. Not a real one.

"I keep getting too dramatic. I know him being in a coma is scary and awful but he isn't dead yet. Your call to 911 probably saved his life. Don't beat yourself up like I did when I lost your dad. There is still life inside of him; don't let that life go." Her words struck something in me. My carefree, jokester of a mother was being serious and it made sense to me.

"What did you do while you were grieving?"

"Well, I'm always going to be grieving a little bit but when it gets really bad, I like to do everything he loved. I've been hiking, I've been to the theater. I even went skiing. I hate skiing, but he loved it. I recreated our first date, I went to our first house we bought together. I try to find him in everything that is still around." She smiled at me, something small and sad.

I had never seen this side of her. This nostalgic, determined person. For years, she had tried her best to shove all of that away to deal with my dramatics. "Thanks." I hugged her tightly, thinking about what she'd said. I got up and slowly went up to my room. As I entered, the first thing I saw made the tears flow once again.

The wall across from my door held an array of photos. From real to virtual, all of our greatest memories rested on that gray paint. Alex and I at Smithville Lake; Somnus and Mirage at the virtual lake. Alex with his crocheted crab resting on his shoulder; Somnus with Jessie and her little bow. Everything we'd done together. Everything from flesh to pixels reminded me of him. I knew how I could reconnect to him.

After sleeping fitfully for a few hours, I headed out to my car. My mom was still asleep, so there was no painful conversation to be had. I got in my car and pulled out of the driveway. As I neared the interstate, I saw the McDonald's we had once eaten at. The mere sight of the restaurant caused me to tear up. By the time I reached the interstate, I couldn't control my tears. I couldn't focus on the road because I could barely see through my glazed eyes. So I didn't cause an accident, I found an exit and turned around.

Fear, anger, and disappointment swirled in my gut as I went home. I knew if I tried to go to Dave & Busters, a similar reaction would take place. The only place I could be safe was in VR. I couldn't get seriously injured with just a headset on. I could cry my eyes out while still connecting with Alex. In some ways, it was perfect. We spent a lot of time together in *Echoes*; it was our second home. If he couldn't come home to Velouria, then I would spend enough time there for the both of us.

At the same time, Alex wasn't safe even in VR. It was in this game where I had watched him practically die. Finding Alex here when he wasn't *here* would be difficult but I'd do anything to find our connection again.

I started in the town. Tears fogged up the lenses of the headset as I walked through the town square. I tried to blink them away but eventually I accepted that my vision would just be blurry. This town was where I had first met Somnus. Where he had once grabbed my hand and drifted with me above the clouds.

After at least an hour of sitting around in Wysteria, I finally headed to the Plains. I walked through the fields of flowers aimlessly. I just floated through the Plains, a ghost ignoring everyone and everything. I had no real goal, I just wandered. All I wanted was to find Alex. Any trace of him. Any sign that he would be okay. Part of me believed he could be in the game too. I hadn't known he even played for half of the map, why couldn't he be here now?

By the time I reached the small town, I had one goal in mind. No matter how pointless it was, I would search for Alex. Alex, Somnus: it didn't matter what his name was, I would try to find him. I knew I never would, but I would still try. I had to try. I couldn't give up on him. Even if he didn't survive the coma, his memory lived on in this world.

I went into Sonique's Sweets to stock up on some pastries. If I didn't fight anything, I needed some way to regain my health. After ordering enough food to heal me now and later if I needed it, I left the town behind and headed to the mountains.

I didn't bother calling on Jinkx. I needed to check everywhere. I couldn't do that from the air.

I began my climb. The path was littered with thick trees and large rocks that I had to maneuver around. I checked behind every stone, bush, tree, and waterfall. Nothing. No trace of Alex. At this point in the trek I had given up calling him Somnus. That was his name here, but I was looking for Alex. As I walked across the mountain, I would whisper his name every few minutes. No response.

After passing the small clearing on the mountain, it was almost time to enter the valley. My regard for paths and order was gone. My love was gone, so why did anything else matter? I had a new obsession. He was the order I was missing. It wasn't a path, an algorithm, or an equation I was searching for. No "correct way" could dictate my movement. Only the wind that blew through the holes in my heart could push me. I could only hope it would push me back into his arms.

I stumbled down the rest of the steep rocks and landed in the vast grassland. The valley was healthy, just like we had left it. Even if the heart had been returned to the valley, mine was still missing.

After checking every house and store, I gave the valley up as a lost cause. It was too open for him to be hidden away here. I had to move on. It was almost 11:00 pm when I finished in the valley, but I didn't care. I would stay as long as I had to if it meant reconnecting with Alex. Even if he wasn't there, I needed to find him. Somehow.

The forest was the worst. The high up houses and different areas blended together, creating a confusing mess of a search. I took the ziplines up to the treehouses and scoured the mushroom dwellings. Of course Alex was too tall for the houses, but maybe he was there. Maybe he wasn't in a coma in real life.

Maybe he had just shrunken down here. Maybe he was still awake. Maybe he would live.

After passing shops, houses, and countless NPCs, I reached the small shop in the Amethyst Woods. The store that allowed me to save Alex's avatar. The store that allowed me to leave when I needed to most. I bought ten more escape potions, practically clearing out my coins, and headed for the palace.

CHAPTER TWENTY-FIVE

Saturday, February 23rd

By the time I reached the palace, it was already past midnight. I still didn't want to give up; I had a whole map to check for my boyfriend. The palace hurt the most. This was where we had first met in the game. Where I first saw his dragon in real time. Where my dreams had become a reality. It felt like a symbol of everything that had been taken from me.

I couldn't bear to go into the palace. I couldn't see the place where we had met, where he saved me, where everything I had dreamed of came to fruition. I couldn't see that place but not find him there. I decided to stay outside. I passed through the flying crystals, ignoring the local fauna and goblins. I had put away all of my weapons so I had nothing to worry about. I passed the little creatures as they clawed at my legs. I was strong enough that they didn't hurt me; I barely even noticed their presence.

After checking the courtyard, I headed to the lake. I sat

there for hours. This was where we had our first adventure together. Where I first saw his real charm. I couldn't leave too soon. I sat there for hours, then made myself get up.

The beach was even worse than the palace. I had thought it couldn't get worse, but I was wrong. The beach was where I fell in love with Somnus. Where I got to see his caring, kind soul. I was already falling for Alex in real life, but our time at the beach made me love him here, too. I sat down on the sand, but only felt my rough carpet. The shells littered across the pure sand made my heart ache even more. I reached up to grab my shell necklace, but it wasn't there. The goblins must have taken it. I didn't think they would have bothered me, but they must have. I got up from the shore and headed back to the palace.

There, in a circle, were five goblins. I didn't even think, I just grabbed my sword and killed all of them in one swing. I didn't care. They weren't real, not like Alex. No one had shown him mercy, and he actually felt the pain he endured. It wasn't fair. They took the only real trace of Alex I still had.

Once they all dissolved into the ground, my necklace was left on the ground. I bent down, grabbed it, and quickly wrapped it around my neck. A wave of relief washed over me. While it took off the burden of the missing necklace, it didn't make me feel better. Finding the jewelry only restored me to my already rigid state.

With my shell returned to my chest, I went back to the beach. I sat on the beach for several more hours. I ignored the players that came up to me as well as the NPCs who offered me coconut drinks. I didn't eat, I didn't leave the game, I never took off the headset. My hands became one with the controllers. I couldn't tell where the headset stopped and my face began. I didn't sleep, how could I?

In search of my love, I had truly become a sleepless knight.

. . .

After sleeping fitfully for a few hours, I headed out to my car. My mom was still asleep, so there was no painful conversation to be had. I got in my car and pulled out of the driveway. As I neared the interstate, I saw the McDonald's we had once eaten at. The mere sight of the restaurant caused me to tear up. By the time I reached the interstate, I couldn't control my tears. I couldn't focus on the road because I could barely see through my glazed eyes. So I didn't cause an accident, I found an exit and turned around.

Fear, anger, and disappointment swirled in my gut as I went home. I knew if I tried to go to Dave & Busters, a similar reaction would take place. The only place I could be safe was in VR. I couldn't get seriously injured with just a headset on. I could cry my eyes out while still connecting with Alex. In some ways, it was perfect. We spent a lot of time together in *Echoes*; it was our second home. If he couldn't come home to Velouria, then I would spend enough time there for the both of us.

At the same time, Alex wasn't safe even in VR. It was in this game where I had watched him practically die. Finding Alex here when he wasn't *here* would be difficult but I'd do anything to find our connection again.

I started in the town. Tears fogged up the lenses of the headset as I walked through the town square. I tried to blink them away but eventually I accepted that my vision would just be blurry. This town was where I had first met Somnus. Where he had once grabbed my hand and drifted with me above the clouds.

After at least an hour of sitting around in Wysteria, I finally headed to the Plains. I walked through the fields of flowers aimlessly. I just floated through the Plains, a ghost ignoring everyone and everything. I had no real goal, I just wandered. All

I wanted was to find Alex. Any trace of him. Any sign that he would be okay. Part of me believed he could be in the game too. I hadn't known he even played for half of the map, why couldn't he be here now?

By the time I reached the small town, I had one goal in mind. No matter how pointless it was, I would search for Alex. Alex, Somnus: it didn't matter what his name was, I would try to find him. I knew I never would, but I would still try. I had to try. I couldn't give up on him. Even if he didn't survive the coma, his memory lived on in this world.

I went into Sonique's Sweets to stock up on some pastries. If I didn't fight anything, I needed some way to regain my health. After ordering enough food to heal me now and later if I needed it, I left the town behind and headed to the mountains.

I didn't bother calling on Jinkx. I needed to check every-where. I couldn't do that from the air.

I began my climb. The path was littered with thick trees and large rocks that I had to maneuver around. I checked behind every stone, bush, tree, and waterfall. Nothing. No trace of Alex. At this point in the trek I had given up calling him Somnus. That was his name here, but I was looking for Alex. As I walked across the mountain, I would whisper his name every few minutes. No response.

After passing the small clearing on the mountain, it was almost time to enter the valley. My regard for paths and order was gone. My love was gone, so why did anything else matter? I had a new obsession. He was the order I was missing. It wasn't a path, an algorithm, or an equation I was searching for. No "correct way" could dictate my movement. Only the wind that blew through the holes in my heart could push me. I could only hope it would push me back into his arms.

I stumbled down the rest of the steep rocks and landed in

the vast grassland. The valley was healthy, just like we had left it. Even if the heart had been returned to the valley, mine was still missing.

After checking every house and store, I gave the valley up as a lost cause. It was too open for him to be hidden away here. I had to move on. It was almost 11:00 pm when I finished in the valley, but I didn't care. I would stay as long as I had to if it meant reconnecting with Alex. Even if he wasn't there, I needed to find him. Somehow.

The forest was the worst. The high up houses and different areas blended together, creating a confusing mess of a search. I took the ziplines up to the treehouses and scoured the mushroom dwellings. Of course Alex was too tall for the houses, but maybe he was there. Maybe he wasn't in a coma in real life. Maybe he had just shrunken down here. Maybe he was still awake. Maybe he would live.

After passing shops, houses, and countless NPCs, I reached the small shop in the Amethyst Woods. The store that allowed me to save Alex's avatar. The store that allowed me to leave when I needed to most. I bought ten more escape potions, practically clearing out my coins, and headed for the palace.

SATURDAY, FEBRUARY 23

. By the time I reached the palace, it was already past midnight. I still didn't want to give up; I had a whole map to check for my boyfriend. The palace hurt the most. This was where we had first met in the game. Where I first saw his dragon in real time. Where my dreams had become a reality. It felt like a symbol of everything that had been taken from me.

I couldn't bear to go into the palace. I couldn't see the place where we had met, where he saved me, where everything I had dreamed of came to fruition. I couldn't see that place but not find him there. I decided to stay outside. I passed through the flying crystals, ignoring the local fauna and goblins. I had put away all of my weapons so I had nothing to worry about. I passed the little creatures as they clawed at my legs. I was strong enough that they didn't hurt me; I barely even noticed their presence.

After checking the courtyard, I headed to the lake. I sat there for hours. This was where we had our first adventure together. Where I first saw his real charm. I couldn't leave too soon. I sat there for hours, then made myself get up.

The beach was even worse than the palace. I had thought it couldn't get worse, but I was wrong. The beach was where I fell in love with Somnus. Where I got to see his caring, kind soul. I was already falling for Alex in real life, but our time at the beach made me love him here, too. I sat down on the sand, but only felt my rough carpet. The shells littered across the pure sand made my heart ache even more. I reached up to grab my shell necklace, but it wasn't there. The goblins must have taken it. I didn't think they would have bothered me, but they must have. I got up from the shore and headed back to the palace.

There, in a circle, were five goblins. I didn't even think, I just grabbed my sword and killed all of them in one swing. I didn't care. They weren't real, not like Alex. No one had shown him mercy, and he actually felt the pain he endured. It wasn't fair. They took the only real trace of Alex I still had.

Once they all dissolved into the ground, my necklace was left on the ground. I bent down, grabbed it, and quickly wrapped it around my neck. A wave of relief washed over me. While it took off the burden of the missing necklace, it didn't make me feel better. Finding the jewelry only restored me to my already rigid state.

With my shell returned to my chest, I went back to the beach. I sat on the beach for several more hours. I ignored the players that came up to me as well as the NPCs who offered me coconut drinks. I didn't eat, I didn't leave the game, I never took off the headset. My hands became one with the controllers. I couldn't tell where the headset stopped and my face began. I didn't sleep, how could I?

In search of my love, I had truly become a sleepless knight.

CHAPTER TWENTY-SIX

Sunday, February 24th

The next day came and I decided to purchase a boat. I used the last of my coins to get a small dinghy and headed for the open water. I didn't bother to move it manually, just let the water move me as it pleased. I didn't have Alex's boating skills and I didn't bother to try. The sea didn't calm me, instead it only made me mad. I should be here with Alex, on a real beach, enjoying his company. Instead, I was on a tiny boat in a pixelated ocean while machines kept him alive.

I was done with it all. I jumped out of the dingy and swam back to the shore. I didn't want to check Dove Skies. If I did, I would probably jump off of the island in hopes of dying. Death in this world wouldn't bring me any closer to Alex. I headed back to the palace. I crossed the drawbridge and entered the blue castle. The first room was the same, boring and quiet. I found the stairwell and headed up to the second floor. Similarly, nothing was there.

After winding around the spiral staircase, I reached the old boss room. Below the aperture, a large oak tree sat. Around it were white lilies sprouting from a golden liquid that flowed from the roots. The tree itself glowed a similar gold to the pools. It felt so familiar, and looked more real than the rest of the room. As I pulled my tired body to the tree, I saw a figure.

It was him. "Alex? Is that you?" I tried to move quicker..

Before me was Alex. Somnus. It was his avatar. Curly hair and tan skin: it was definitely him. He spoke, but it didn't sound like him. "Zack, you need to stop. You've been in this game for three days straight."

"I've," I started losing my breath. "I've been looking for you." I collapsed.

I was flying again. Somnus's dragon, Swift, was carrying me through a black void, flapping her white wings aggressively. I heard a siren sound through the darkness. It felt far away from me and I didn't let it bother me. I just let myself be carried through the darkness.

CHAPTER TWENTY-SEVEN

Tuesday, February 25th

I awoke in a gray room. I squinted against the harsh LED lights. A light, annoying beeping was coming from some-where in the room. There were small tables next to my bed; one held a plate and the other had two vases of flowers. I was in the hospital. I didn't know what day it was or how long I'd been here but my body still felt exhausted. I forced myself to sit up, pulling the electrodes off my chest. The beeping stopped. I pushed myself out of my bed, grabbing onto my IV stand.

I shuffled out of my room, closing my door lightly to muffle the sound. I looked around the hallway; I was in the ICU, which meant Alex was nearby. As swiftly as I could, I made my way to the hallway Alex was in. The sign on Alex's door read 'TESTING.' I assumed they were doing some blood work or a scan. I didn't care what test they were running or if there was anyone in the room; I just opened the door. No doctors or nurses stopped me. I made my way slowly to his bedside.

Looking at him made my eyes well with tears. Someone had cleaned most of the blood off his face but he was still bruised and still unconscious. Purple traced his lips and cheeks. His neck was held in a brace and his arm was wrapped in a cast. In my mind, Alex was always smiling. Now, there wasn't even a hint of a grin on his features. He didn't look like he was feeling anything other than pain. I reached for the hand not wrapped in a cast; he was so cold. My tears fell onto his face. "I love you. I love you. I love you. I love you. I love you." I kept repeating it until blackness overtook my vision again and I fell backwards onto the cold tile floor.

MONDAY, MARCH 3

I was discharged on Friday, but my first day of school without Alex was about to begin. My mom dropped me off; she had been feeling incredibly overprotective the last few days and hadn't let me go anywhere by myself. I walked into the front desk area and saw Mr. Wills waiting for me. "Hey Zack! So great to see you. I'm not one for romance, but I heard about everything that happened." Embarrassing. Why would he bring it up to me? "There's some make-up work but I've given you extensions on everything so don't worry." This was the nicest I had ever seen Mr. Wills.

"Thanks, that means a lot." I wondered if the rest of my teachers would be so accommodating. He patted my shoulder and walked me to English. As I walked in, I saw Connor laughing with his friends. As soon as he saw me, his laugh shifted into a sneer and his eyebrows narrowed.

I took my seat behind him and waited for his inevitable comment. He turned to face me. "Aw, so the little fag-" I didn't let him finish, I just punched him. I'd never punched anyone in real life before but it was the most satisfying thing I had ever done. He reached up to cradle his nose, which had started to drip blood. "What the fuck?"

"Excuse me? What is happening over here?" Mr. Wills turned Connor to face him.

"Oh nothing, he's just a rude ass bitch." I didn't care that I shouldn't be swearing in front of a teacher.

Mr. Wills took a few seconds then responded. He looked conflicted. "You know, I -" He cut himself off before continuing. "This isn't okay. You two need to go to the office, come on." We followed him to the principal's office, and both of our parents were called in. As we waited, Mr. Wills patted my shoulder again, "It'll all work out, Zack." I got the impression that he had also wanted to punch Connor more than once.

The meeting dragged on forever but Mr. Wills vouched for the fact that I had been provoked. Luckily, I didn't get suspended at all but Connor's parents didn't want me in class with their son anymore. After a tiring deliberation, the principal and my mom decided to move me into virtual school. I would come in for the AP exams in May, but I didn't have to go to in-person class anymore. I had no issue with this settlement since it meant I would get to do the work at my own pace. With how I felt emotionally and how tired I still was, that was probably for the best. I even had some clay at home to finish off my projects for 3D Art.

Despite my eagerness to go home, I had to visit Ms. Bash first. Before I could even say hello, she wrapped me in a warm hug. "Thank god you're okay. I was so worried. I heard about what happened. Is Alex okay?"

My face probably said everything she needed to know but I still answered. "He's alive, but he's not awake yet."

She patted my cheek. "Well, it's only a matter of time." She walked to the back of the class to grab a tub of my projects. "Here you are, and I added in some extra clay for you."

"Thank you so much. I'll see you next year." I hefted the tub in my arms and turned to leave.

She stopped me as I headed out of the door. "Wait! You might want this." It was the sculpture Alex had made for me. I couldn't keep it together anymore. I just started crying. Again. I slumped to the floor - the same floor we used to eat lunch on - and bawled. She set the bust down and kneeled down to comfort me. "It's okay, Zack. He's not gone, and this is proof of it. Even if he doesn't wake up soon, you'll always have him with you." It was obvious that she didn't know exactly what to say, but her words still calmed me down.

"Thank you." I took a deep breath and tried to dry my eyes on my sweater. "Could you help me bring it out to the car?" I didn't want to risk dropping it.

"Of course, anything you want." She picked up the clay sculpture and followed me out to my mom's car. "If you ever need anything, you can call me." She handed me her number on a piece of paper.

"Thanks." I hugged her again and then got in the car. When I looked in the right rearview mirror, Ms. Bash was still standing there watching my mom's car drive away.

THURSDAY, MAY 5

I looked at my many weapons collected on my desk. I had finished off my portfolio for 3D Art and was ready to submit to the AP Digital Portfolio. I took pictures of each piece. Some were boring: depictions of enemies or controllers. The weapons were the true centerpiece of the portfolio. I started with Selene's staff. Her staff represented a united sense of whimsy and purpose but also power. I connected it to her personality in real life.

Lali's sword was next. Her sword stood for loss and replacement. How we all go through grief and will lose what we love, but out of that loss, something even more beautiful can be created.

Sylvia's staff represented elegance even in childish behavior. How her carefree attitude contributed to an effortless strength. It showed that instead of being rigid, letting go and just living can be the best route to success.

I had put Apha's and Rufus's weapons together. The shelled and feathered gauntlets embraced, showing how our world is connected through sky and sea. How all parts of the earth can be one. How even the most opposite of creatures can find solidarity.

Rampi's rod was the hardest to finish. Its translucent look was difficult to capture using clay, but I did my best. Her piece was meant to display how energy is needed in leadership. How care and determination are necessary to yield a powerful product.

The most important piece was the last. It showed love. The love between Alex and I; the love that transcended worlds. It featured our two similar yet different swords crossing blades. Just like how we had crossed paths and our love had crossed into two different planes.

I finished typing the last word and hit submit. Every word I had written about the symbolism of each piece felt like complete bullshit. I hadn't even been back to *Echoes* since I was hospitalized. I didn't expect very high scores on the portfolio. As I breathed out a sigh of relief at finally being done, my phone began ringing. I scrambled to answer as I recognized the number for the hospital. "Hello?"

"Is this Zack Catrone?" The voice on the other end sounded bored.

"Yes, what is this about?" I asked, my entire body tensing up.

"Alex Greene is awake."

CHAPTER TWENTY-EIGHT

Wednesday. February 26th

"It looks like he's waking up." My eyes blinked open. Maia came into focus, standing above me. She held a small balloon in her right hand. It was one of those "Get Well Soon" balloons they sell at the grocery store. I skipped over the pathetic balloon to what Maia was holding in her left hand.

"Hey Maia," I croaked. "Hey Sierra. Nice to finally meet you."

Sierra blushed and dropped Maia's hand. "Oh, so you recognize me?"

"Yeah? I mean I'm not dumb. I do follow you on Instagram."

"Not dumb? I would beg to differ," Maia scoffed. She grabbed the cup of water next to my bed and shoved it at me, nonverbally insisting that I drink. My throat felt instantly better once I did. "You didn't sleep, eat, or drink water for three days then tried to leave your hospital bed. Not really the actions of a smart person."

"Whatever." I shrugged. "So are you two together now?" I asked, even though the answer was obvious.

"Yeah, duh." Maia walked over to the table with the flowers that I had noticed the last time I woke up. "Ah, these are from Rampi and Lali. I guess they called the florist I sent them." The thought of their kindness warmed my heart but the feeling was cut short by my next thought.

"Did they send any to Alex?"

"I think they tried, but the nurses didn't let them through. Something about attracting bugs." Maia rolled her eyes.

I could feel my eyes growing heavy again. "Well, thanks for coming. I'm going back to sleep." I fought off sleep as the couple exited the room and left me alone. I reached for my phone, which was on one of the tables next to me. I wanted to check my notifications. I had some boring ones like DoorDash and Settings, but a specific message caught my attention. It was from Bostyn.

"When are you getting back? Connor has been bothering me all week. I need you here."

I sent back my honest answer, which was, "I don't know, I am so sorry." I didn't know how to explain anything else. Almost as soon as I hit send, sleep stole over me again.

CHAPTER TWENTY-NINE

y heart stopped. "What?" I couldn't believe it. After all these months, he was finally awake. I had never stopped trying to see him. Every Friday, I showed up with flowers, but was always denied a visit. Now, I would get to see him. Hopefully even talk to him.

"Yes, he is awake and talking. He's been asking for you."

"I'll be there soon." I raced downstairs to find my mom. "Ma! He's awake!"

She shot up from the couch. She didn't say anything, just hugged me and then ushered me out to my car. On the way to the hospital, my mind raced. Was Alex really okay? Was there any permanent damage? Would he still love me?

I didn't put on any music and my mom didn't try to talk to me. I drove straight to the hospital in silence, trying to concentrate on not getting in an accident on my way there.. I reached the hospital and parked as close as I could to the doors. "You can't park here." My mom protested jokingly, gesturing to the "No Parking Fire Lane" sign. "Give me the keys, baby, go see Alex."

I smiled at her and took off, leaving the door hanging open behind me. I rushed inside, running the familiar route to Alex's room as fast as I could. I couldn't wait any longer to see him. I finally reached the door.

"Alex?" I practically yelled as I burst through the door.

"Mirage?" My heart fell out of my chest. Did he really only remember my name from VR? "I'm just messing with you, Zack." His smile was back, brighter than ever.

"I'll let you two have a moment." The nurse that had been looking at Alex's chart left the room. I just stood for a moment, taking him in. He looked so much better now. The bruising had all cleared up and they had removed the plaster cast from his arm.

"I love you." I started crying. It was the only thing I could think to say.

"Hey, hey. Why are you always crying? It's okay. I'm okay and I know you love me."

"I just never got to say it. I feel so bad about that." I sniffled.

Alex grew serious. "I don't want you to feel bad about anything. You saved me. *Again*. If you hadn't called 911, I would probably be dead." That didn't help me stop the tears. The thought of an alternate timeline where he didn't survive only made me cry more.

I wiped my tears as best I could and pulled a chair up to his bed. "Can we not talk about you being dead? How do you feel?"

Alex smiled brightly again. "Great. Over two months of sleep is amazing. I highly recommend it!" His positivity would never cease to amaze me. He had just been through hell but he was still happy. I had to smile with him.

"I'm so happy you're awake. You have no idea how scared I was." I clutched at his hand.

"I have some idea. The nurse told me that you went a little crazy for a few days and stayed in VR for like three days. She said that you'd said something about looking for me? I'm flattered you tried, but I am not sure what you expected to find." He started to laugh at me, but was interrupted by a coughing fit. "Sorry. Gotta start exercising again. My muscles are basically gone."

"Don't worry, you're still cute." It was my turn to laugh at him. He pouted slightly then pursed his lips like he wanted to kiss me. I leaned forward then stopped, wrinkling my nose. "Wow. your breath is not the best."

"Sorry? I can't control how well they treat me when I'm asleep." He looked at me for a few seconds. I wondered if he had dreamed about me during his coma. "Can we watch *Drag Race*?"

I laughed at the odd question, "Interesting first request, but sure." I gingerly climbed into his bed with him, trying not to crush him. I held my phone where he could see it as I rested my head against his pillow. We watched two episodes without interruption, resuming where we were in Season 13.

"Sorry to bother you guys," the nurse was back. "I just have to go over some things with you, Alex. Can we talk about them now?" She looked nervous.

Alex nodded. "Go ahead. He can hear anything you have to say to me."

The nurse made a noise of acknowledgement and then continued. "This isn't easy, but your mother made some arrangements while you were asleep. She said that if you were to wake up, you couldn't come back to live with her." She cringed as she said it, bracing herself for Alex's response.

"Oh." He sounded defeated, but not surprised. He turned to look at me. "Can I live with you?"

I was shocked. "What kind of question is that? Of course."

"Well, then I'll make sure to send patient care instructions home with you as well. Generally, he needs to eat gradually for the first few weeks, building back up the amount of food he eats. Make sure he has lots of protein and carbohydrates in his diet."

"Got it." I would make sure he made a full recovery.

"There's more. With the severity of Alex's concussion, we have determined some limitations. Zack, before you got here, Alex told me all about you two." Alex started blushing. "I think your story is beautiful, but it raised some concerns for us. With the damage to the head, we feel it is unsafe for Alex to return to VR. The proximity of the eyes to the lenses is too risky. He could have a seizure, which could be life-threatening. I am so sorry."

So that was it. We would never defeat Syphon. We couldn't go back to our dual-wordly love. It was all over. As I started spiraling, I noticed Alex's face. He looked horrified.

"No, no. That can't be. There's no way." He kept shaking his head, like he couldn't accept what the nurse had said.

I placed my hand over his. "Hey, it's going to be okay. I won't go back either. We can just exist here, in the real world." That didn't do much to calm him, so I turned to the nurse. "Thank you, ma'am."

The nurse nodded and left us alone. I pulled Alex in close, letting him hide his face in my neck. He didn't stop crying for hours.

CHAPTER THIRTY

Monday, March 3rd

I was discharged on Friday, but my first day of school without Alex was about to begin. My mom dropped me off; she had been feeling incredibly overprotective the last few days and hadn't let me go anywhere by myself. I walked into the front desk area and saw Mr. Wills waiting for me. "Hey Zack! So great to see you. I'm not one for romance, but I heard about everything that happened." Embarrassing. Why would he bring it up to me? "There's some make-up work but I've given you extensions on everything so don't worry." This was the nicest I had ever seen Mr. Wills.

"Thanks, that means a lot." I wondered if the rest of my teachers would be so accommodating. He patted my shoulder and walked me to English. As I walked in, I saw Connor laughing with his friends. As soon as he saw me, his laugh shifted into a sneer and his eyebrows narrowed.

I took my seat behind him and waited for his inevitable comment. He turned to face me. "Aw, so the little fag-" I didn't let him finish, I just punched him. I'd never punched anyone in real life before but it was the most satisfying thing I had ever done. He reached up to cradle his nose, which had started to drip blood. "What the fuck?"

"Excuse me? What is happening over here?" Mr. Wills turned Connor to face him.

"Oh nothing, he's just a rude ass bitch." I didn't care that I shouldn't be swearing in front of a teacher.

Mr. Wills took a few seconds then responded. He looked conflicted. "You know, I -" He cut himself off before continuing. "This isn't okay. You two need to go to the office, come on." We followed him to the principal's office, and both of our parents were called in. As we waited, Mr. Wills patted my shoulder again, "It'll all work out, Zack." I got the impression that he had also wanted to punch Connor more than once.

The meeting dragged on forever but Mr. Wills vouched for the fact that I had been provoked. Luckily, I didn't get suspended at all but Connor's parents didn't want me in class with their son anymore. After a tiring deliberation, the principal and my mom decided to move me into virtual school. I would come in for the AP exams in May, but I didn't have to go to in-person class anymore. I had no issue with this settlement since it meant I would get to do the work at my own pace. With how I felt emotionally and how tired I still was, that was probably for the best. I even had some clay at home to finish off my projects for 3D Art.

Despite my eagerness to go home, I had to visit Ms. Bash first. Before I could even say hello, she wrapped me in a warm hug. "Thank god you're okay. I was so worried. I heard about what happened. Is Alex okay?"

My face probably said everything she needed to know but I still answered. "He's alive, but he's not awake yet."

She patted my cheek. "Well, it's only a matter of time." She walked to the back of the class to grab a tub of my projects. "Here you are, and I added in some extra clay for you."

"Thank you so much. I'll see you next year." I hefted the tub in my arms and turned to leave.

She stopped me as I headed out of the door. "Wait! You might want this." It was the sculpture Alex had made for me. I couldn't keep it together anymore. I just started crying. Again. I slumped to the floor - the same floor we used to eat lunch on - and bawled. She set the bust down and kneeled down to comfort me. "It's okay, Zack. He's not gone, and this is proof of it. Even if he doesn't wake up soon, you'll always have him with you." It was obvious that she didn't know exactly what to say, but her words still calmed me down.

"Thank you." I took a deep breath and tried to dry my eyes on my sweater. "Could you help me bring it out to the car?" I didn't want to risk dropping it.

"Of course, anything you want." She picked up the clay sculpture and followed me out to my mom's car. "If you ever need anything, you can call me." She handed me her number on a piece of paper.

"Thanks." I hugged her again and then got in the car. When I looked in the right rearview mirror, Ms. Bash was still standing there watching my mom's car drive away.

CHAPTER THIRTY-ONE

"Alex? Are you ready?" I knocked on his door. We had turned one of our guest rooms into Alex's bedroom "Come in!" I opened the door and blinked rapidly, unsure of what to focus on first.. "Which swim trunks do you think look better?" He was currently wearing swim trunks with bright pink flamingos on them but was holding another pair patterned with even brighter neon pineapples. He was also shirtless. I averted my eyes to the Rupaul poster that hung next to his bed.

"First off, put a shirt on. You know my mom's rules. Second, I think the flamingo ones are really cute. And I'm not just saying that so you won't strip down right now. I really do like them."

"Okay!" He threw on a shirt and grabbed some jeans. He raised his eyebrows. "You gonna watch me change or leave?"

"Right, sorry. My bad." I closed the door and skipped back to my room. I hadn't told Alex where I was taking him, just to pack swim trunks with his regular clothes. I grabbed my suitcase headed downstairs to wait for him.

My mom was waiting for us in the kitchen. "Are you ready for your trip? I'm just so thankful I don't have to give you the pregnancy talk."

"Ew. Mom, that was unnecessary." I scrunched my nose in distaste.

"I'm just messing with you, no need to be so uptight. Do you have your Switch?"

"Yes, why?"

"*Mario Kart* has online play."

"You can't survive for two days without *Mario Kart*?"

"I heard something about *Mario Kart*?" Alex came bounding down the stairs with impressive speed for someone who was still supposed to be recovering from a coma. Everything about him was impressive. In just over a month he had regained his strength, abs, and attitude.

"Oh, nothing. She's just addicted to it." We carried our luggage out to the car and climbed in. I was too nervous to speak as we approached our first destination. Looking in the rearview mirror, I saw Alex's eyes grow wide as we pulled into the drop off area at the airport.

"Wow you really meant a trip trip." I hadn't told him we were flying to our location, just that he needed luggage. We grabbed our bags out of the car and then hugged my mom goodbye. Originally, I had wanted to say goodbye at home and drive Alex here myself but my mom didn't want to pay for airport parking. She kissed us on the cheek and told us to have fun.

I led Alex inside, guiding him to our terminal. I placed my hands over his ears every time our location was about to be said. After safely shielding him from signs and announcements of our location, we boarded our flight. I was quick to throw headphones onto his head and force him to watch *Everything Everywhere All at Once.* Luckily, he fell asleep pretty quickly and didn't find the screen that showed a live map of where the plane was headed.

After three hours of Alex's head on my shoulder, we landed. We deboarded and collected our luggage quickly before heading to the staging area to request a rideshare.. We didn't have to wait long until our car arrived and took us to where we would be staying: a beach house.

Alex's nose was practically glued to the window the whole drive. As we got out of the car, Alex looked around in amazement. "Zack, where are we?"

"Florida."

"What? Don't they kill gay people here?" He shot me a wide-eyed look.

"Um. I think that's everywhere."

"You're right, my dad did almost kill me in Missouri."

"Hey!" I shot him my own look.

"Right, no talk of *that* while we are on our trip." We got to the beach house - a cozy one bedroom - and put away our luggage. We changed into our swimsuits and headed straight for the sand that stretched out behind the house.

Alex tackled me onto the soft sand, sending me rolling towards the water. "Bitch!" I laughed as he grabbed my waist.

"What? Do you not love me anymore?" He teased.

"Hey, I didn't say it, you did."

"Wow! You stayed for a whole coma but you leave after this? I am absolutely stunned." He smiled at me and kissed me.

"I thought they killed people here?" I gestured vaguely around us.

He shrugged, unapologetic. "At least we would die on a beach."

"That's fair." I smiled at him, abandoning our banter in favor of leaning in for another kiss.

He kissed me again, this time wrapping his arm around my neck. Abruptly, he pulled back. "Wait, look what I have." He reached into the pocket of his trunks before pulling out a little pink crab. "Jessie is here too."

I rolled my eyes playfully, "You and that damn crab."

My comment made him tense up, his smile dropping. He stared directly into my eyes as he pressed the crab to my shell necklace. "I never want to forget our time in Velouria together. I love this crab because it's proof we loved *there* too."

It now felt a little absurd that we talked of Velouria like a separate world. It had once felt like our second home but it was just a fantastical reflection of our real world. We had once separated the flesh and pixel worlds, but now, when he held me in his very real arms, I found that only one world mattered. Velouria would always be special to us because we had found each other there; but though Alex and I may have had to close that enchanted chapter of our lives, we would always have each other.

As we stood together on a real beach, in the real world, the root of my torture became clear to me. It was never Alex who was dying, it was Somnus. It was our fairytale that had died, not the true love's kiss. My knight in shining armor had been sacrificed, but not in vain. We had given up the fantasy but I knew that his kiss would save me forever. No one could take that away from us.

As Mirage and Somnus or Zack and Alex, our love would always be real.

The End.

GUILD

<u>Mirage</u>
Dragon: Jinkx
Weapon: The Spring's Vigor
Race: Elf
Class: Knight
Role: Support

<u>Selene</u>
Dragon: Dawn
Weapon: Amethyst Staff
Race: Elf
Class: Mage
Role: Tank
Pet: Holly

<u>Sylvia</u>
Dragon: Bianca
Weapon: The Lake's Blessing
Race: Sylph

Class: Mage
Role: Support
Pet: Teddy

Lali
Dragon: Syd
Weapon: The Sapphiric Blade
Race: Elf
Class: Knight
Role: Tank

Rampi
Dragon: Raja
Weapon: The Thunder's Fury
Race: Elf
Class: Mage
Role: DPS

Rufus
Dragon: Noel
Weapon: Ravenous Fists
Race: Orc
Class: Brawler
Role: DPS

Apha
Weapon: Shelled Clench
Race: Druid
Class: Brawler
Role: DPS

Somnus
Dragon: Swift

Weapon: The Spring's Vigor
Race: Elf
Class: Knight
Role: Tank
Pet: Jessie

ACKNOWLEDGMENTS

This project has become more than I ever believed it could be. More than just an idea, more
than a couple drafts, more than me.

Which, ironically, is how it has always been, more than myself. Every character is inspired by
somebody in my life, some experience, and some conversation. Everything within this book was
inspired by a friend, enemy, or failed romance.

I would like to first thank Journey, Sydney, and Noel. Journey, you were the first person to
show me kindness in my new home, the first person I came crying to about a man, and the first
person I shared this story with. You have done more for me than I think I could ever voice.

Sydney, you have always been there for me. No matter how long we go without talking, we
always click right back to being best friends. You are my longest friendship, and I hope to keep
that truth for as long as I can.

Noel, I owe the most to you. You came to me at my darkest point, and you showed me that I
could be myself, no matter what anyone else thought. I never even came out to you, we just
started talking like you already knew, and that indifference brought me unimaginable relief.

All of you shape every best friend, every powerful woman, and every kind stranger I will write

from now to forever. I love each of you, and so many others, so much.

It was Noel who introduced me to my wonderful paperback artist, Lily (@lilyybellee), who has

been amazing at working with my demands. You perfectly encapsulated what I wanted in the

discrete cover.

Then, Pinky (@Pinky.kei) came in with the most beautiful hardcover, all thanks to the

kindness of Jazzy and the Indie Forge team.

Indie Forge was the only publisher willing to give this silly little teenage dream a chance, and

their support has been life changing. No matter what happens with my career, the kindness of

the Indie Forge team, and their ability to make me feel like family, will be carried with me forever.

Speaking of family, I have to express appreciation for my virtual family. Rampid and Lala, you

shaped my high school years. I joined your guild and no one asked my age, and it never

mattered. You treated me like an equal, and we went on amazing adventures together. You

made me feel like I had a home, an escape, when my own home was a nightmare. I am forever

indebted to you two, the original Sleepless Knights.

Last but never, ever, ever least, I have to thank Grace. You showed me safety, kindness, and

a belief in me that I didn't have in myself. You so kindly edited this sloppy piece made of my

dreams and nightmares, and turned it into something sensical and beautiful. I'm forever indebted to you, the school librarian who quickly became a close friend.